PEN

THE GREA

Simon Mason was born in Sheffield in 1962 and attended
Silverdale and High Storrs, local comprehensive schools, before
going on to Lady Margaret Hall, Oxford, in 1981. In 1984 he
graduated with a degree in English and joined Oxford University Press, where he currently works as an editor in the paperbacks department. He lives in Oxford with his wife Eluned.

SIMON MASON

———

THE GREAT ENGLISH NUDE

PENGUIN BOOKS

PENGUIN BOOKS

Published by the Penguin Group
Penguin Books Ltd, 27 Wrights Lane, London W8 5TZ, England
Penguin Books USA Inc., 375 Hudson Street, New York, New York 10014, USA
Penguin Books Australia Ltd, Ringwood, Victoria, Australia
Penguin Books Canada Ltd, 10 Alcorn Avenue, Toronto, Ontario, Canada M4V 3B2
Penguin Books (NZ) Ltd, 182–190 Wairau Road, Auckland 10, New Zealand

Penguin Books Ltd, Registered Offices: Harmondsworth, Middlesex, England

First published in Great Britain by Constable and Company 1990
Published in Penguin Books 1992
1 3 5 7 9 10 8 6 4 2

Printed in England by Clays Ltd, St Ives plc

For Eluned

Waiting so long for death has put me in poor spirits.

Of course, it has only been a few days since I resolved to kill myself, but they have been the longest and most uncomfortable days of my life. The succession of unforeseen delays, the drawn-out waiting for the proper moment to arrive, the time-consuming practical difficulties involved – all these things have so depressed me as almost to make me change my mind. Almost, but not quite. Then why, you ask, am I not busy knotting the noose or fitting the shiny rubber tubing to the exhaust of my car? Why am I writing this instead?

This is, in a sense, my suicide note. No inarticulate fearful scrawl penned as the alcohol and aspirins paralyse the brain – I have my standards – but a detailed account of my last two weeks as a human being, the History of my Martyrdom. I shall never again have the chance to make art out of such promising raw material.

And why commit suicide?

I will be brief. My wife has betrayed me. This is admirably brief, is it not; perhaps I should leave it at that. But no, I will not cheat myself of what I can never have again, a last recollection of the awful details of my wife's infidelity. Even she would not want me to waste the memories, the vicious, the dull, the inexplicable, the heart-scalding memories, as I sit here in this draughty, meanly-furnished bedsit, ministering to myself this final unction.

The bedsit, by the way, although it sounds unlikely, having about it rather too much of the starving artist's garret, is not an invention. I am really here. A few days ago, I packed two small bags, left the home in which my wife and I had lived for the eleven months of our marriage, and walked the last stretch of

7

my Via Dolorosa to reach, two blocks away, this bedsit, my final station. I had taken the room without seeing it, caring only that it had a desk and chair. It has, in fact, a three-legged stool and a broken folding card-table, but I don't mind. The point is that she won't find me here, not until after. I am close enough to share the neighbourhood with her, to look out over the same streets, perhaps even to catch sight of her car as it shuttles between home and the local police station, but there will be no chance of her interrupting me until I am, literally, finished.

In fact my original plan had been to kill myself immediately on arrival back in this country. I had flown back alone from Majorca, you see, where we had been holidaying and where my wife had, at last, confessed her infidelity to me. However, arriving back home and thinking the matter through, I felt that it would be more polite, more intimate, to wait for her to return and then kill myself. Besides, I was sure that she would be following me home on the next available flight, no doubt to beg the forgiveness I had deliberately withheld. Night after night I sat up waiting for her, preparing myself for death with whisky and my favourite book, holding myself in readiness. The book, incidentally, an illustrated critique of *fin de siècle* paintings, those ghostly pictures of death and decay, was brilliantly suited to the occasion. Alas, although it provided me with an enormous fund of images concerning the final effects of fatal illnesses, in particular tertiary syphilis – putting me wonderfully in the mood for my own demise – in the absence of my wife my reading was a pointless exercise. I was forced to change my plans yet again.

In a mood of icy self-abhorrence known only to the very disappointed, I scribbled a note to her, not a suicide note – she will have to wait a while longer for that – but a simple message of farewell. There were other letters too, to be sent to relatives, and the editors of the journals from whom, since I left university last year, I have earned my living as a freelance writer on the arts and theatre. All these letters stated boldly that I would not be around for a while, and hinted, rather ponderously, at the notion of precipitate foreign travel connected to a literary project (I invent alternative truths with surprising facility when I have to). Then I bought a local newspaper with two columns of accommodation ads down its inside back page, made my brief phone call, packed my bags, and moved out.

It seems I have begun my story at the end, but why not, it is closer to hand. Indeed, the end – the End – such as it is, is more vivid to me even than those earlier, rather spectacular events, my wife's lustful escapades.

I knew all about them, of course, even before she confessed them to me. I am not blind. I knew, beyond all doubt, that for a whole week before we flew to Majorca she had been betraying me with a friend of mine. My *friend*, oh yes, that should raise a chuckle. But, please, don't be too quick to assume that my wife's adultery timidly conformed to type. This cuckolder of mine was my friend but he was not, as he would have been in cheap fiction – or the imitations of it that occur in real life – my *best* friend. He is not the honest Iago of the piece, the smirking recipient of my blind trust. Really, I call him a friend merely because we had known each other for a number of years. I never particularly liked him, even before I knew he was fucking my wife. He was always, I thought, a singularly unattractive man; very ugly, ill-tempered, anti-social. My wife, it must be admitted, displayed quite appalling taste.

We were staying at his country house, the two of us and several other friends. It was, as he styled it, a 'house party'. My wife called it a reunion, and we had not, it is true, seen these friends for some time, not since we left university last summer. I was caught on the one side by his glib benevolence and on the other by her sense of the social occasion, and between the two my own reservations were dissipated. A week before our holiday in Majorca, my wife and I loaded up the car and drove westward towards the coast to join the party.

Once we were there we descended, almost immediately, into a kind of Marlovian 'savage farce'. As is the convention in such nightmares, identities were swiftly reversed: I assumed the role obviously intended for our host, one of ceaseless good humour and old-fashioned courtesy, while he unapologetically made love to my wife, fucked her I mean, more or less continuously, with wonderful energy and appalling ingenuity, to their mutual delight. Had I been the most myopic observer of human drama I could not have failed to notice this. However, reversed roles cannot always be re-reversed. Think of Tithonus, darling of the dawn goddess Eos who granted him immortality but forgot to include perpetual youth, the stupid woman, and could not recall her awful gift, though she herself was horrified to see Tithonus withering and shrivelling through century after century, with Death ever retreating before him. So, paralysed, Hamlet-like, I endured the libidinous display without being able to terminate it – without, even, finding it possible to venture criticism. For six days I watched and twitched, but said nothing to my wife. I was waiting for her confession, her confession would release me. But when at last it came, it was not delivered to me at my friend's country house (I had imagined them appearing before me in the garden, standing beneath the rockery in a shared attitude of quiet determination – though their hands are twisted nervously together – speaking calmly in turn: 'Darling, please try to understand', 'We can't hide it from you any longer, dear boy'); no, the shock was delayed and the *coup de grâce* finally delivered far away from the Scene of the Adultery, in the long, hot torpor of a Majorcan evening.

Our holiday. The bitter fragment of it. What snapshots of memory remain? I do not remember our flight out in much detail, but I recall that we landed at Palma airport at 3.30 a.m., in the cold pre-dawn dark. After sleepwalking ourselves, our passports and, eventually, our luggage through all the official portals of admittance, we faced a choice: either pay some swindling taxi-driver an exorbitant fee to drive us fifty miles to the door of our villa in Sóller, or sit for three hours on the excruciating moulded-plastic seats of the Arrivals Lounge until the buses began running. Choices! I had thought the time of choices was over. Not quite.

Our taxi ride coincided in high romantic fashion with the dawn, a bitter touch. My wife slept or else gazed inexpressively out of the window. Like a melancholy drunk, I thought, though I knew she was pining for her lover. All around us the palely illuminated mists rolled slowly across the ground like enormous stately breakers. Trees and hills and houses appeared out of them, flecked with spindrift concoctions as delicate as the pen-and-wash drawings of William Blake. As we drove on, gradually

10

the mists brightened and thinned, the landscape became harder, more mountainous. Through remaining flights of mists we rose on a steep, winding road towards the small town of Sóller and – I had no doubt – my wife's eventual confession.

When we reached our villa it had already begun to grow warm. The air inside the shuttered rooms was heavy and oppressive, and the dust we raised banging our suitcases about and opening drawers thickened the atmosphere further. By the time we lay down in our dim white bedroom for a nap, we were too hot to sleep. Instead we lay apart on the broad bed, listless and irritable, watching lines of slatted sunlight lengthen across the floor, or the occasional fly spiral slowly in mid-air like a taper-end of drifting smoke. It grew steadily hotter. If I slept at all it was briefly and fitfully. My wife soon gave up trying, and sat reading a paperback. She had taken off all her clothes, on account of the heat, but the poor light did not flatter her. In this way, silent but ghosted by our unspoken conversation, we wasted the rest of the morning. Then, in the early afternoon, I got up to explore the house.

It is ironic that such a beautiful orderly house should be the setting of our messy little farce. It was a traditional Spanish cottage in a terrace lining a narrow street; it looked cramped from the outside, but was surprisingly spacious inside. At a guess it dated back to the turn of the century, but had been tastefully modernised: strip lighting greenishly illuminated the ground floor patio; the dark antique sideboard in the lounge contained stereo and compact disc player; the kitchen and bathroom were equipped with the latest gadgetry. Yet the house cleverly contrived to retain its original dignity. I appreciated the whitewashed walls and tiled floors, unpolished wooden tables and chairs, and I admired the forthright architecture of the hallway, stairwell, and veranda. Only in the living-room had the bold lines and the simple decor been obscured. Here, in every available space, Spanish and Moorish artefacts clung or clustered like overripe fruit – leather water-pitchers, ceramic dishes and jugs, musical instruments, oleographs, statuettes wooden or metallic, glassware and mirrors encumbered with ornate frames. This room, this den of vulgar riches, I made my headquarters, for my sins. Its wild and improbable decoration suited my mood.

11

The only sounds in the house were the ticking of a clock on the mantelpiece in this living-room, and somewhere the infrequent, parched dripping of water. Occasionally I heard a donkey bray harshly from the allotments at the back of the terrace, and once I heard the distant drone of a motorscooter, rising and descending in pitch as it negotiated corners. Otherwise everything was quiet. My explorations over, I waited downstairs with a furtive drink for the rest of the day to disclose itself. Now was the time to wish to be another, happier person, to absorb the quiet peacefulness of the house, to put aside my drink and climb the white stone stairs, release my wife from her itchy, creased bed, and drift with her out onto the veranda where the air was fresher and the humble muted donkey looked up at us like its comical counterpart in the Nativities of the early Italian Renaissance. (I am thinking here of something by Giotto or the Lorenzetti brothers, an altarpiece or a mural. Perhaps you know the type. They have about them a rapt and slightly bemused innocence.) I remained instead myself; the same. It was very hot and past lunchtime already. Rising wearily from my speculations I went into the kitchen, found a meal of sardines and some salad left for us in the double-breasted American-made refrigerator, and took it up to my wife – who refused to have anything to do with it. After we had traded looks of dismay, or perhaps disgust, I went downstairs again to get another drink – a tepid sherry, I think – and after that I went for a run.

It is time to confess that I am something of a fitness fanatic, and I take my running shoes with me wherever I go. I run, I train, I work out. I take these things seriously. Of course, by now, mid-afternoon, it was very hot indeed, but for obscure masochistic reasons I was keen to play the mad dog Englishman. My run was a long one. Too long, perhaps; I rather suffered towards the end of it, no longer caring if I trod on a chicken or kicked dust up into the glasses of café-ridden old men. By the time I got back to the house, my lips and mouth simmered under a crust of salt, my lungs had sucked themselves raw. Inside my wife was waiting for me.

'I wondered where you were, S. J.,' she said, 'you've been gone such a long time. Where did you go?'

I began to describe where I had been.

'Isn't it too hot to run?' she interrupted. I nodded. There was another, longer pause and then she said, 'I think I'll go to bed.' She said it as if she had been wondering for a long time how to phrase it.

'Bed?' I looked at my watch. It was half-past five.

'Tomorrow we'll go to a restaurant or something,' she murmured dejectedly from the foot of the stairs. And departed.

I looked at my watch again. It was now twenty-five to six. The rest of the evening mocked me. My first thought, I confess, was of alcohol. There was nothing to drink in the cavernous refrigerator – and nothing to eat now, either, apart from an egg, a half-empty jar of English marmalade, and a carton of withered olives. There was plenty of ice, of course, which I automatically put in a glass, and as the ice slowly melted I searched the cupboards one by one. Nothing. Beginning to feel that heat, I tried to turn the fan on; the switch seemed to jam. Then I tried to open a window, but it was locked. Such little obstinacies enrage me. I banged my glass down on the kitchen table, ejecting ice-cubes onto the floor, and immediately a lizard shot diagonally up the wall from behind the fridge and froze arbitrarily near a corner of the ceiling, three disgusting inches long, jet-black and completely terrified. I banged the glass a second time and the lizard shot back down the wall and disappeared behind the fridge. Lizards are not my favourite things. I rattled the cutlery tray for a few minutes to keep it frightened, then, thirsty and frustrated, I abandoned the kitchen for the living-room. It was here I discovered the second drinks cabinet.

Saved. Sing Alleluia. In fact most of the bottles it contained were of a dubious age, sticky around the mouth, with dribble-stained labels and semi-silted contents, but there was about half a litre of Scotch left in a relatively presentable state, which I immediately appropriated. I was suddenly content. I fetched my favourite book (the one I mentioned earlier; I seldom go anywhere without it) and settled back to contemplate those charming, sinister dreamscapes of the great European Symbolists, Moreau, Redon, Böcklin, Munch, Khnopff, Kubin, Toorop, and Puvis de Chavannes.

I have already let slip that I make my living by reviewing, among other things, the latest London exhibitions – perhaps you have even read some of my articles? – so it will not come as

13

entirely surprising to find me settling down to the enjoyment of such esoteric pleasures as these rather obscure late nineteenth-century Dutch, German, and French perverts can offer. I can claim professional interest. But in fact art has always meant much more to me than simply a part of my job. I will be frank: it is an obsession. I am, though I say it myself, thoroughly knowledgeable about the broad themes of European art from the Hellenic period to the present day, and I keep myself up-to-date with the latest significant happenings in this post-post-modern period of Radical Bad, *Anachronisti*, Neo-Pluralism, Genderism, Bunker Art, and all the rest of it. Even the most moronic art usually captivates me in the end; there is always, to the observant eye, a detail to redeem the most stultifying show. It is possible, in other words, to rise above what is offered and seize the unexpected. I have grown quite ecstatic at the sight of an interesting mould, tenderly rendered, on the skin of a single grape buried in an otherwise lifeless still-life; I have needed restraint on discovering a rivet hanging wonderfully loose from one of Anthony Caro's lacquered, girdered nonsenses. Such details compel a kind of worship. The detail, I find, is nearly always greater than the sum of the whole. It is truer.

Art-lover though I am, I am not, however, an artist. No, I have never attempted to paint or draw or sculpt. All my creativity, what is left of my original meagre fund of it, is diverted into my magazine work. Once, it is true, I thought of myself as a serious writer, a poet – and in fact while I was an undergraduate I had a slim volume of prenticepieces privately printed and circulated among friends. But I long ago renounced poetry for journalism. I preserved my sensibility to allow me the pleasures of objective appreciation I have already described.

All this sounds rather well organised, does it not? An unfortunate misapprehension. Because works of art fascinate me, I am often drawn to the artists who created them. Dead artists pose no problems; I simply read the biographies. Living artists can be disastrous. I am thinking now of a particular and pertinent example – my friend, the seducer of my wife. It was because of my regrettable weakness for his work that I first got to know him, and more recently had allowed myself to be persuaded to join his 'house party'; I had hoped to be diverted by his art, not his versions of life. This, at any rate, was the basis of the tragedy I am claiming, although there were also certain distressing complications which I will come to later. It is enough for the present to return to my whisky and book – the impressively titled *Cold Caresses of the Sphinx: Feminine Evil in Fin-de-Siècle Culture* – which kept me sane at a moment when I might easily have become rather desperate. The pictures are perfect. Whoever has seen Alfred Kubin's 'The Turkey', a key work of the period, or Arnold Böcklin's 'Island of the Dead', will understand what I mean. I was, at that moment, standing dubiously between the certain horrors of the recent past and the probable calamities of the future, and these pictures, with their delicate, dangerous women and weird animal-life, in which the imagination ripens and sickens and falls into a deathly state just short of death itself, seemed to point the way I was shortly to go. I was much calmed by my study of them. The whisky too played its part in this.

After a few more Scotches, say half a dozen, I became rather philosophical. Irrevocable disaster still stared me in the face, but instead of railing against it I began almost to accept it, to contemplate it at any rate. Lying on the sofa, with my book on my lap and my drink in my hand, I felt myself becoming slowly calm, reasonable, even sweet-tempered. When the illusion was complete I rose from the sofa and made my way mildly upstairs to our bedroom.

Thus trauma begins, with softly padding footsteps mounting the stairs . . . though to be entirely truthful, my footsteps did not sound soft at all. In fact I was alarmed to hear how loudly they echoed. The wall-lights in the stairwell were already on and my shadow, like the villain's silhouette in murder movies, loomed along the walls. For my own amusement I fitted an appropriate musical score to its silent, sinister progress, the gloomy second movement from Bartok's fifth string quartet. I hummed the last phrase as I reached our bedroom door, then listened in silence to my heart bump while I got my breath back. The door, stupidly, was locked. I rattled the handle uselessly.

'Poppet, it's me. Open the door.' ('Poppet' is not my wife's real name, of course, but it is what I habitually called her, originally out of affection, I think. Old habits die hard.) When I spoke there was a small noise from the other side of the door, though it was impossible to tell if this was a gurgle of plumbing or an incompetently suppressed sob.

'Poppet?' I rattled the handle again but the door remained closed. 'Poppet?' A whisper now. And then, from just behind the door, low down, she spoke.

'Please leave me alone. I can't talk to you now.'

I pondered this in the silence that followed. 'Why?' I asked eventually. No answer. 'Poppet, can you hear me?' My speech was limited to short staccato phrases due to a slight slur. 'Where am *I* going to sleep?'

'There's a bedroom on the floor below. I've made up the bed for you.'

'For Christ's sake, open the door. I'm not sleeping downstairs.'

'I'll see you in the morning.'

It hurt me to think of her sitting against that door, like Picasso's blue waif with her knees hugged up to her chin and a faraway look in her large eyes. Then I heard her get to her feet and move away towards the bed, *her* bed. Anger mingled with my pity. There was a sigh from the mattress as she lay down, then a lumpy creak as she turned over.

'Is it something I've done?' I said. 'Tell me. I swear I've no idea what it is. Talk to me.' I squatted down to squint through the keyhole but it was blind. She must have blocked it up.

'What is it?' I persisted. There was no answer.

Back downstairs, I tossed off another whisky or two and paced up and down the living-room, tempted to smash a Moorish artefact. The clock on the mantelpiece said a quarter to eight, a ridiculous time considering that Poppet was already in bed, and that I hadn't yet eaten lunch. There seemed to be very few options open to me. One of these was evidently drunkenness, into which I had ventured a little way, but it was too hot to drink seriously. I gulped down a last largish whisky and went to have a shower.

I don't think that I have mentioned yet that I take my personal hygiene very seriously. I shower at least once a day – or that is what I do in normal circumstances; in this case I had not showered for nearly a week, which indicates the degree to which Poppet's infidelity had disorientated me. My hair was stiff with scurf, my feet and armpits stank, my crotch was crawling with an itch no savagery of scratching could alleviate. All this of course is recognisable as a classic symptom of stress. I must have stayed under that shower for approximately an hour, rubbing, scrubbing, flushing, sluicing, until eventually I was more or less clean. I stepped from the shower, buffed myself briefly with a towel, and brushed my teeth five times. Pausing briefly to investigate the bathroom mirror, a complicated hinged triptych in which I was intrigued to see myself reflected from three different angles at once, face on, left profile, right profile – curiously reminiscent of Venetian portraiture of the sixteenth century, and also of the police identity photographs of our time – I then dressed and returned to the living-room, clean and refreshed.

It was now half-past nine and beginning to get dark, but a number of Spanish and Moorish artefacts unexpectedly proved to be table lamps, and together they illuminated the room with a delicate yellow light. I drew the curtains, and settled back with a Scotch and my book. But this time the caress of the Sphinx was withheld. Immediately I felt depressed again. Poppet's voice seemed to echo smugly in my ear: 'I've made the bed up for you,' she was saying, 'the bed downstairs, your bed, out of the way . . .' I began to pace again. What to do? Once, mid-stride, I paused by the digitalised telephone installed in an alcove, picked up the receiver and held one hovering finger over the dial as if to call somebody. But there was no one to call. After a moment or two I realised this and replaced the receiver. I began to pace again. It would be tedious to describe the anguish I felt, the circumstantial horror, the farcical improbability of my position. It is enough to say that I went on pacing – until suddenly a solution occurred to me, that splendid thing, or rather to be precise not so much a solution as My Own Back. I slammed down my empty glass on a table, or perhaps even dashed it to the floor, and, without bothering to collect my jacket, strode manfully out of the house.

Cool air pressed itself to my face. The twilight sky reflected darkly in the windows of the cottages. The one opposite ours was shuttered for the night, but a faint glow from an upstairs window was just visible. I saw all this quite clearly, as if sober.

At first I thought my knocks would go unanswered. Then I heard a scuffling upstairs and the light there grew brighter. For a while nothing else happened, and then, just as I was about to leave, the door gave a click and shuddered open an inch or two. The house was still in darkness but I could just make out the cropped silhouette of something vaguely resembling a face in the dark crack between doorjamb and frame.

'*Perdon*,' I said, with all the romance intonation I could muster. '*Momento por favor.*' The door swung open another inch and I discerned the rudimentary features of an elderly woman.

'*Bien*,' I said gratefully. '*Soy Ingles* (I am English). *No hablo muy bien el Español* (I speak terrible Spanish).'

I had reckoned on this burst of language being more or less conclusive, but in the inscrutable silence that followed I suffered a collapse of confidence and blurted out several questions in English. 'I'm on holiday,' I added lamely. Slowly the door began to close, but with the greatest possible rudeness I wedged my foot into the closing gap, startling the poor old woman who disappeared momentarily into the darkness of the background. I grovelled to make amends.

'*Perdon, perdon*,' I blathered. '*Por favor. Ingles. Momento. Emergencia.*' The door reopened and the woman barked out an unfamiliar angry word. '*Mucho gracio*,' I said humbly, '*Ingles.*' I tapped my chest emphatically. '*Emergencia.*' I looked as despairing as possible. Probably any self-respecting Spaniard would have wept in such a situation, but I had no such resources. I could see the old woman more clearly now, and she was very old and stooped and cross-looking. As I hastily attempted to placate her and explain my predicament, I was seized by the fantasy that she was not only unsympathetic to my fumblings with her language, but also deaf. I raised my voice and bellowed at her in demotic Catalan. She said nothing in reply except, once, the same unrecognisable word as before, uttered curtly like a command. It sounded something like *Righto*. Perhaps it meant sod off.

At last, in the midst of my incoherence, a meaningful phrase came to me. '*Necesito* (it is necessary),' I said, '*une escalera* (a ladder).' I pranced daintily as if climbing a ladder, my hands mounting invisible rungs. 'I have locked myself out,' I said slowly, 'and I *necesito une escalera* to get in through the window.' My hands dithered mid-air with imaginary shutters and I gave

18

a little wriggle to indicate successful entry. The old woman immediately began to laugh, toothlessly and silently but with obvious mirth. Delighted, I wriggled again and dived head first through my theoretical window. She laughed harder, and I began to giggle myself. Soon we were both roaring with laughter. It was then that I looked up and saw, standing behind the old woman, another figure slightly taller: an old man. He opened the door wide and stared at me in astonishment. Evidently this was *Righto*, her husband.

'Hello,' I said chummily, '*Ingles.*'

'Ah,' said the man thoughtfully. He looked at his wife, smiled, then turned back to me. 'I have English,' he exclaimed proudly. 'Ah yes. *Englishman!*' He gestured courteously, retreated with his wife, and I followed them into their home.

I got my ladder without any problems. My Spanish neighbours were unbelievably courteous, feeding me brandies as if I were an invalid, and offering me sticky old boiled sweets from a battered tin marked *Candy*. They seemed to assume that all Englishmen like boiled sweets, and I received mine like the sacrament and smacked my lips politely to simulate enthusiasm.

'Mm,' I said, 'good. *Bien*. In English we call this . . . *a boiled sweet*.' My hosts put on their astonished faces for no apparent reason, then burst into laughter. It was almost with a sense of disappointment that, some fifteen minutes later, I left, taking their ladder with me. '*Mañana, mañana* (tomorrow, tomorrow).' 'Is OK,' they said, waving their hands. Interpreting freely, I took this to mean that I didn't need to return the ladder until the following day.

I found my way to the back of the house via the allotments, breaking, I fear, a great many vegetables and flowers. Luckily the donkey was absent; I do not like donkeys at close range. Eventually, by using the ladder as a kind of rudder to keep my balance, swinging it from side to side as I outmanoeuvred knee-high grey-green cacti, patches of aloes, troughs and buckets, I gained the ground floor patio, and soon after that, the house-side. I placed the ladder silently under the window (it was the only window on that side on that floor, so I knew it was the right one), and slowly began to climb. I was not unaware of the irony of having to break into my own bedroom on the first night of what was originally planned as a romantic holiday ('A second honeymoon,' was the phrase we idly bandied between us) but all my thoughts were taken up with the difficult details of my ascent. By now it was quite dark. The rungs of the ladder were no more than whitish blurs in front of me, and the bedroom window was much higher than I had thought. By now, too, I was fully aware of my drunkenness, and I felt the whiskies and the brandies mingle together and set up a gentle swell in my stomach. The dark grainy stone of the house wall rose inch by inch to meet me, emerging out of my own speckled shadow. It appeared strangely soft and yielding in the dark, as if the ladder might sink into it, as into suet pudding. When I reached out and touched it, however, I found it to be cold and hard. Like the patio below. Far too afraid to stop, I climbed on until I reached the very top of the ladder. From here it was a short reach to the window ledge. I cautiously put up my right hand to fumble with the shutters, and they slowly swung open. My hands encountered no other resistance. Managing, mercifully, to think about nothing at all, I hauled myself upwards and inwards and, upside down, I crumpled onto the dusty tiled floor of the bedroom.

Poppet didn't wake up. I raised myself to a crouching position, and in the pitch dark moved stealthily forward to the bed. I put out my hand to wake my sleeping beauty – and discovered she was not there.

I found her in the living-room. I had just reached the bottom of the stairs when I heard her voice, low and conspiratorial, coming from down the hallway. I crept along, all ears, but could only make out a few discontinuous sentences: 'It's worse. I don't know what will happen. No. Tell me what to do. Please tell me.' Then I burst in through the door and found her crying by the telephone. The conversation was over. Evidently she had heard me coming.

'Phoning the underworld?' I asked.

'What do you mean?' she replied in alarm.

'Nothing,' I said, 'nothing. A joke. Relax.' My tone was deceptively nonchalant. 'Do you want a drink?'

She nodded miserably, and I remembered how little drink there was. 'It's whisky,' I said. 'Hot or cold?' As it happened I had left the ice-cube tray out in the humid kitchen, so we had our whisky warm and sticky.

At Poppet's suggestion we now took our drinks, and the bottle, up to the second-floor veranda which, by means of potted plants, wall-creepers and hanging baskets, had been converted into a miniature jungle. Here, sitting at a table in a tiny clearing, we at last began grudgingly to talk.

'Beautiful, isn't it?' Beyond the distant hills the last vivid flecks of sunset were fading.

'Beautiful.'

'Nice to be out here.'

'Yes.'

'Can you tell me what's wrong?'

'No.'

'Would you like another warm drink?'

'No.'

An indubitable heart-to-heart. A little brief perhaps.

I took out my cigarette packet, a provocative gesture on my part. Poppet disliked me smoking. I had taken it up only recently, but had already learnt to toss cigarettes into my mouth from an arm's-length away, a rather pathetic little accomplishment you might say, but I never failed to be impressed. I threw one up now and caught it deeply, rather too deeply, a swallow-job in fact, if I may make use of the appropriate jargon. I removed the soaking cigarette from the back of my throat unabashed and replaced it raffishly in the corner of my mouth. I smiled falsely as tricksters do, into the din of imagined applause, and reached for the whisky bottle.

'Nice out to be here,' I said, mismanaging the words slightly.

'You're drunk,' Poppet retorted, 'you've drunk nearly the whole bottle.'

It was then that I lost my head and did a very regrettable thing. I seized Poppet's hand and started violently to kiss her wrists. Why did I do this? I do not know. I was simply overpowered by a desire to smother her with passion. Like some demented clockwork Casanova I pecked and gobbled along the underside of her wrists and up her arms, moaning to myself, mounting slowly to her narrow shoulders. Frequently I muttered her name, Poppet, Poppet, Poppet, Poppet, not her proper name of course, as I have said, but the term of affection we commonly used. It was deeply embarrassing. I have no idea what came over me. And when the crazed impulse passed I

21

found myself stranded high and dry with my lips battened onto Poppet's collarbone.

It was actually Poppet's sense of humour that rescued me. I felt her neck swell under my lips and then she began to giggle. 'What on earth are you doing?' she asked.

I had no idea. Perhaps it had been an unconscious attempt to recall her to old ways and feelings. It was all so useless.

Abruptly Poppet got up and walked round the table. She seemed not to want to remain near me. Her dressing-gown clung to her buttocks as she walked. I knew every inch of those buttocks, every tender shift of weight, each sheen and shadow across her skin. We had not made love for a number of nights. Since discovering her in bed with my ex-friend I had consciously repressed my own desire and resisted hers (if it was desire and not habit), knowing that we would never make love again. Now I somewhat regretted my principled chastity. But it was not love that aroused me now; opportunistic lust, perhaps – let me be frank about this. Poppet shifted her position and I saw her in profile. Her breasts were flattened by the fold of her dressing-gown: the thick knot of the belt sat softly on her belly. As she moved to rub a yawn out of her eyes, a part of me was aroused, animal that I am.

'Let's have sex on the veranda,' I said casually. If I had expected her to start with alarm at the suggestion, I was disappointed. She smiled, and without turning to face me, said, 'Too hard.'

'What do you mean, too difficult?'

'I mean, hard on the knees.'

I tapped the tiled floor with the thick sole of a running shoe, and considered. Possibly she was right, but I resented truth being on her side. 'Not if we stand up,' I said cunningly.

She smiled again and moved away, blending with shadows. When she reached the low wall of the far edge of the veranda, she sat down. 'I can hardly keep my eyes open,' she sang softly through the darkness, 'let alone stand up.'

I helped myself to the last of the whisky, a messy, clinking manoeuvre. My hands were no longer steady. 'Then I shall force you,' I said loudly. Naturally I intended to do nothing of the kind. It was a joke, ha ha. 'Hide-and-seek,' I said. 'I shall count to fifty with my eyes closed, and then, with my eyes

22

open, I shall hunt you down like a wild rutting beast. One, two, three, four, five . . .' I thought she might hide to amuse me. It was no more than I deserved. I imagined her crouching invisibly behind a short, fat cactus with its leathery, pudgy limbs and phosphorescent spines, the neckline of her dressing-gown falling forwards so that I could see the divided pale luminosity of her hanging breasts, and, below them, the soft gleam of skin moulding her ribs, and, below that, the dark, vulnerable undulation of her belly as she breathed, and below everything, a hint – no more – of the sheltered pubes. I was afflicted by erotica, as I sometimes am, there is little point in hiding it.

When I had finished counting, although the veranda was conveniently crowded with obstacles, it took me less than two minutes to ascertain that Poppet was no longer about. The door to the bedrooms, still swinging on its hinges, rather gave the game away. It creaked as it swung; three croaks, how biblical. At least this time I was not locked out. As I entered the room, I saw Poppet standing by the window opposite, with her back to me, skinny, skimpily dressed, like one of the Lautrec's washed-out prostitutes. She had taken off her dressing-gown and I was distressed to see that she had put on a lacy nightdress that we usually reserved for moments of special intimacy, I mean of love, or at least sex – not of anger, as now.

I didn't want the tender feelings that nightie burdened me with, and I disliked the necessity of approaching her, as I did, softly and amorously on tiptoe, resentfully taking gentle hold of her from behind and then circling her with my arms. She didn't turn, but bowed her head and trembled a little, presenting me with the delicate hot skin at the back of her neck and shoulders, to which I moistly pressed my lips. Murmuring inarticulacies, I palpated her belly through the gauzy pink material with the palms of my hands, working gradually upwards over her padded ribs, one by one, and upwards further.

A moment later I slipped the dress's straps off her shoulders and drew the whole thing over her still submissive head. Her nakedness was frightening and beautiful. She turned, looked up, and began to cry angrily. Between sobs I made out her stuttering, beaten, desperate heart's truth: 'Leave me alone. I don't love you. I hate you. Doing this. Leave me. Please, leave.'

23

This was how it began, or, if you like, how it ended. Whatever I said to her during those endless hours of argument her violent outburst provoked, I suppose I should regret, but I don't. What *she* said I should like to forget: I can't. Luckily the briefest summary of it all should serve my purpose in this account, viz., that with my special coercion and the demands of our mutual fate, Poppet eventually made a full confession, enabling me to divorce myself from her for ever. She also made the incidental claim, if I understood her correctly, that I no longer loved her, a shot in the dark if ever I heard one.

It all sounds rather simple as I write it down, but in reality it was horribly complicated and protracted. We must have talked (I mean raged and wept) for about five hours, pausing only once when Poppet fell asleep, and I, eventually noticing this, broke off what I was saying and took the opportunity to sit down for ten minutes or so. Then Poppet woke up, or I woke her up, and we continued as before. Her behaviour throughout was unusually erratic and violent. Mine was efficient and insulting. We were both images of our altered passions; in fact when I knew that everything I had imagined was true, I realised we were altered entirely, not into strangers (novelistic glib inexactitude) but into our true selves, as Shakespearean characters disclose their real identities in the final act. However, while Poppet and her lover had joyously abandoned their masks, mine was ripped from me against my will. Naturally I was not overjoyed to recognise myself as the cuckold of the piece, an idiotic Hamlet betrayed as much by his own lack of perspicacity as by the eager venery of friends. I had not quite seen things this way until that night in Sóller. Then I understood how Poppet and I had changed: certain assumptions no longer counted; mutual understandings had ceased to exist. I couldn't ask her to explain why she wasn't happy (obviously she was extremely unhappy) because that wasn't my role any more, and she no longer had any business to explain her emotions to me. Instead we confined ourselves to accusation, denial, and confession. Only once, towards the end, did I show any signs of curiosity in the workings of Poppet's affair:

'Why him?' I screamed. 'Have you *no* taste?'

'Do you really think he loved *me*?' she screamed back. '*Me*?' Inarticulate sobs obscured the rest, and, lapsing into silence, she fixed me with a hateful stare. What she said, if I have got it right, was of course meaningless, I merely record it. Her confession, the definitive version, followed shortly afterwards, I need hardly repeat it here, it was entirely predictable – but I suppose it served its purpose as the inevitable and indeed overdue dénouement. There was nothing now for me to do but leave Poppet sobbing, and begin to pack.

I was in a taxi again and travelling south almost before I knew it. Evidentally I had been at my most decisive – and once I had decided to go, never more to darken her illicit fun, Poppet had been irritatingly acquiescent. I do not remember her trying to stop me leaving once. It seemed that one minute I was dragging my suitcase out of the wardrobe, and the next I was negotiating my passage in incomprehensible Spanish with the taxi-driver – whom I recognised, to my horror, from our trip to the villa only hours before. And then, exasperated into silence, I was whisked away through the narrow dark streets, peevishly refusing to look back and therefore not seeing my fat suitcase standing in a pool of yellow lamplight outside our door.

This, I must remember, was the character of my furious escape. The taxi windows were misted over, making it difficult to see, for the second time in swift succession, the first light of dawn fringing the hills. Scratchy English pop blared from the radio, teenage voices chirruping to me in my own language of love and fun and money, while I sat in a daze, fingers tapping on the seat, unable to let out the howl I felt swelling slowly deep inside me. When we reached Palma airport I realised that I had left my suitcase behind. Hurling myself out of the taxi to be met by a freezing blast of wind (Why are airports always windy? Do aeroplanes still need a good breeze behind them?) I gave my driver a lethal smile and an enormous tip, intending major insult. He took both smile and tip without the slightest acknowledgement, and drove slowly away. Even before I had reached the Departures Lounge I felt my first headache beginning to pulse in my temples.

There was no relief for me in the airport. The bar was closed. I could not, though I tramped miles through the wincingly bright corridors, find a duty-free shop. In any case, as I discovered later attempting to buy a coffee, I had given all my

25

money to the surly taxi-driver. There was nothing to be done about my atrocious sobriety. I surrendered myself to the plastic moulded seats and, hugging my holdall to my chest, planned my revenge. By this, of course, I refer to the revenge I was plotting against myself – I had already done what I could to hurt Poppet. The first inklings of suicide began to buzz in my brain.

And yet, both in the airport terminal and later on the plane, even while I occupied myself with thoughts of my future (radically abbreviated though it was to be), details of the tawdry drama I had forced to a climax only a few hours earlier kept returning to my memory. Set speeches still rang in my ears, faces loomed.

First there was Poppet's face, wearing the expression it had worn at the moment when she fatefully confessed her love for her seducer. She was looking directly at me for perhaps the only time in our long argument. I could see how wet her face really was, every detail of it soaked through: her eyes, usually a flinty grey, seemed to have completely dissolved; her mouth was a three-year-old's, blubbery and vividly red; a bubble of snot, inflating and collapsing as she breathed, blocked one nostril – a shame, as her nose, pert and delicate, was her best feature. But strangely enough I felt neither pity nor disgust for this face in front of me, I merely registered that it was Poppet's and that it was making too much noise.

Then there was the face of her erstwhile lover, my friend, whose grinning features, I think, had haunted us both while we argued. He was one of those people whose faces are too big for their heads. It overlapped his skull at every point; it hung from his chin and jaw and piled up around his mouth and under his eyes, dividing his features with deep shadow. And the look of disdain that was his usual expression seemed to exaggerate this fleshiness, as if he wanted to overpower everyone with his sheer physical weight. The effect, however, was not so much intimidating as unfortunate; when he smirked at you with his camel-lips distended, you did not feel overawed, you felt either disgusted or amused. What I am trying to say is that he was not, in any sane sense of the word, an attractive man. This was for me one of the most painful and curious details in the whole painful, curious affair. Simply by recalling

26

his awful ugliness, I was again initiated into the full mystery of my wife's love for him, why she so joyously sacrificed herself to his pasty, sluggish body, his atrocious manners, his BO, scummy hair, eczema and wind. What was his attraction? I was not unaware of the irony that this man's appearance held me as spellbound as it did my wife, though, I need hardly assure you, the fascination was of a different character.

Finally, I saw a third face – my own, as I had happened to see it reflected in a mirror during my final argument with my wife. It had been like this:

Poppet and I are standing in our bedroom in Majorca, facing each other across dark shadow. Our gestures, staccato and unfinished, are stiffly lit by twin shafts of moonlight passing through two windows high in the wall to my right. *Why did you sleep with him? Why so often? Why, Poppet why? Speak, say something for Christ's sake.* But she can't speak. All she can do is weep, hiding her face in her wet hands so I won't see how scrunched up and helpless it is. *You don't love me.* By the viciousness in my voice I can tell we are nearing the end of the argument. *You love him.* She is trembling, and I understand that she longs to run from the room, but is transfixed by her fear, like Daphne touched by Apollo. And then there comes a sudden moment of silence, a moment of fragility which exposes to me her awful meekness; unbearable. And so I flinch away, and unintentionally catch sight of myself in the mirror above the dressing-table.

This is it. I see my face within the mirror's circular frame, blandly, perfectly composed, regarding me without the slightest sign of animation or interest. It is, I have to admit, a handsome face. Admiringly I note the purity of its features, the large, bright eyes, the strong nose, the small but sensuous mouth, the pale smooth brow that contrasts so strikingly with the crinkled hair which rises above it. But though the face is expressionless now, I can easily imagine the shapes it might adopt: the forehead buckled by a crease of anger, lips compressed into a sneer, a cheek drilled by the classic twitch of fading self-control. I like these alternatives; rage obviously suits me. I watch my quiet face as if it were the face of an actor, wondering what transformations might be rising angrily to the surface. Then, remembering myself, I turn towards Poppet, to shout more

27

effectively. *Have you no bloody taste?* Again, I see her dash her face into her hands. Really, how appallingly inessential this scene is, how pointless and unforgivable. I am faintly surprised that we don't stop immediately, and continue with something more interesting . . . But when I look towards the mirror again, it is from a different angle and the glass is full of unfathomable shadow. There is only the sound of my voice thrashing on in the darkness.

Three faces in a triptych, mine, hers, his. A triptych I can make no sense of: is this really all I have salvaged from the past?

I have delayed as long as I could, but it is unfortunately impossible to continue without formally introducing my wife's lover. His name was Henry Hippolytus Fluck. An unusual name, is it not? And let me remind those who foolishly maintain that a name bears no definite relation to the person who bears it that, on the contrary, both life and literature thrive on unusual names. Silas Tomkin Comberbache, Smelfungus, Humbert Humbert, Englebert Humperdink, Henry Hippolytus Fluck – these people are not normal, their lives are curlicued by the same twists as their names, they eschew the decent obscurity upheld by the rest of us. It is interesting to note also how often the possessor of a ridiculous name belongs to a family of the English upper classes. Fluck certainly did, though in him ancestral distinction had faded in every respect but the pretension of his name. It is not, however, my aim to offer a psychology of nomenclature. I introduce Fluck because he is regrettably essential to the story of my wife's affair, though by the time my wife confessed this to me, the affair was over and he was dead.

Yes, dead. Surely I have mentioned this before, at least in passing? Perhaps not. *Mea culpa*: his death has some bearing on the rest of the story. It was when he died, in fact, that I realised I had lost my wife's love for ever.

The morning of the day Poppet and I flew to Majorca, the body of Henry Fluck was found on the beach below his cottage. He had drowned a few hours earlier, according to the autopsy, and his corpse had duly floated ashore and deposited itself on solid ground. The judgement of the inquest, as I heard later,

28

was death by misadventure, i.e. a combination of extreme inebriation, natural clumsiness, and an inability to swim, but I do not believe it. It is my opinion that Fluck killed himself. The reasons for his suicide may be obscure, certainly, but I have a strong feeling that Fluck, the Great Abuser, finally inflicted on himself the ultimate abuse, preceding me in this, as in all other things.

The day that his body was discovered I cannot remember in any great detail. The night before, at a party given by Fluck to mark the end of our holiday with him, I had been insensibly drunk, and in accordance with certain laws of biology, the following day I was almost insensibly ill. It was in fact a day of the fresh and sprightly sort, with blinding blue skies and high, loose cloud and a smack in the blustery breeze – but I spent most of it indoors, periodically vomiting and querulously asking the others what was going on as we endured successive waves of ambulancemen, police, relatives, and assorted hangers-on. I understood, of course, even in my weakened condition, that Fluck was dead, and of course I should have triumphed, but I did not. I sank into the most awful depression. This dead Fluck was permanently elusive and unpunishable. And I knew that Poppet's lust for him, still unsatisfied – such was its size – would linger on, acquiring in time a kind of faded poignancy like a memento of pressed flowers kept between the leaves of a favourite book.

First to arrive were the ambulancemen. Glassy-eyed and gloomy, I watched from an upstairs window as the ambulance drew up outside in a brisk shimmer of dust, and its white-coated occupants set off with their collapsible stretcher down the path to the beach. They were led by Poppet, who knew the way. I remember the ambulancemen struggling over unfamiliar bumps and craters to keep up with her unusually quick, knifing strides. She seemed small and frail beside them, like an elf leading humans to the underworld. When they disappeared from sight I tottered off to bed and was apparently still there long after the party returned bearing Fluck on a stretcher, and drove him, or it, away to a hospital for tests.

The police arrived next. There were two of them. Someone fetched them tea and some sandwiches left over from the night before, and I was dragged from my sickbed, a little blue in the face, but conscious, and breathing fairly normally. My testimony was naturally going to be useless because, like many of the other post-party-goers assembled in the living-room, I remembered very little from the night before, though this didn't prevent me, along with everyone else, suffering vividly from an imcomprehensible sense of guilt. I suppose that's what policemen do to you. The mere presence of them seemed to inspire the most extraordinary urge to confess something – anything. During the interview I also had constant difficulty keeping down whatever remained in my stomach – it couldn't have been much, perhaps it was the stomach itself.

We all entered the room decorously. I refused tea and avoided looking at the canapés and sausage rolls. I seated myself near the door in case of unexpected accidents. There were about eight of us: Poppet and me, Moyra and Myra, Angel and three people I dimly recognised from the party but whose names I did not remember and who affected not to remember me at all. Of those assembled, I was in the feeblest physical condition.

The policemen – who were no more animated than us – sat behind a battered gate-leg table at the far end of the room, conversing in quiet, weary voices. As soon as we had settled down, the interview got under way. One of the policemen (he was short and chubby, with bristling red hair and a soft voice) swallowed tea, belched agreeably to put us at our ease, got to his feet and explained why he was obliged to ask certain questions. The situation, he told us languidly, was grave, but his sympathies, he added, were with us. We mumbled acquiescently, ready to cooperate.

'First of all,' he said, glancing round, 'I'll need a statement from the person who found the body.'

Although this was a reasonable request, it produced only a nervous silence. 'Am I wrong,' he asked, 'in thinking that someone here found the body?' He slowly sheafed through his notes. We all looked at Poppet. Poppet looked at me. I was the one who had found Fluck's body. I cleared my throat.

'I found him,' I said. Everyone swivelled round. 'With Poppet. We were together.'

This was a difficult thing for me to say, because I rightly suspected that my discovery of Fluck's body was not widely known by the people in the room. Poppet knew, of course, she

30

had been with me, but because she had been the one to announce the discovery and alert the authorities and so on, everybody rather assumed that she had found the body herself. In my weakened condition, when I could hardly speak let alone defend myself, this misconception was marvellously convenient. In fact I almost wish Poppet had sustained it for longer, it would have done her no harm; but no, ill though I was, she chose to expose me when I was least able to articulate the precise nature of my discovery.

'It was me,' I repeated in a tone midway between abject horror and haughty indignation. Public scrutiny does strange things to one's tone of voice, not to mention one's levels of nausea. As I spoke, as nine pairs of eyes fixed on me, boggling cartoonishly with astonishment, I fought to ignore a rising knot of acid in my stomach; fought also to quell the sudden, bitter sense of outrage I felt, at the way Fluck's week's worth of guilt seemed, in a single moment, to have been neatly transferred to me.

'I found him,' I said uncertainly, 'or it; I mean, the body; Henry's . . .' I began to hiccup. Immediately a glass of water was brought to me which I drank in sloppy emotional gusts. 'We both found . . .' I said catching my breath in deep sobs, '. . . on the beach. It was . . .' I gulped '. . . just there . . . on the sand . . .'

My topographical inexactitude must have been frustrating, but at last the mood of the room started to change, thank god. People began to murmur sympathy. I may even have cried a little – with shock, you understand – which would have helped. The interview was temporarily suspended. Behind their desk the policemen lounged and ate canapés while I lay on the floor with someone's cool hand, perhaps Poppet's, on my hot brow until I felt strong enough to sit back in my chair. 'All right now?' asked the red-headed policeman at last, with his mouth full, and handing us a couple of official forms, he advised both Poppet and me that we could make written statements if we preferred.

After this initial contribution, I did not participate further in the interview but instead devoted my attention to my official form. It would be nice, I thought, to write Fluck's obituary as I might have done for one of my regular magazines, or to be

31

more ambitious, for *Artforum* or *Village Voice*. 'Henry Hippolytus Fluck, who was among us in the Village only briefly, has died. His achievements are not particularly numerous. Exhibitions: none. Features: none. Sales: none. Seldom has an artist died with less recognition. But let us not forget that, in the end, he put his genius not into his work but into his life. I refer to his brilliant and bold seduction of . . .' No, I could not write his obituary. In any case, all the form had room for was a couple of extended sentences concerning discovery of the body. I didn't have a lot to say, it is true, but there was not much that could be said in two sentences. The first sentence came easily. 'Intending to dispel my blinding headache and perhaps also to purge my general nausea, I walked with my wife down to the beach and there discovered the bloated corpse of Henry Hippolutus Fluck whom I loathed and despised above any other human being.' Did I smile at this? Certainly when I looked up, Poppet was frowning at me angrily. I returned Poppet's look with equal hostility, and as she turned away I saw that her cheek was streaked with tear-tracks. The second sentence of my statement, I decided, would be as dully factual as the first. 'The face of the corpse was so swollen and corroded as to be almost unrecognisable, but when we at length realised who it was, my wife and I were extremely distressed, which indicated her inability to grasp essentials and my failure to avoid them.'

I did not last much longer in the interview. About ten minutes later I was abruptly obliged to leave it. Naturally, I was afraid that such suspicious behaviour as bolting from the room would be the final self-accusatory act necessary to my immediate arrest, but, strangely, I received a spontaneous show of sympathy and the red-haired policeman even rose to his feet to offer assistance – the most energetic thing he had done all afternoon. Regrettably I was unable even to acknowledge him in my rush for the door.

It was, perhaps, during the long hour I subsequently spent on my knees, back teeth afloat, weepily embracing the toilet bowl that I realised the full implication of Fluck's death. It wasn't just that I could now never revenge myself on him, nor that Poppet would never cease loving him (and by implication hating me); I felt the first dim recognition that my own life had lost all purpose and was as good as over.

Eventually I returned to bed. For the others, however, there were 'interrogations', and as I discovered later from various sources, the police were provided with a number of interesting points of information. One of my friends, the last to see Fluck alive, told them that Fluck had been 'drunk and boisterous' at his party, which is perfectly true as far as I remember, though he had been boisterous all week, for other reasons. Apparently the two of them had talked together just prior to Fluck leaving the cottage for the beach, ostensibly to study the effects of moonlight on the water for a painting he had in mind. As he was a painter, this was not unlikely. My friends stressed the drunken Fluck's unusual high spirits, erratic conversation, and physical unsteadiness – all, in my view, symptomatic of a suicidal state of mind. Fluck's drunkenness was especially significant as he did not normally drink. Everyone testified to this, although only Poppet suggested a reason for his sudden intemperance. According to her, Fluck had planned to show a number of his pictures to a gallery owner that night, but he, like most other invitees, had failed to turn up to the party. The pictures, which Fluck had spent hours fixing to the walls of all the downstairs rooms (including the lavatory, can you believe it?), went unnoticed except by the faithful few, I mean ourselves, who had already seen the pictures countless times, enduring Fluck's loquacious explications of their numerous beauties and profundities. Poppet also mentioned – in passing, as it were – that recently her beloved Henry had suffered almost constant denials and rebuttals of his genius (from whom?), and since an unsuccessful sojourn in Bohemian Greenwich Village, New York, a year earlier, his confidence had been low. Frankly, if this is true, it merely supports my argument for suicide.

In the end I imagine the immediate circumstances of his death revealed most. Firstly, Fluck was incredibly, preternaturally clumsy. There was little he could be expected to do without falling over. If he had really planned to go clambering over slimy rocks in the middle of the night, then I can only express surprise that the calamity was confined to his own death. He could easily have dragged, smothered, or crushed to death any number of other living things in his wake. Secondly, he was very drunk, drunker than the eye-witness reports suggested. An empty bottle of whisky was apparently found in his overcoat pocket. Thirdly, perhaps most importantly, Fluck could not swim, as everyone knew. It made him a rather bizarre figure, especially as he lived by the sea, but he enjoyed being bizarre.

These points, as I imagine them detailed on a police memorandum, led to a conclusion so plausible as to be completely tedious: Fluck killed himself, either by accident or by design. But these details suggest nothing more than the bare workings of a particular fate. What do they express of Fluck's sexual gloatings, or Poppet's eager submission, or my constant self-conscious, irrelevant grief? Nothing. They bypass the whole appalling drama. Imagine a performance of *Hamlet* in which Claudius dies peacefully of natural causes halfway through the first act. It is for me to return now to rediscover the real story, give it essence and meaning, without which Fluck's death and (to anticipate a little) my own – and what I hope will be Poppet's undying misery – will be no better than itemised inferences on official notepaper.

There are a number of things to add to my account of that breezy, queasy, policeman-infested day, not least my actual discovery of Fluck's body. I do not now remember what trivial summary I concocted for the purpose of my official form, I expect it was apposite, consistent, concise (of course), and evasive of essential truth. I did not lie, God forbid, but I omitted to be all-inclusive. Here, then, is a more extended version.

I did not want to wake up at all that morning, not after that dreadful party, not after those wretched few hours' sleep on the dining-room's freezing parquet floor. My neck ached, both knees were crushed, my temples throbbed. In my mouth were the salty remnants of something I couldn't identify. Worst of all, my right hand was bruised and swollen; inoperative. I had not realised before how remarkably difficult it is to rise from a prone position without the use of one hand. At my third painful attempt, I managed it, and limped clear of the surrounding detritus of glasses, beer cans, ash trays, sleeping bodies. Eventually, by chance, I found myself in the conservatory, where I was overtaken by the exigencies of my condition. With unexpected clarity I remember the sudden steam rising off the terracotta tiles, and the pattering of liquid on the broad unresponsive leaves of a potted plant. Then Poppet accosted me in somewhat disapproving tones, and after this my memory becomes confused until some time later when she had led me outside. I suppose it must have been difficult for her, carrying me. It may have taken her several minutes.

We sat on the garden wall and looked out to sea. Waves were barely visible through a hanging veil of mist which filled the middle sky, but which was already being dissolved by sunlight, a shattering brightness above grey fizz. Gulls screamed inconsiderately; the wet breeze jarred against me like a slap. My bad hand bulged tenderly into my lap. Breathing deeply, I tried to calm my queasy stomach by focussing my mind on the distant waves; but the whitecaps that rose and descended and spilt as I counted reminded me of froth on lager, endless quantities of it, perpetually swaying and sinking, and before I had counted beyond twenty I turned aside and vomited indiscreetly over a bog violet which was handy in the rockery. After that I felt much better.

'Shall we walk now?' asked Poppet. Her voice was oddly strained. Perhaps, like me, she had a hangover. The wind twirled her hair about her face, obscuring it in a strangely unnerving way, and I noticed that her arm was about my waist, presumably for comfort or support. Beckettian, we tottered off together, often stumbling when our platform shoes encountered an irregularity in the path, or the flapping flares of our trousers encumbered our steps.

Perhaps at this point our dress requires some explanation. It is simply that the theme of Fluck's party the night before had been 'The Culture and Style of the 1970s'. It was his little joke. Dress, music, dancing and even food were limited to 70s styles. We played Slade and T Rex and Gary Glitter, those dinosaurs of glamrock, and stomped sweatily through half-remembered versions of the jive and the twist and the 'Bump'. When exhausted, we sat out and drank filthy cocktails the colour of lipstick and the consistency of phlegm, and smoked cheap cocktail cigarettes. In Fluck's opinion, only certain periods of the eighteenth century had been quite so frantically tasteless. 'Louis XIV invented glamrock,' he said. 'We are the inheritors of the Enlightenment.' We had curled our hair in imitation of the page-boy cut, painted our cheeks with blusher, fabricated side-burns out of cotton wool dyed black, and dusted our foreheads with glitter. Poppet and I wore the relics of our teenage years, years from which I remember only a little, but with definite distaste. It seems remarkable, but between 1973 and 1979, the years of my secondary education, I cannot remember a single occasion when I was happy . . . But I digress. Poppet and I had brought with us costumes of identical absurdity: decorated shirts, slim-fit tank tops, flared trousers, and platform shoes. The colours of our costumes (gold, lilac, crimson) clashed badly, but this we considered *de rigueur*.

That we might wake up the morning after, hungover, in this fashion apparatus and that it would so deepen our misery and make our locomotion so difficult, was not something that had really occurred to us. However, crippled though we were, we maintained a lame stumbling forward along the path. Whenever we came across a particularly hazardous section, Poppet held me firmly by the hand. The gesture, once commonplace, now obsolete, puzzled me, as did numerous other small demonstrations of care. On one occasion she fixed me with a searching, tender look, and said, 'First we have to walk it off. We have to do that first,' she repeated, 'before we can begin to do anything else.' In my weakness, I responded to her with thoughtless gratitude, sometimes even stretching out my hand towards hers, always expecting ready support. And so we proceeded, clinging together around the twists and over the switchbacks of the path that ran along the bluff between high gorse hedges and blown heather towards the sea, each lost in our own thoughts.

Only when we reached the tangle of crab apple trees halfway down the dramatic descent to the beach, did I begin to look about me with any interest. I was beginning to feel slightly less moribund by then. It was among these trees, I remember, as we were resting, sitting on a mossy bank, that a butterfly came down suddenly through shafts of light and shadow, and landed on Poppet's head. It seemed a rather poor specimen to me, dizzy and jaundiced; perhaps it had been drinking. It soon took off again, and we watched its erratic glancing flight until it disappeared amongst the trees. I noticed then that my hand was in Poppet's, apparently had been in hers for some time, her cold fingers softly moulding my cold knuckles. For a moment we stayed like this, perhaps mutually surprised at the

36

simplicity of these, our hands, and then I slowly withdrew mine, and we rose without a word and continued on our way.

I did not want to remember the night before, but could not help myself. Fluck's party had been the most miserable experience of my life. Somehow Poppet and Fluck must have thought that the general jollity would camouflage their amour, not realising that partygoers are by habit principally occupied with the observation of others. Everyone saw them. I myself saw them constantly, even after I had begun to avoid them, fleeing their frivolous entwining gestures and smoothly interlocking smiles. They were, to use an old and inadequate word, brazen. Had they fallen to the floor and rutted openly, they could not have been more explicit. On several occasions, it is true, they saw fit to retreat upstairs for lengthy periods, returning later with the one satisfied smirk on both their faces, but these retreats were not prompted by modesty. Oh no. Once I tried to follow them and had to turn back, not because they were elusive, but on the contrary because they were so ostentatious. I could not bear the thought of rounding a corner and tripping over them. It was my fate, I suppose, to be merely accessory to their goings-on, a skulker, if I may grow Keatsian for a moment, alone and palely loitering.

After such behaviour the night before, Poppet's tender ministrations this morning were unexpected and unsettling. At first I could make no sense of it, although I considered it with care – such care as I was able to muster. Some way beyond the crab apple trees, she took a deep breath and opened her mouth to speak, and I was suddenly convinced she was about to make a full confession of her infidelity – a histrionic, tender, abject confession. I was mistaken.

'It's not the platform shoes,' she said, 'that are making you stumble. You're still drunk.'

Now that our pace had picked up on the downhill, my gait was even wilder than before. I was also hampered by the fact that the skyscraper sole of one of my shoes had come adrift.

'You drank so much last night,' she went on, 'I'd be surprised if you remembered anything.' She sighed. 'But you were funny,' she said, 'in the games.'

This was a comment of such ambiguity as to be redundant. I could not remember anything about games. We walked on for

37

a while in silence. Now that we were nearing the shore, the breeze had grown brisker and damper, and some degree of self-control began to return to me. I unhooked my hand from Poppet's and walked, or rather hobbled, unaided. This small measure of independence was, of course, symbolic as well as practical, and I noticed that Poppet began to look at me anxiously. I turned away from her pretty face, not wanting to be a prey to feelings that were now obsolete and, properly speaking, should have been dead. Eventually – we were about to cross the narrow stretch of shingle between path and beach – she spoke again.

'Henry finished my picture last night.'

We began to crack and slither our way across the loose pebbles, causing a noise which prevented further conversation. Ahead of us, above the white crusts of waves breaking crisply far out at sea, the mist was rapidly dissolving. Gulls bobbed delicately or scrambled in the breakers, screaming idiocies. I saw one of them bank abruptly from the water, trailing a sliver of silver from its beak, to be immediately pursued by three other gulls cursing it loudly; and silently, with great concentration, I willed all four birds to plummet from the air and vanish with a gurgle into the sucking mouths of tiny, revengeful fish. They didn't. Instead a dog appeared in the distance, cavorting alone on the beach. Perhaps it was mad. Its barks floated across to us. It seemed to be heading, like us, for the isolated group of rocks that stood in the centre of the beach. Then Poppet and I reached the end of the shingle and she began to talk again.

'Did you hear what I just said?' she asked. 'Henry's finished my picture. I thought you were interested in his pictures.' I shrugged.

'He's going to show it to us today,' said Poppet brightly. I scowled, trying to be off-putting; I clutched my stomach and groaned.

'He finished it last night at the party,' she repeated. 'He kept calling me away every few minutes to pose for him; I didn't want to go, but he was so funny telling jokes, I went anyway. He's hilarious,' she said, 'don't you think? I don't know what it is, but I can't stop laughing at him. I don't think he knows he's being funny half the time. It's just him. Do you know what I mean?'

'No,' I said.

'You'll be interested in the painting,' she went on, changing tack. 'I don't know anything about it, but you'll know. It's painted in a mixture of oil and something else too. He told me, sounds like gauche or gosh or . . .'

'Gouache,' I said. There was a pause and she frowned at me. 'Thickened watercolour, basically,' I added.

'That's right. I knew you'd know. You're so clever about these things.' As she finished speaking, she attempted to engage my hand again, but I quickly stuffed it in my pocket.

'Sulky boy,' she said in a childish voice usually reserved for love-play, 'just because he drank too much last night and he's got a headache.' I began to say that on the contrary I felt much better, but the lie stuck in my throat, curse it.

'What do you call the little trowel thing he uses?' she asked.

'Palette knife,' I said shortly, but adding, despite myself, 'Cézanne used it quite frequently.'

'He's the man who did mountains, isn't he?' she said. 'Tell me about him.'

But I did not tell her about him. I was thinking about Fluck painting Poppet.

Fluck's ambition to paint the Great English Nude, sparked off by Wessellman's series of paintings, Great American Nude, was well-known among his friends – 'In order to reclaim Art for Pornography,' he used to say. 'The girlie mags are mere ephemera. I'm interested in a permanent affront to polite society.' Like everything he did, he said this to shock. He loved pretending he was frivolous when he was in earnest. I had seen him at work, watched him scream and cavort round his easel like a jester, jabbing at the canvas with cavalier flourishes, poncing backwards with a hand on his hip to squint comically at his handiwork, all to entertain his sitter, but I knew that in spite of everything he was perfectly serious in his ambitions. 'These,' he said to me once, gesturing towards his paintings, 'are the Images of Our Age. You won't find better anywhere.' He believed this absolutely. With my wife, his sitter and his lover, he had his great chance. 'Nudity is knowledge,' was another of his catchphrases, and now – my heart wept – he knew.

And so it was not difficult to imagine the scene. Fluck talked continuously while he painted, told jokes, indulged in the niceties of power. I could imagine his bulky figure squatting on his painter's stool behind the enormous easel and canvas, while his shrill, smug voice floated over the top of it to my wife. 'It's a question both of ethics and aesthetics,' he was squeaking (there was, incidentally, something wrong with his voice; perhaps he had a hormone imbalance). 'If you don't take your clothes off, the picture will be a calamitous failure, and naturally there will be an element of blame.' His voice rose and broke into hiccups. 'Off, off, you lendings!' he declaimed. 'Come, unbutton here!' snorting and wheezing, and then suddenly silent. 'Don't look now,' he warned in a stage whisper, 'but one of us is stark naked!' And his voice rose and dissolved into a wail of demonic hilarity. Then, without warning, brisk and business-like. 'Chin and left tit up; don't droop, dear. How beautiful you look, both art and artefact, my Naked Maja and my Duchess of Alba. Incidentally, do you know the story of Goya and his mistress?'

Yes, I could imagine the awfulness of Fluck at work. It was much more difficult imagining Poppet's part in all this, posing and listening, and occasionally giving a simper. I did not want to see her in some coy compliant posture, as for a centre-page spread; but, curse my vigilance, although Poppet didn't know it, I had already seen the painting with my own eyes. Imagination – what need was there of that paltry thing? I *knew* what she had done.

'. . . He paints very quickly,' Poppet was saying. 'He jabs at the canvas like that.' She demonstrated.

'Stippling,' I said briefly, 'it's called stippling.'

'You know it all,' she said brightly. 'I like talking to you about painting.'

Up ahead, across the pinky-grey sand, I could see the rock pools, towards which we were headed, standing isolated in a crescent in the middle of the beach like the wrecked feet and shins of Ozymandias. Boundless and bare the lone and level sands stretched far away. Shelley drowned too. The sand nearer the sea was damper. I watched it wrinkle and moisten under my feet. Soon, when she confessed, Poppet's face would do much the same thing.

'And then,' she went on, 'he gets out his palette knife and he strops it on his shirt-tails like a carving-knife or something, so funny. And then . . .' Her eyes were shining, but not with tears, no, with enthusiasm, with, if I can bring myself to use the word, joy! 'Sometimes he sings while he paints,' she said. 'He can't sing, but he sings anyway and rocks from side to side like that man on television, what's-his-name. Once he nearly fell off his stool. I thought I was going to die laughing. Poor Henry.'

I thought I was going to be sick. Clearly they were united by something more than Fluck's lust. Poppet's pity for him bound them together too.

'So you kept an eye on him,' I said grimly, 'while he painted.'

Poppet looked confused. 'Oh yes. Well, you couldn't hide Henry, could you? I mean he's so, you know, large, and, well, what's the word?' She giggled. 'Bobbly, that's it. When he moves, he bobbles; do you know what I mean?'

Jesus Christ, I thought, the woman is obsessed with him. She talks about him as if he were a teddy bear. Yet strangely, distressingly, I found myself looking at her without distaste. The eyes, especially the eyes; I had forgotten how large and clear and bright they were. Grey irises spiked with greeny-yellow at the centre, the colour, I had always thought, of innocence. Of course, she was not *wholly* beautiful; in the early morning, staggering from bed, her face was as round as a little girl's and waxy with a residual sheen. And yet, 'There is no excellent beauty that hath not some strangeness in the proportion.' There were certain moments. When she laughed, she opened her eyes incredibly wide as if the laugh itself were giving her a totally unexpected jolt of pleasure. And, even funnier, when she frowned, her tiny eyebrows failed to meet; when she sulked she was tomboyish and rude, and her mouth puckered like dried fruit. It was by these moments I had to measure how much Fluck had stolen from me. For him, now, she made her special faces; she walked alongside me, with the sunlight in her eyes, talking and thinking of him. Suddenly I remembered her naked, putting her breasts into my mouth. *His* mouth, now, battened on her body. Enough. No more of this. I prattle like Polonius.

I lurched across the beach, saying nothing, towards the rocks

41

and rock pools with their dark damp cargo. Gulls, apparently nearer now, perhaps disporting themselves in those same rock pools, set up a mocking cry which mingled oddly with the sound of Poppet's voice, as she twittered on about Fluck's 'amusing conversations'. The mad dog was also nosing around the rocks, running in furious circles. How strange to think that at that moment Fluck himself, or rather his inanimate form, was almost within sight, straight ahead of us, lodged securely in its watery crevice. As if he was still drawing us to him, exerting his influence.

It may be useful, as they loomed towards us, to give a brief description of these rocks. In fact, to follow certain twists in the narrative it is actually quite important to comprehend the idiosyncrasies of their appearance. They rose abruptly from the flat sand, a high, dense mass of rock and seaweed and barnacle, about twenty feet in length and sheer at either end. The only way to mount to the top was to scramble up one of the slippery sides. But it was worth the trouble; scattered between jutting shelves of seaweed and tussocks of rock were about a dozen of the finest rock pools along that stretch of coast, broad and deep and teeming with marine life. At high tide the sea covered the rocks, replenishing livestock. Also, the view from the top of them was very pleasing, the rocks being situated almost exactly mid-way along the beach, directly opposite the narrow mouth of the bay. A good point of vantage for a painter. But, in my opinion, the most fascinating aspect of the rocks was their strange formation. They formed a perfect crescent, horns pointing out to sea. If I was a painter I would have painted the rocks themselves, a kind of amphibious Böcklinesque 'Island of the Dead', sometimes circumfluous, sometimes landlocked. Fluck did not paint them. His tribute was to die among them. Böcklin would have loved *that*.

We approached them slowly. Poppet talked; I, chokingly, kept silent. Suddenly, when we were about twenty-five yards off the rock pools, I mismanaged my ruined footwear, stumbled and fell, screeching, and twisting my ankle quite badly. Immediately, Poppet was at my side. Calm in a crisis, she handled my foot keenly like a trained nurse, extricating the wreckage of my shoes from my trouser flares, and then restraining me while I groaned aloud and heaved from side to side like a fish in a bucket. When at last I stopped squirming I seemed to be in an awful tangle, lying motionless in Poppet's lap with my legs knotted and my arms round her shoulders for support. In this position we formed a *pietà* – both Virgin and Martyr dressed in multi-sole, two-tone platforms, flares, and pastel-coloured shirts with decorative work round the collars. How foolish, you will say. And yet there was briefly a moment, as we lay tangled together, when our foolishness resembled a kind of peace and we were almost gentle with each other, almost, dare I say it, unvindictive. Then we hauled ourselves to our feet and staggered towards the nearby rocks.

'Over there,' said Poppet, 'you can sit down over there. Are you all right? Can you walk?'

I could not walk. I was not all right. Her face, it seemed to me, was closer to mine than it had been all week; I could see the tiny golden hairs on her upper lip. I felt again, with a lurch of the heart, Fluck's theft.

'Oh, I'm fine,' I said grittily. I clung on to her, and we tottered slowly forward.

After this we sat quietly on the rocks listening to the sea and the gulls. The dog seemed to have disappeared. I thought of nothing but the pain in my ankle, unless I was occasionally mindful also of the spreading misery of my hangover. After a while Poppet showed signs of uneasiness again, staring out to sea (the wrong direction, in view of Fluck's position among the rocks), and cuffing wet sand from the knees of her trousers. She seemed to be making a great effort, to do something or not to do it. Eventually she spoke.

'How is your writing going?' she asked.

'What?'

'Your story.'

'My *story*?' I remembered, of course, the idea that I might write a story while we were on holiday. What amazed me was that Poppet was obviously in earnest – smiling even – without an inkling of the gross insensitivity of her question. There was no story, as Poppet could not have failed to notice, and in the sense she meant it, there could be none. Not ever. What should I have written about did she think – fidelity, honesty, the lovely slow maturing of mutual trust? A romantic idyll? Something with a happy ending, naturally. I laughed out loud. 'My story!' I could not help a sneer.

Partly to relieve the tension of my feelings and partly to test my ankle, I rose, unsteady but effective, and hobbled over to another rock. Evidently I was not permanently maimed, not in my ankle anyway. A twinge of pain, and then I was seated again. In this new position I faced Poppet directly; also, as it happened, I had placed myself just below the rock pool which contained Fluck's waterlogged body. I cannot be sure, but I would guess that all or part of the corpse was visible to Poppet whenever she looked in my direction. The arms, I guess, were sprawled across dark bunches of seaweed that clotted the rim of the pool, and the pale hands must have been quite obviously displayed. Unless they were discoloured, of course. I do not remember. I am not a doctor, I am ignorant of the effect of seawater on decomposing flesh. But in any case Poppet's eyesight was not equal to the occasion.

'What's wrong with you?'

This was a new initiative on Poppet's part. 'What do you mean?' I asked eventually.

'Something's wrong with you.' Her voice was sullen and accusing, quite extraordinary.

'I have destroyed one of my ankles,' I said evenly, 'there's a pain in my head, and another worse pain in my stomach. It's eight o'clock in the morning and I had two hours' sleep last night. I am apparently welded into some crippling costume, and I have lost the ability to walk normally.'

'What's wrong?' asked Poppet again, as if she hadn't heard me. 'I'm getting frightened, S. J.' Now she looked up and her cheeks were damp. She always cried easily.

'You tell me,' I said bitterly, and turned away from her. I had forgotten how much I disliked confrontation. I always forget until it actually happens.

'Is it us?' To answer this I obviously needed to know exactly who 'us' was, and I didn't. 'Something's wrong, S. J.,' she went on regardless. 'All last night you avoided me, and every time I caught your eye you just stared at me with that horrible blank stare you have, and I was so frightened, S. J., why were you trying to frighten me?'

This was nonsense, or at least innaccurate and badly

44

expressed. I shuffled further round on my rock to face out to sea, concentrate on the soothing monotony of waves and light and gulls, which wasn't at all soothing, just as it hadn't been earlier.

'I don't think you talked to me once.'

Despite myself I could not help wondering if this was true. Damn my memory, I couldn't think of a simple example with which to refute her. 'Of course I did,' I said.

'You never came near me. Not once.' She was weeping quite openly by now, and sniffing loudly.

'You've obviously forgotten.'

'When, then?'

'Don't be stupid. How can I remember when I was so drunk?' If only my stomach had been calm and my head quiet, I wouldn't have felt so ill when I shouted.

'If you'd just tell me what's wrong,' said the voice over my shoulder. 'You've been like this all week.'

'Not now Poppet. Later.'

'Is it us? Tell me, S. J.' Again the indelicate question. 'You seem so sad,' she said. 'Everyone asks me what's the matter with you, but every time I try to talk to you, you just won't, so what can I do? Why won't you tell me what's wrong?'

All the time we spoke, or did not speak, Fluck's blackened body presided over us from its damp vantage-point, like an umpire. No other role could have suited him quite so well. He was omniscient at last. I only wish that he had been more visible, or that Poppet had cleared her eyes of tears for an instant, and seen him, thus curtailing our ridiculous interview. But she saw nothing and the interview continued.

'When I found you this morning you were weeping,' she said through her own tears.

Weeping? Unfortunately I could not deny it. I had woken up weeping, a great surprise, but of negligible importance compared to the general pain of my condition. At the time I think I hardly noticed the tears. It was quite wrong of Poppet to attach significance to a slight case of weeping.

'And look at you,' Poppet went on, 'you're crying now.'

Literally speaking, this was also true. It is disgusting how one gets caught up in other people's emotions – and without the slightest inclination to share their grief. It may even have been

45

that I was myself becoming a little upset, even letting out the occasional sob and burying my face in my hands.

'What's wrong with us?' cried Poppet, suddenly shrill, dramatic in a way I had not thought possible. 'Why are you crying S. J.? Please, please, tell me why you're crying.'

And then she was rising and rushing towards me, and I had risen too, and I remember the wide gesture of her arms as she made to embrace me –

But there was no embrace. She stopped dead, arms outstretched, a queer expression on her face. And in this frozen moment I heard above me a sort of snarling noise, as of a dog worrying a bone, and as I turned, or rather cringed, to look, Fluck's corpse, suddenly dislodged, careered towards my head, dark and solid. Poppet screamed, though not so loudly as I. With the briefest of glimpses I took in the death-mask face coldly looming from the enormous overcoat collar, one congealed eye cocked ludicrously in my direction, with the dark round barrel of his body swiftly following, and then, with helium under my heels, I spun slowly into the Fluck-thickened air towards collision.

When I came to for the first time, I did not feel well. Opening my eyes with a sickening wrench of the lids, I saw Poppet peering down at me, looking white and ill. Pushing her away, I rolled to one side, threw up, and blacked out again. When I woke up for the second time, with the cold, hard beach sticking into my back, I knew exactly what had happened, who I was, and what I had to do.

'Are you OK?' Poppet asked tersely.

'I'm dying,' I said at last.

'Not you,' I heard Poppet say, and then cold salt water hit me in the face and, choking, I sat up. Poppet was sitting on a rock a few feet away, wiping her wet hands. We looked at each other intently.

'Did you see . . . ?' she began. I became aware of gulls bickering greedily in the rock pools behind her. There was no sign of the dog – but I did not look very carefully.

'No,' I said firmly.

Poppet rose to her feet. 'Get up,' she said flatly, 'you've got to come with me. Henry's dead. I think drowned. A dog . . .' She was crying, and I also began to weep, whether out of grief

46

or fear or helplessness I don't know. I let myself be led by Poppet like a child, and we started to limp slowly back across the beach.

When we were halfway back to the cottage, under the stripy shadows of the crab apple trees, I said, 'Perhaps he isn't dead. If we hurry we can get help.' I lied easily and persuasively because I felt so bad.

Fluck was cremated two days afterwards at a local Chapel of Rest, apparently at the time when I was slowly making my way home from Heathrow, busy with thoughts of my suicide. I discovered this from a message left by a friend on my answering machine during the few days before I moved to this bedsit. The message was surprisingly detailed. Apparently the service had been conducted almost entirely by Fluck's father, an ex-actor who recited Hamlet's famous soliloquy – without intended irony, hard though it is to believe – and his youngest son Pip, who scraped the violin. The vicar, when he finally got the chance to speak, turned out to have a terrible stutter which turned Fluck's name into a quavering obscenity, a nice tribute. It seems that there were only a few people present at the cremation. Naturally. Fluck had very few friends. *I* was not really his friend, as I think I have mentioned already; nor were the others who had stayed the week with us at Fluck's cottage and who eventually made up the numbers at the funeral. They were friends of Poppet who had since met, and been appropriated by, Fluck. It was an extraordinary and rather sad thing for him to have invited a group of distinctly casual acquaintances to stay with him during his last week on earth, but Fluck was an extraordinary and sad person, as was fairly well-known. When I say sad, I mean pathetic. I did not know then that he was also capable of breathtaking viciousness. This ability was well-practised, but more often than not cunningly concealed.

I must confess that I had been acquainted with Fluck at university, in fact we were members of the same college, although we studied different subjects, I literature, he, obscurely, modern history. Initially, as freshers, we were somewhat thrown together, though we never attained the easy compatibility that marks real friendship, and in due course we

47

drifted apart. Our backgrounds being as different as they were, this was hardly surprising.

By the time we separated I had already begun to see Poppet, and I suspect that Fluck kept in touch with me for her sake. He had never attempted to disguise his admiration of her. 'So gay a popelote,' he used to say, quoting Chaucer delightedly. 'A lovely little thing. Full of . . . what's the expression . . .' (squinting at me slyly through lazy eyes) '. . . ah, yes – fun.' But it was not Fluck she came to see, and soon, as I say, Fluck and I drifted apart. My marriage to Poppet, a few months after graduation, completed this process. Our temperaments had always been very different. After coming down from university Fluck abruptly left for New York, ostensibly to take the art establishment by storm. Poppet and I received postcards from time to time. These were nearly always addressed to Poppet. 'The Americans are delightful,' he wrote at first, 'beautifully house-trained and ideally unintelligent. I am thinking of keeping a couple as pets.' But the Fluckian braggadocio did not endear him to the Greenwich Villagers, and within six months he was home again, complaining bitterly about galleries and agents and the editors of fancy journals who formed, though perhaps only in his mind, a kind of Mafia of Style dedicated to the hindrance of his destiny as the Next Best Thing. We did not hear from him for some months after this, a lovely Fluck-free time of grace. But eventually one Friday afternoon he telephoned Poppet at work and invited himself to dinner the following day. I had forgotten, in the intervening year, how garrulous and vain he was. Afterwards Poppet said that she thought he had changed, into a sadder though not necessarily wiser person, at odds with himself and his abilities, but I saw no such contradiction, nor any sadness; I simply heard, over and over and over, his voice, that shrill insectile whine, and his anecdotes, those awful tawdry dramas of self-satisfaction.

From then on he would phone Poppet every couple of weeks or so, or meet her for a drink if he were visiting a nearby gallery; I was never asked, or else I declined the offer. At first his visits to Poppet irritated me, but in time I came to appreciate that Poppet effectively kept him from me, and for this I was duly grateful. Then we received his invitation to spend a week with him at his country cottage.

I remember Poppet coming into my study (causing a neat pile of typewritten pages I had carefully left on the sofa, my latest article, to cascade onto the carpet) and telling me the news.

'He wants us to stay for a week.'

'Impossible. When?'

'July.'

'We'll be in Majorca.'

'It's the week before.'

'Impossible. Do you mean the week *immediately* before?'

'Yes.'

'Absolutely impossible. How can I take a whole fortnight off work?'

'Because you're freelance.'

This conversation rather cleverly indicates the precise nature of the relationship between Poppet and myself. I stand for instinct and passion, she for logic and perseverance, a brutish combination against which I never quite got used to breaking myself.

'Are you sure you can manage it?' Poppet persisted after I had reluctantly given way.

I threw my diary across the room. What questions she was capable of! But looking back, my guess is that Poppet was already in love with Fluck, and was already foresuffering the contingent guilt.

A month later we made the laborious journey to Fluck's cottage, which is situated in a particularly remote region of the countryside. The drive took us five and a half hours, and on the way Poppet took the opportunity to relate superfluous details about Fluck's family background.

I should immediately make it clear that Henry Fluck was a very wealthy young man. He had no need to work, and indeed I very much doubt if he was capable of it.

It would be convenient but probably erroneous to damn Fluck's parents for their repellent son. His mother is permanently absent, nursing a nervous constitution in Monaco, and his father exists only to indulge his dilettante passion for amateur dramatics (and amateurish actresses), taking little notice of his two sons. Old-fashioned family values, if you like. It is said that the fortune he inherited and is so diligently squandering derives from a vulgar range of lavatory accessories popularised by a more industrious Fluck in the middle of the last century. Despite his father's profligacy, Fluck's education naturally included a top public school and one of the most prestigious universities – both of which seem to have done little but confirm him in his role of self-appointed genius. He was spectacularly unpopular at school and gloried in it, deriding his fellow students and sneering at his teachers. As a result he was often beaten up, sometimes with the obvious connivance of the masters, who must have found it difficult not to exult in the passage of natural justice. But Fluck recalled these occasions with a sort of inverse pride; he told me on several occasions that a school jingle existed to commemorate him: 'If you're ever out of luck, take it out on Henry Fluck.' He chuckled as he recited it, the bloody fool. And: 'Brute aggression is the tribute mediocrity pays to genius,' he used to say. He had a habit of echoing Oscar Wilde at his most unendearing. Yet, after all, what else could Fluck have expected, but beatings? Although he was vicious with his tongue, and his talent for verbal aggression was incredibly refined, he was physically feeble, like a Wyndham Lewis trapped inside the body of an Elizabeth Barrett Browning, and he made an obvious target for anyone he offended. At university too he achieved immediate notoriety for his arrogant attitudes and unwashed appearance, though he was beaten up less often. Instead he was simply ostracised, quite a rare event for someone from such a prominent public school. For a time I found it possible to marvel at his eccentricity – but I was not sad when he suddenly took himself off to New York, and I was not sad to hear from him so infrequently afterwards. To be quite frank (and it's a matter of now or never) I always hated him, always.

We arrived at his cottage at eight o'clock in the evening, very weary. I didn't feel up to Fluck. 'I know he's looking forward to seeing you,' Poppet said, as we climbed stiffly from the car.

Not true, of course; Fluck was eager to see *her*, however much he pretended otherwise. I have already mentioned that Fluck openly approved of Poppet, but I always suspected that it was more than this. For one thing, as I have said, he was forever trying to persuade her to pose nude for him. 'For historical reasons only,' he insisted. 'It's a great tradition, rather difficult to ignore, you see. I'm going to paint the Great English Nude.

Someone's got to do it.' His behaviour too, in her presence, was ludicrously blatant. 'Why don't we leave these dullards and go and fuck?' he would say loudly. By these and other subtleties of behaviour I came to realise that he was to some degree attracted to her. Now, of course, after everything that's happened, I could easily spend all the short time left to me speculating on the postcards and phone calls they had exchanged previously, those occasional lunch-dates, after-dinner drinks, all darkened now with a seedier meaning, but why dissipate the drama I have been given? I simply introduce the notion of Fluck's existing passion to substantiate the background to the consummation displayed for me later, rather as, in sixteenth-century profane painting, playful putti decorate the spectacle of Venus and Mars majestically fornicating in grottoes and along riverbanks. (In the background Hephaestus hobbles out with his mesh of magic steel to catch them at it.)

'You're going to have a lovely time,' said Poppet, a moment before the front door was opened to us. No comment from me was necessary, nor did I give one; but her words form a kind of sardonic epigraph for the rest of our story. In a sense they were the last words she ever spoke to me. Everything afterwards merely represented the survival of a habit.

The door was flung open, exactly on cue, and Henry Hippolytus Fluck stood before us, entirely filling the doorway.

'S. J.!' he cried. 'You're here. At last!' Someone in the hall behind him gave out a half-hearted cheer. 'We thought you would never make it.' I opened my mouth – but Fluck at once drew breath with a sound like bellows and continued unstoppably. 'Have you brought us anything by the way of alcoholic refreshment?' he shouted. 'We're simply dying of thirst in here, *nunc est bibendum* etc., you know Horace of course, marvellous man, lousy poet. I'm afraid I shall have to ask you to hand over all drink before entry.' He flapped his arms as he said this, like an enormous grounded bird.

'S. J.'s got a bottle of cognac,' said Poppet blithely, slipping past Fluck to greet other friends in the hall.

'Good man! Splendid chap!' shouted Fluck, and then, before I knew what was happening, he had me in a hearty clinch, Russian style, squeezing my ribs and rubbing his damp bristles against my cheek. '*Lovely* to see you,' he purred. 'Let me look

51

at you. Are you a little thinner, have you lost a little puppy fat?' He prodded me indelicately in my midriff and guffawed. 'We'll soon do something about that, don't worry, a strict diet of suet and thick custard. Now, no arguing, *please*. And do come in, don't hang around out there like a lesser angel at a Botticelli Nativity.' He turned suddenly and retreated, and I followed his vast shambling form inside, my arms full of suitcases he had not offered to carry.

My initial reaction was to marvel at how much fatter, dirtier, louder, and uglier Fluck had become. But I was mistaken. He had always been that fat and dirty and loud and ugly, it was just that I was no longer used to it. Let me describe him. He was about six feet three inches tall, and weighed around eighteen stone. Whenever he walked more than a few yards, which was not often, his body seemed perfectly uncontrollable, setting up alarming rhythms of its own, quite independent of the momentum of his walk. Even when he wrapped himself tightly in his large tweed overcoat, as he did most of the time, his body resisted any predictable notion of order, bulging from unexpected places when he moved.

Facially, his looks complemented this impression of formlessness. Let me reacquaint you with them. Like a baby's, his face seemed as though his bone structure had not yet grown into it; his cheeks, jowls, chins, and even the fleshy nub of his nose quivered under pressure of the slightest expression, so that for all its pendulous weight, his face was oddly defiant of gravity. When he smiled – which he seldom did, preferring to roar with open-mouthed laughter – his jowls bunched, his chins stood on tiptoe and he revealed, rather coyly, a few bad teeth, grey like the shadows of proper teeth, inside the crumpled shape that was his mouth. When he roared with the usual open-mouthed laughter, all the parts of his face flew, they hurtled, whirled, danced. I do not exaggerate. They were, alas, to be observed mostly in this aspect of unrest.

Pictured in a photograph, Fluck might conveniently have been dismissed as a cartoon character, but his dirtiness and smelliness imbued him with reality. As I have said, his teeth were bad. His breath was worse. His BO was worse than this, and did not so much emanate from particular areas of his body, as wrap him completely in a miasmal mist. His smell lingers in my nostrils still. His dirty habits too I remember, and his dingy demeanour. Dressed in threadbare corduroys and old dress shirts, he would sit at the dinner table and pontificate about style and manners while stuffing food into his mouth. Occasionally he craned a hand above his head and, with long, blackened fingernails, combed his slippery hair. This hair was the colour of putty and several shades more robust than his complexion. A different kind of hair, gingery and sparse, adhered to his chins and jowls.

This, then, was Henry Fluck, the man who was shortly to engulf the petite form of Poppet in riotous sex. But enough of that for now.

'I think you know everyone,' said Fluck as we entered the living-room. Of course I did, they were my friends, not his. 'Angel, S. J.: Moyra, S. J.; Myra, S. J. S. J. has cognac, but refuses to deliver it up, I suggest we extract it from him by force.'

'You're two and a half hours late,' said Myra flatly, whose habit it was to be precise. 'Trust you to be late.'

'How are you?' Moyra asked. Her voice, unlike her sister's was breathlessly soft. She stood, as always, in a curvaceous, comfortable slouch, glass in one hand, cigarette in the other. Occasionally she held both glass and cigarette in the same hand and ran the other through her dark, tangled hair. I was glad to see *her* at any rate. Angel, who had clearly been drinking heavily already, merely inclined his glass and his eyebrows. He was not a garrulous type. His real name was Gabriel, but that was now lost to posterity.

I unzipped one of my bags, removed from it the bottle of cheap cognac, and presented this to Fluck.

'Ha!' he shouted needlessly, and disappeared with a flourish into the kitchen. Have I mentioned that he was wearing an enormous slop-stained white pinafore? Naturally it looked ridiculous, but more ridiculous still was his tall chef's hat which he continuously adjusted, as if in an unnecessary attempt to draw our attention to it. As he left the room he informed us loudly that he was about to add a 'soupçon' of something to '*le dîner*'. Angel offered me a drink.

'And how are you?' he asked. 'You've lost weight. Marriage wearing you out?'

'Leaner and hungrier,' I said, slipping into our usual bantering tone, 'though I can't say the same for you.'

'Fatter and thirstier,' Angel said affably, refilling our glasses, 'but I'll be challenging you to a game of squash later.'

'I'm ready for you,' I said.

We drank quietly after this outburst. Angel is not a frantic conversationalist. We finished our drinks and then poured ourselves some more, which we drank in silence. When I say that he is no conversationalist what I mean is that he is virtually a mute. Long sentences seem to alarm him and he rarely attempts them.

'Did you bring your kit?' he asked after a while, playing a gentle air stroke with the palm of his hand, gestures being for him what sub-clauses are for everyone else. I nodded silently, not to be outdone.

'And my bathing trunks,' I confessed, after another, longer pause. He nodded; smiled. I regarded him over the top of my glass.

'And a beach ball?' he asked. 'Water-wings?'

'Fuck off,' I said. 'Water-wings? Fuck.'

As Angel and I joked in this carefree way, Fluck reappeared to take Poppet and me on a tour of the house. I did not want to leave Angel or the brandy so soon but Fluck's ideas of hospitality were inflexible. The more I think about it now, the more I am persuaded that he deliberately sought to separate Angel and me. Angel is one of those people from whom it is possible to derive strength and comfort. Now, in my present plight, if I were the confiding type I might confide in Angel who is the type to be confided in. But I have put all that behind me now, *noli me tangere*, it's too late for such intimacies, and not even Angel, sympathetic and sincere though he may be – even, in many respects, my closest friend – could relieve my suffering now. But enough. On with the story, what there is of it.

We, my wife and I, were mustered at the bottom of the staircase, where the tour was to begin. 'Come on now!' Fluck shouted sharply. 'Quickly, or you'll miss it.' I remember throwing a last, despairing glance at Angel, who shrugged and blandly raised his glass. Frankly, Angel cuts an odd figure, amiable and urbane though he is, and perhaps, in the interests of setting the scene, I should describe his appearance. Spiky blue hair, yellow string vest, zebra pants, silver motorcycle boots; all these seemed comically incongruous on a man whose manners are those of a tame butler. He is stuck in the Punk era. Somehow I have never got over this. Somehow I could never equate Angel with the way Angel looked. But this is the old dilemma, is it not, the falsity of representation, the illusion of reality, noumena and phenomena, as dear Emanuel Kant would say. Quite a little sub-theme to my maunderings, as it turns out.

'Isn't he lovely?' said Fluck sarcastically to Poppet's blank face. 'Always dawdling but *how* can you be cross with him. Now, I can hardly believe that you haven't been here before, but you tell me it's true, so I think we should start with the ground floor and slowly defy gravity, always something of a thrill, don't you think?' He laughed immoderately and then led us along the hall to the dining-room.

The house has impressed itself on my memory, but not our Fluck-conducted tour of it. I suppose, like Poppet, I was fairly quick to register that it wasn't a cottage at all, but a good-sized house. There were four bedrooms, three reception rooms (living-room, dining-room, games room), kitchen, bathroom, two lavatories, a conservatory, a cellar, and an attic, where Fluck, I discovered later, painted.

'Do you ever use the attic?' I asked, as we passed the ladder to it on the top landing.

'Of course,' Fluck replied shortly. I had forgotten the infuriating elliptical manner he sometimes employed in an effort to contrive moods of meaningless mystery.

'I suppose you paint in it,' said Poppet innocently. Fluck glared at her and we descended meekly, without further conversation. It was only later that he would tell us all about his attic studio, his early morning vigils waiting for the dawn to force an entry through the sooty skylight. By special consent I was once allowed to visit this studio. It was an appalling mess, a cramped, filthy hideaway, stinking of turpentine and oils and human sweat, an aroma in which Fluck was patently at home, expounding eagerly the naff theories of medieval architects or twentieth-century deconstructionists, which he professed to find 'charming', and even, with grosser affectation, *'bijou'*. His respect for other artists was, in fact, negligible. I do not remember my brief visit in much detail. Fluck's conversation had this numbing effect.

For the moment, however, as Poppet and I trudged behind him down the stairs, we were not favoured with his anecdotal self-explanations. We were shown to our room and there left in peace for about three and a half minutes.

'What's that?' asked Poppet with her head in the maw of a suitcase. A gong was sounding somewhere in the recesses of the house, a thin tintinnabulation.

'Fluck struck,' I said wittily. It was, of course, the gong for dinner. Plainly we were to be allowed no time to ourselves. Another strategy. As was the dinner itself, which, like the subsequent dinners served up by Fluck, was dominated by the double display of his appetite and anecdotes. I made myself very nearly ill in the impossible endeavour to avoid both the sight of him eating and the sound of his voice. Drinking to excess blurred the spectacle, but could not entirely obliterate his terrible monologues. I did my best, of course.

He sat at the head of the table, looking like a master in a prep-school dining-room. 'You be father,' said Fluck to Angel, sitting on his right. 'And S. J. can be mother,' he added, laughing.

Was this funny? Have I missed a joke? No one laughed with him except Moyra, who tends to laugh at the slightest provocation, the silly bitch, beautiful though she is. She sat opposite me, giggling into her wine glass which she held in an outrageous manner by the base. Here it would be as well, I think, to get a small confession over with straight away. I find Moyra very desirable. Purely in a physical sense, of course – her conversation, her half-formed ideas and mumbled thoughts I find utterly inconsequential, but I have to admit that her physical presence is for me a constant erection. There is no harm in this, except perhaps a temporary ache in the testicles, and it has only the slightest bearing on the rest of the story. But perhaps the scrupulous reader might like to keep it in mind in the interests of accuracy. On the other hand, those whose imaginations lack discipline will ultimately be disappointed.

Conversation round the dinner table wound on. Angel and I encountered few problems in becoming drunk, but when the authentic Fluckian monologue finally got under way, some time

56

during the fish course, it was immediately plain that we would never be able to drink enough to escape his ineluctable drone which effortlessly smothered everyone round the table. He talked of many things, of oil paint techniques, the poetry of the Marquis de Sade, the Nature of Creativity, the history of the French Empire in the Sudan, the fruitful relationship of art to pornography, the novels of William Gerhardie, Wittgenstein, and Nudity. I select merely. Nor do I do justice to his devouring style of oratory, which, like a plague of locusts, engulfed all before him and left it blanched and empty. We could not resist. Whenever I grew tired of trying to subvert his monologues, I studied the table or gazed round the dining room. It had been tastefully rusticated. The walls were roughly whitewashed and the ceiling was the colour of old meringue. The furniture was plain and solid ('Roughly hewn,' Fluck had commented during our tour, his posh accent at its most proprietorial). The floor should have been stone-flagged, but – here the inevitable touch of ostentation – it had instead been laid with expensive, over-varnished parquety which squealed softly whenever a chair leg was pressed across its surface, just loud enough to be heard in the infrequent intervals when Fluck was forced to pause for breath. Always my gaze returned to the enormous mirror hanging above the sideboard on the wall opposite me, in which everyone seated at the table was reflected, the fronts of myself and Poppet and Angel, the backs of Moyra and Myra, and the mobile, deliquescent profile of Henry Fluck.

I watched Fluck's mouth move as he soliloquised. How frightening laughter would be without sound. (How ridiculous it is with it.) Whenever he wasn't actually speaking, and often when he was, he stuffed food into his mouth or around it. Polite disregard of this proved impossible; the very first course left a green trail of cream of courgette and cambazola soup glistening snail-wise across the fluff of his chins. Later this was embellished by subsequent courses. In a way this puzzled me, as Fluck's mouth was so often open, and so widely open, that I could not see how he succeeded in avoiding it. Nevertheless he continuously besmirched himself, scoffing, gobbling, guzzling, chomping, grabbing titbits with buttery fingers and indiscriminately discarding bones and gristle onto the table cloth and even, once, into his wine glass where the grisly item turned his untouched Soave to gravy. Perhaps this sounds comical, but it was not. It was a tragedy of manners. Nabokov, the Russian-American novelist, held the view that tyrants are destroyed precisely in these, the risible aspects of their involuntary behaviour, the picked nose, the vacant gaze, but he is surely wrong. It is by such signs that tyranny is perpetrated; the belches and farts of absolute power suffocate the tyrannised.

Occasionally we struggled to initiate our own mild conversations. Thus Myra attempted to engage me in a discussion about Special Overseas Investments. As she talked, hissed rather, I regarded her closely. Alcohol, in its early stages, tends to stimulate such superficial curiosity. She hadn't much changed.

'This country doesn't know what's hit it,' she said. 'Investment's up, the exchange rate's up, interest rates are the lowest they've been for years – and productivity's nowhere.'

It is amazing that Moyra and Myra are twin sisters. The one is so sultry and dozy and sexy, the other all bones and gristle and flickering temper. It would be interesting to have the opinion of an obstetrician on those two.

'Take Afghanistan,' Myra said. 'Now there's an interesting country. Absolutely awash with foreign investment. Why? Just watch. In about two months' time the dollar's going to sky-rocket.'

Myra works for a merchant bank somewhere in the City, though I am not sure at what level. She gives the impression of seniority by the humourlessness of her conversation.

I asked her whether it wasn't rather risky to put your money into Afghanistan, even for a short time. 'Risk is what it's all about,' she replied briefly, flaring her nostrils, an unfortunate habit, her nostrils being so large and winnowy. She seems to live on her nerves. Her hair is naturally bottle-blond and her breath smells, alas, of bowels. Try as I might I could never be impressed by her knowledge of finance. It is a failure of mine to be unable to separate the opinion from the person.

In Myra's case I date this back to an incident which occurred three or four years ago, when I happened to be at a party with her, and she made a pass at me. It was especially embarrassing as I had actually taken Poppet to the party, before I knew her very well, but had unaccountably got drunk and lost her in the crowd. It was a college summer ball, and all the men were in

DJs and the women in fancy gowns. Myra, very unfancy, strangely blurred in appearance, suddenly stumbled upon me out of a thicket of revellers and caught me round the waist. Her speech was clear and memorable.

'Careful,' she said, somehow breathing up my nostrils. 'Steady, easy does it, you're drunk.'

We swayed together, and at close range I regarded the front of her dress which had inexplicably come adrift. She wore no bra. Her breasts were pale and small, pear-shaped, discoloured at the tips as if by extreme cold. Even in my drunkenness I had no desire to touch them.

'Where's Poppet?' she said next. 'I saw her with another man.'

'This party's full of men,' I told her, but she just smiled, unusual for her, a jagged, lascivious smile, and utterly chilling. I let her go, and fled. Lacking the support of my arm she seemed to fall to the floor; I felt her plunging away from me as I left. Perhaps she had forced me to give her a slight push. It was an unremarkable incident, but although Myra and I never mention it to each other, it hangs between us forbiddingly.

We were, by now, approaching the conclusion of the dinner. For dessert there was a chocolate mousse. Poppet, a great lover of the stuff, had my helping as well as her own, and then declared she felt sick. More wine appeared, a little grudgingly I thought, and then, at last, coffee, port, and cigarettes. At this point Fluck began to talk about the week ahead, our holiday.

'If the weather remains fine,' he said, 'I expect you will want to go to the beach. I don't object. There is only one beach within easy reach, but it's perfectly adequate for that sort of thing.' He waved a pudgy hand apparently coastward.

'What if the weather isn't fine?' asked Poppet.

'And it's almost bound not to be,' said Myra.

'I expect you'll go to the beach anyway,' said Fluck. 'I harbour no illusions about holidaymakers by the sea. Umbrellas and mackintoshes are kept in the hall.'

'But isn't there anything else to do here?' asked Myra.

'No,' said Fluck, 'not for you. You might find something in the nearest town but that's about an hour's drive away.'

'But there must be *something* to do?' Poppet was being characteristically persistent. 'Television, books, board games?'

Fluck treated her to a sneer. 'Of course,' he said, 'you are right. I was forgetting. There is a television in the living-room, rather small, I'm afraid, but functional, and a collection of books in the games room. There are no games. Incidentally, anyone is free to come and keep me company in my studio, at my labours, you know, though I dare say you'll find it intolerably tedious. I do my best but I can't make any claims to be entertaining, I'm no Whistler, I'm afraid.'

But a Whistler is exactly what he wished to be. Soon he was describing to us his latest pictures, pontificating richly on their various merits. It seemed that although we were on holiday, he was not, and our presence was not to interrupt his work; rather, we were to become his subjects, together or singly, clothed or nude, for a series of life-studies he wanted to make. This was depressing enough, though there was more, worse.

'You'll hardly notice me,' he said peremptorily. 'I'll simply flit among you making my little sketches.' Fluck as Nijinsky was a particularly ridiculous notion. He was not capable of flitting. He had problems merely walking.

'Won't you miss out on the swimming and things?' said Moyra, drawing heavily on a cigarette, slant eyes on him quizzically. She sounded genuinely puzzled, the poor dear.

'Can't swim,' said Fluck cheerfully. 'Besides, I have to paint, it is my calling, you see.' He spread his arms wide as if in benediction. 'And while you're here I'm going to paint all of you. All except you, S. J.,' he added softly.

'What do you mean?' I said. I should have been pleased but I was indignant. He laughed.

'I hear on the grape vine' – giving a nod towards Poppet – 'you have a little project to keep you busy.'

I looked at Poppet. I imagine my expression was what is usually termed filthy.

'I knew you'd hate me for it,' she said, 'but you said you needed the time. You can write your story while Henry paints. Isn't that a good idea?'

'Your story,' interrupted Fluck. 'You will write your story, and I will paint, and there will be – ' again the arms were spread wide ' – a wonderful cross-fertilisation of the arts. These other persons can enjoy themselves in Porlock. It's beautifully simple.'

I dislike open confrontation, it is so embarrassingly crude. I smiled and nodded and vowed to do nothing that Fluck suggested.

'What story are you writing?' asked Moyra. I ignored her.

'There is a desk in your room,' Fluck went on, 'and I've put a wad of paper in the top drawer. I'm afraid I can't offer you a word processor, but pens are available if you need them. Do you prefer nib or ball-point? Or quill?'

'Very kind,' I said. 'I write in pencil.'

'Ah, like Hemingway,' he murmured.

'Not at all like Hemingway.'

'What story are you writing?' asked Myra, who always seemed to fight her sister's battles for her. But before I could reply – presuming I intended to – Fluck, full of surprises, leapt to his feet.

'I've had a wonderful idea! We can make a game of it, S. J., a competition. A Decameron of the modern age! I'll paint my pictures of everyone, and you can write a story about us, and on the final day we'll have an exhibition and a reading, the two of us, just like old times. What do you say?'

'Absolutely not. I might not be able to finish a story in a week.'

'You can read what you've written.'

'I might not write anything at all.'

'Nonsense. The terror of the reading will be ample incentive.'

'Please, S. J.' Poppet has a comical, appealing expression she uses with scant regard to the seriousness of a situation. It drew a slight murmur of approval from the others. I did not know at the time why she so much wanted me to write. And had I really intended to write a story? What a bore it sounds. I think perhaps I may have concocted the idea for Poppet, to account for the long periods I liked to spend alone. The fact is I need time to myself, I am an only child, I am the thoughtful type. There may have been a plan, a synopsis of a story, some time previously, but even if it existed I fear it had languished beyond revival.

'Please, S. J.,' said Moyra and Myra simultaneously, and laughed.

'It is decided!' roared Fluck.

Soon after this the dinner party broke up. Someone, perhaps

Poppet, immediately went to bed feeling very tired, hopefully guilty too; the other girls followed shortly afterwards. Fluck, Angel, and I retired to the living-room to smoke and drink and generally decline into a stupor.

I remember little of our conversation; probably a blessing. My general impression is that Fluck did most of the talking (of course). I expect I was sulking. Fluck kept referring to me as 'our budding Chekhov', and asked me a lot of irrelevant questions about my non-existent *opus* – 'opuscule' he called it.

'Do you write every day?' he asked. 'How much do you write?'

I told him I wrote a thousand words a day, but that only five hundred of these were new. The other five hundred, I said, are the same as those written the day before, but in a different order. This had a ring of authenticity, and I was pleased to have said it. Fluck merely snorted, and quoted Latin in a ponderous Etonian accent.

'You know Juvenal, of course,' he said. '"Many suffer from the incurable disease of writing."'

'Naturally,' I said. I know no Latin whatsoever.

'"And it becomes chronic in their sick minds,"' Fluck continued. 'How marvellously precise, don't you think? I fail to understand the critics who complain about Juvenal's melancholy and misogyny; they completely miss the point. I'd choose Juvenal over Martial every time, wouldn't you?'

'Possibly,' I said, looking at Angel, who reclined on the sofa in a thoughtful pose, like Sir Brooke Boothby in the famous picture by Joseph Wright of Derby, though more vivid and more slovenly, with his motorcycle boots up on the arm-rest.

'Yep,' said Angel. He was at his most vibrantly witty.

We lifted our glasses solemnly and drank, and Fluck began to talk about Roman society under Domitian. I don't think Angel or I spoke again until we were obliged to crawl to bed.

'Goodnight, goodnight,' called Fluck from behind us when he realised we were making for the door. 'I have enjoyed our little chat, S. J., just like old times. Goodnight to both of you, dear boys.' We stumbled with relief into the silence of the hall.

In bed I tried to make love to Poppet, and failed.

* * *

62

What did Fluck mean when he said that our evening together was 'just like old times'? It is puzzling, in a trivial kind of way. But then nostalgia is a common enough form of untruthfulness, and I suppose it should not surprise me that Fluck invented the past, he was so used to inventing the present and the future. The facts, however, as always, stand apart.

I met Fluck at college, associated with him for a while, then let the association drop. The period Fluck over-enthusiastically refers to must be related to the time we shared college rooms together, a rather shabby little suite above the porter's lodge, overlooking the main quad. We shared these rooms, in fact, for the full three years of our undergraduate life, right up until our break, which occurred at the end of our final year, as such breaks should. I suppose living with Fluck was a form of solidarity; you see, we were somewhat thrown together by circumstance. Most of the other members of college seemed to hate us, or at least they hated Fluck, and this hostility they extended to me by association. To be perfectly frank, I did not care. My background – comprehensive school, Northern industrial – was anathema to those from the shires or the *nouveaux riches* enclaves of Hampstead or Holland Park. Have I mentioned that my college days where the unhappiest of my life? Let me summarise: I belonged to no dining societies, no debating clubs, no sports teams; I was never seduced to any political persuasion or religious belief, in fact, never seduced at all, by débutante or Nigerian princess – or if I was, it was unmemorable and probably accidental. I never rowed the college to victory in Eights or Torpids; I never stood for the Union or was invited to dine at High Table; I was never caught red-handed in the act of some wilful famous misdemeanour involving gambling, drugs or drink; my name was never posted in Schools for Scholarships or Exhibitions; it never even appeared on the most insignificant of college noticeboards. And I was never, at any point in my undergraduate life, approached by the KGB. But so what? It hardly matters, or at least it matters only in so far as I am trying to suggest that sharing rooms with Fluck was an act of social necessity, not choice.

Our interests, it is true, coincided to a degree. Fluck of course loved to play this up. '"We have the same life,"' he used to misquote Robert Lowell in a lousy American accent, 'the generic one our generation offered.' And again, 'You want to write. I want to paint.' He had the idea that we would one day collaborate on a book, a Blakean union of word and image, the bloody fool. Perhaps he thought I believed in it too, perhaps I neglected to deny it as strenuously as I should. Of course any collaboration quickly proved, thank god, impossible, but this caused its own problems. I don't know why, but it became a source of uneasiness between us. Naturally we drifted apart then, as we would have done sooner or later anyway. There was no final row or recriminations, I remember, no drama at all, until now.

As you would expect, I often wonder what Fluck thought of those three years once they were over, the years before our break, before my marriage, before he went grumbling off to New York. Very different thoughts from my own, I suppose. You never dip your toe in the same river twice; like the present and the future, the past is continuously changing. Memory alters all. And in any case everyone has a different toe to begin with. No, Fluck's memories were, I'm sure, ideally unique. When he spoke of the 'good old days' he was referring to his own personal property. Certain concrete facts I could no doubt recognise – my book of poems, *Prohibited Caresses*, which he helped with when it came to be printed; the drawings he made of me and later presented to me, in a rather sneering way, on the eve of his departure for New York – some things, like these, I could prove to have existed. But who is to say what such things meant to Fluck, what images he squeezed out of them? Who is to describe the memories that are curled around these images, clinging like candy-floss to the stick, a confection of colour and air, and a fantastic hoax? Nevertheless, it grieves me sometimes that I was not as plain with Fluck as I might have been.

Waking on the morning following our drunken dinner, I was instantly made aware of having been outmanoeuvred. Firstly, I remembered the ridiculous competition which Fluck had devised, for although I had not specifically accepted his challenge, I had not made an effective refusal of it, and I felt its dead weight on me even before I had anticipated the difficulties it would cause. Secondly, I suffered a vague foreboding I could in no way define but which, it proved later, was entirely justified. Thirdly, I had an appalling headache. I had not yet learned to connect such dissatisfactions with my wife, but I was already aware of her collusion with Fluck in the matter of the competition. Had she not convinced everyone that I needed time alone in which to write my story, stupid mistake on my part it was ever to have invented it?

'Don't be cross,' she said to me later that morning, 'you'll thank me for it when you are a famous writer.' There was a hint of humour in her tone. She even had the gall to remind me of my sportsman's agreement with Fluck. 'I know you can do better than him,' she said, 'you're so funny and clever. I can't wait to hear you read, I'm going to be so proud of you. Now, help me find my swimsuit, you did pack it, didn't you?'

No one seemed to care or even realise that whereas I was to be confined to a desk, Fluck could accompany the others to the beach whenever he felt like it, on the simple pretext of sketching his portraits – *en plein air*. Or alternatively – and worse – he could retire to his studio, with, say, Poppet, for an afternoon experimenting with formal poses.

Of course I have said earlier that I crave solitude. But I do not *enjoy* being on my own, I never mentioned enjoyment in relation to my craving. Like any other civilised human being I suffer to some degree from a confusion of primary impulses, of desire and fear. This is hardly uncommon, and indeed wouldn't be worth a mention at all if it wasn't for the fact that Henry Fluck, like some gross imp of Fate, had already begun to manipulate circumstances beyond my control. More of this later.

That morning I got up at about six o'clock, very early, as is my unnatural practice after a heavy drinking session the night before (I do it in order to regain some sense of self control) and left Poppet sleeping under the twisted pale pink eiderdown. As its tormented configuration suggested, we had had quite a night of it. The eiderdown itself had immediately disgusted me, drunk though I was when I finally stumbled to bed in the early hours of that morning. The room was pitch black, so I was not at first aware of the eiderdown's hideous pinkness, but I swore viciously as soon as I engaged its slippery nylon folds. Fluck had provided us with nothing else, no sheets or blankets, just the eiderdown, plump and pink and clammy.

'What's this?' I roared, grabbing a handful of it. Poppet woke up.

'What is it?' she cried into the dark.

'What's this?' I repeated angrily.

'Where?' she shouted in a panicky voice.

'This!' I yelled, tugging at the eiderdown. 'Here!'

'In the bed?' she screamed, leaping out of it. 'Oh god, there's something in the bed, S. J., help me, S. J., please, help!' The light came on, and with it, stunned silence. Poppet was crouched in the corner, under the light switch, her knees up to her chest, her arms round her knees. She was staring at me wildly, mouth open.

'This eiderdown,' I said coldly, 'I can't sleep with this eiderdown. Where's the rest of the stuff. I can't sleep with just this.'

Poppet closed her mouth and got to her feet. Folded her arms. 'You're drunk,' she said.

'Just look at it, just look at the colour of it. And feel it. Christ!'

'Go and clean your teeth and drink plenty of water,' she said.

'But he's meant to be rich.'

'Go and clean your teeth.' Her face was firm. Her fingers waited by the light switch. Poppet and I have – or had – an unwritten agreement concerning drunkenness. The sober one of us looks after the drunk one. Perhaps due to the sheer force of routine, this has the necessary calming effect. Soon I, or sometimes Poppet (not often), lapse into a childish grumbling obedience, the penultimate stage of drunkenness, which eventually gives way to friendly oblivion.

'Wait,' she said, 'take off your socks. You know I can't bear it with them in bed.' I began to shiver violently. The room was chilly. 'Off.' Poppet commanded, and off they came. I remember how cold and lumpy the bed was as I slid into it; the eiderdown was a gaudy rag, it sickened me, but worse, towards the bottom of the bed, where my feet twitched and shrank into themselves, it was insidiously damp. I set up a shrill wail which Poppet, climbing into bed after me, angrily curtailed.

'I want to go to sleep,' she said, 'it must be two o'clock.'

The dark engulfed us. I sneezed, and Poppet turned sharply away from me, trailing eiderdown and leaving me exposed, tensely foetal, staring gloomily into the dark V of her narrow trapezoids. It was about another half hour before I could rouse her sufficiently to be made love to, and then, as I have said, it was a failure. The bed remained cold, and the ludicrous eiderdown slithered this way and that as we tossed and turned. Through the sleepless, sobering hours, I kept trying to work out what time it was, two o'clock, three o'clock, half-past four, had I been to sleep? I didn't think so; quarter to five, five o'clock, ticking and breathing with awful regularity, but no sleep.

I was up at six, dishevelled and pained. The room was filled with a watery grey light as I dressed and slipped out into the hall, tiptoeing down the stairs, afraid for some reason to break the silence. Actually, it is not in my character to break silences if I can help it. I am rather timid by nature. In the kitchen I drew back the curtains and made myself a cup of coffee. I didn't realise, of course, that over the next few days I would be making exactly the same trivial trip innumerable times, alone and silent, for coffee, or beer, or just to escape my room with its bare and barren old desk at which I would injure my idle fingerends with my busy teeth, and utterly fail to work. All I had now was a vague feeling of discontent not entirely distinct from the torment of my hangover.

Fluck's living-room, I noticed as I walked around that morning, drawing back curtains and sipping coffee, was crammed full of incongruous furniture. I had not realised this the night before. At the centre of the living-room a tiny monochrome TV rested on a splintering tea chest which, I guessed, had been found on the beach. Facing the TV was a three-piece suite from the 1970s with black leather upholstery and tubular aluminium legs and arms. The left-hand seat of the sofa had collapsed. Behind the TV was an eighteenth-century walnut writing desk, heavily polished. On either side of this, and round the rest of the room, were scattered an odd assortment of battered scullery-type chairs and stools, each standing in distracted isolation, as if abandoned there. Finally, as might be expected, all available wall space was taken up with Fluck's pictures.

I have admitted that Fluck was a genius, and it is unfortunately true. Fluck had the greatest natural talent of anyone I have ever known. Inevitably this complicated things a little – I am an amateur art critic, after all, and I could hardly overlook genius; it tends to assert itself. I could not fail to notice the familiar signs, the flashes of inspiration, the furious revelations, the pure, the incomparable style of his art – a style, I might add, that had no counterpart in Fluck's personal life. Does this sound as though I was jealous of his achievements? It was not so. I always viewed his pictures with a strictly dispassionate awe, and I never let my recognition of Fluck's genius obscure my loathing of him as a person. It was just that there were moments when, looking at one of his pictures, I almost found myself thinking that perhaps all the misery he caused was justified – just to have produced one of his wonderful pictures with its lucid draughtsmanship and singing colours and that unmistakable character of assurance, as if it could not have been painted any other way or by anyone else. But I did not often think like this, thank god – I couldn't have withstood the strain of such forgiveness. Mainly I was able to love the pictures and loathe the man, which was the most graceful compromise I could achieve.

That first morning I took the time to study the pictures carefully. They did not pale under scrutiny as other, better known contemporary works of art have done; rather the opposite, they flourished. Most of the pictures I studied were seascapes, and most seemed to depict the same scene, though they did not at all resemble one another. Fluck's style was idiosyncratic and restless; there seemed to be no constant in his work, and the themes and moods and even the character of the brush strokes changed from picture to picture. Not that this was a sign of mere immaturity, of course not; this ability to adopt, as it were, different disguises was the hallmark of a special expertise. His pictures resembled a series of dazzling and unpredictable card-tricks performed one after another by a fluent and flawless card-sharp.

A few of the pictures I knew already. As a matter of fact they had been exhibited at the Annual Art Students' Show held at the university the year before – although Fluck wasn't, strictly speaking, studying art, he had somehow managed to get a number of his pictures accepted by the exhibition committee. Coincidentally, the arts magazine *Artspeak* had asked me to cover the exhibition. It was my first journalist's assignment. There wasn't much good work there, I remember; Fluck's was about the best. I didn't, however. give it a mention. It is a peculiar fact that the better one knows something, the more difficult it is to talk about. I found myself in just this predicament with Fluck's pictures, and because I could devote only a small space to them anyway, I decided to avoid mentioning them altogether. I think it was best that way. Fluck would have understood; he cared so little about such things, in any case.

Not all the paintings in the living-room were seascapes. There were a couple of self-portraits and one of these caught my attention and held me, spellbound, for several minutes. I remember this well, for I found in that painting the first echo of that ominous feeling I had suffered since waking.

In the picture Fluck was laughing the open-mouthed belly-laugh I have already mentioned. This had the effect of inflating most of his face, and his brush had brilliantly captured the straining chin and stretched mouth, the porcine, twinkly eyes and puffed cheeks, and at the centre, the pale diminished nose, squeezed thin by all these other risen features. Mauve shadows flickered over all, darkening the pink canthi of the eyes, ginger chin-fluff and yellowish complexion. The interior of the mouth, the true focus of the painting, was a rich purple. Fluck had evidently borrowed from Cubism (the formal dislocation of perspective) and also from the Viennese Secession (nervous surface texture, discontinuous line), and there was also a trace of the influence of the mad Expressionist Richard Gerstl, by way of pastiche, in the picture's general composition – but in all other respects it was fantastically original. At the very least you had to admire Fluck's lively sense of the grotesque. His picture exactly mimicked the awful reality of his laughter, the fluid brush strokes suggesting a long peal of rising notes. For a moment it was as if I actually heard the familiar shrill noise, the hiccups and whistles and salivary snorts. This was too much for me. Almost with my hands over my ears I hurried from the picture.

Only to return to it a few minutes later. It seemed to draw me back. And it was then that I realised that I had been the victim of an illusion. The figure in the picture wasn't laughing at all. He was screaming. I mean, screaming as in screaming-in-pain, or possibly screaming-for-help. Perhaps terror had something to do with it as well. But the scream was absolutely definite, it was obvious from the eyes, which were sharp and panicky, and

69

the mouth, a shocked black zero. The whole face, in fact, was horribly jolted out of shape. This was something of a shock to me. To be frank, I became somewhat confused and, stepping back in alarm, I stumbled over a low-slung, glass-topped coffee table I had not noticed before, squealing loud enough to wake the whole house. Typical of Fluck, of course, even at one remove to engineer such an effect. We both knew, he and I, the efficacy of Art. I removed the coffee table from between my knees, rose, and looked at the painting again – and with a sinking feeling I saw the familiar smiling eyes and toothy joyful mouth. It was absurd. I retreated to the centre of the room where I could view the picture more coolly, but from that distance it was impossible to see either the laugh or the scream, or, indeed, the face. From that distance the picture appeared to be entirely abstract.

It was a technical trick, merely, I have no doubt. An illusion, like *trompe-l'oeil*, to bewilder those stupid enough to trust their eyes. I do not usually fall for such tricks, but I was tired and hungover and the dim early morning light abetted Fluck's virtuosity. At least, these are the reasons I provided myself with as I searched in vain for the cunning mechanism that turned laughter into agony in a blink, as if a double-faced coin was spun in front of me, flashing alternately the masks of tragedy and comedy. I did not yet think of Fate which arranges things so teasingly, leaving clues to be discovered only when it is too late and the future has irrevocably turned into the past.

Looking back now, I see that the moment at which I stood nose to nose with the portrait of the screaming, laughing Fluck was a crucial one. It was crucial in the sense that it anticipated certain themes developed later in my story – and it is in this, most strongly, that I see the hand of Fate. You do not believe in Fate? Well, I turned on my heel, strode out to the staircase, and there bumped into the yawning, shambling figure of Fluck, who immediately affected a grotesque attitude of wide-awakeness, and harangued me with matutinal banter. I stared at his mouth, the instrument of so much distressing noise, and realised that I had gone straight from the painted image to the thing itself, from fear to the vivid animation of my fear. Is it not enough to make you believe just a little in Fate? It was half-past seven, apparently the time of Fluck's early morning stroll.

'Join me,' he said, 'build up your appetite, why don't you, you really have become terribly thin, dear boy.' He made calf-eyes of sympathy at me, an expression disconcerting enough to put anyone off their food.

'At this time of year,' he went on, 'I always take exercise before breakfast. It is the most perfect time for cerebration. During the course of a half-hour walk I can compose half a dozen paintings in my head. When I return, I eat a light breakfast, empty my bowels, and paint out my ideas for the rest of the day. What could be simpler?'

I yawned, hoping to irritate him as he elaborated on the theme of his genius and his bowels, and he broke off what he was saying.

'You say you slept well,' he observed with great emphasis on 'slept', 'and yet you seem unduly tired.'

I dismissed this with a flippancy to the effect that I was getting old.

Inexplicably, he found this amusing and began to laugh. 'Oh dear,' he said, at last, breathless, 'do you remember my big oil painting of you as Ganymede? Evidently I shall have to update it, what do you think, I'll get rid of most of the hair and dress you in that lovely stretch-fabric orthopaedic underwear.'

The picture to which he referred, let me assure you, does not exist. I refuse to admit to a large-scale oil painting. Drawings, yes, I have already confessed to drawings, it would be impossible for me to deny the hundreds of chalks, pastels, ink-and-wash, drypoint and charcoals that Fluck made of me – often, I might add, when I was unaware of it, at my most defenceless, sleeping or reading or slipping into a drunken faint. My basic problem was that I was never able to make it clear to Fluck that I resented being his model. He took no hints and was insensitive to rudeness. 'What do you mean, S.J.?' he would ask, looking up from his board and paper. 'I'm not stopping you from taking a bath. I can draw you equally well in the bath as out of it.' – But no, I will not accept the notion of this big oil painting of Ganymede. Fluck was being fanciful, he must have said it to provoke me.

We shambled out of the house and into the garden. Fluck's dressing-gown billowed obscenely in the breeze, aerating his pink, pudgy body. I moved upwind. Now, patting his belly, regarding it with a pleased expression, he began to talk volubly about himself, his voice a loud bray. I expected it would wake the whole house, and I was horrified at the thought of it. Already I resented the idea that Fluck and I had ever had anything in common, and I did not want to be seen in conference with him. Also, he seemed to have certain problems walking. I mean by this that his body showed absolutely no interest in the usual procedure. He would take a few steps forward, stop, perhaps to make a conversational point or to examine a weed in the garden, then shuffle on the spot, make as if to sit (though there was nothing to sit on), right himself, shuffle again, and finally come to rest a few yards beyond his original starting-point. I wondered at first if these were special exercises, but the thought of Fluck doing exercises was inconceivable. He seemed to be simply incapacitated. It is curious, is it not, that Coleridge, another monologue specialist, suffered similarly. A slight deformity of his inner ear permanently affected his balance and turned an ordinary stroll into a kind of choppy gallop, rather disconcerting to his companions. Even so, he at least sounds more energetic than Fluck. Later, however – unpleasantly – I was to discover that Fluck could be considerably more mobile when he chose to be.

'Do you know,' he said now, concluding some satirical observations of the New York art world, 'I always thought you would sell out and go and work in the City. Myra reminded me last night. When I was in New York, especially after I got your letter – your only letter – I used to wonder about this. Everyone else sold out, didn't they? They all went off to grub money in the Stock Exchange. I thought you would have been the first, how strange that you weren't.'

I reminded him that I had always wanted to write for my living; I was referring to my journalism, but he wilfully misunderstood me.

'Oh yes!' he shouted at once, clapping his hands enthusiastically, 'your wonderful stories, how could I forget them! I can't wait to read the one you're going to write here. Didn't you tell me last night what it was going to be called?'

'"A Portrait of the Artist Enslaved by his Art",' I said.

This is a shade over-grand, is it not? I had certain misgivings myself but the title had occurred to me as a sardonic response

72

to Fluck's dreadful monologues of the night before, and although there might never be an actual story I was keen to play Fluck's game, up to a point.

'Excellent,' said Fluck. 'You've found your one true subject. Myself.'

I scowled as he guffawed. 'Only teasing,' he tittered.

A few minutes later we reached the end of the garden. 'Here,' he said, indicating a stone seat in front of him, 'this is where we stop. We'll have a little rest, then go back.' I looked behind us towards the house. We had come perhaps fifty yards. It had taken us almost ten minutes.

He squeezed himself into the small seat like bread dough into a loaf tin, and I stood, a little sullenly, to one side, there being nowhere else to sit – I was not going to sit on Fluck's lap. I think perhaps we were silent for a minute or two while we looked over the garden, a vivid tangle of flowers from our feet to the house ahead of us, and the famous rockery banking steeply to our right. Eventually Fluck spoke again.

'Why do you write?' he asked. I must admit I was rather taken aback by this. 'Well,' he said, after a pause, 'do you *know* why you write? Any idea at all?'

I did not know. Nor was I in the mood for such an interrogation. I recalled, half-heartedly, certain ideas gleaned from Bulgakov, E. M. Forster, and R. L. Stevenson concerning the beauty and enigma of the world, but found myself temporarily unable to express them. I stared inexpressively towards Fluck's house.

'Never mind,' said Fluck. 'Do you know why I paint?' I shook my head. 'I paint because the world is so dull. Because we are ugly and trivial. Only art makes things interesting, and sometimes, though not often, beautiful. Yes, without art, my dear, the world is intolerably mediocre.'

I thought about this briefly and sensed Fluck expected some kind of a retort. 'But . . .' I began.

'Only my materials interest me,' Fluck went on, 'and what I make of them. Once I have chosen a subject it ceases to have any meaning for me – which is natural enough, you see, because it didn't have any meaning to begin with.'

'None of your subjects interests you?'

'None.' He was bluffing.

'Not even self-portraits?'

'When I paint self-portraits,' he said, beaming, 'I marvel merely at the sitter's co-operativeness.'

I left it at that. Not for the first time I recognised in Fluck a fondness for the droll Wildean turn of phrase, and I realised how awful it must have been to have known Wilde and to have had to suffer those perfectly turned niceties. Curious too, I thought, how like the martyred Oscar Fluck looked. He had the same bulk, the same supercilious gaze, the same lacy gestures with his hands as if continually twirling and juggling silk handkerchieves. The difference was, of course, that Oscar was pomaded and perfumed whereas Fluck was dingy and dirty and smelt vaguely like pets kept in warm hutches.

'The façade is rather interesting, don't you think?' he said next, indicating the house. 'Eighteenth-century, of course. My grandfather put about the rumour that it was designed by William Kent, but unfortunately there's absolutely no evidence to back him up. Note the Serliania window though, pure Palladianism and really rather good.'

As we looked, curtains were suddenly drawn in an upstairs window, and Fluck, the Great Actor, billowed to his feet.

'They're up,' he cried, 'or at least your beloved is. Time for breakfast.'

The denuded window glinted black in the sharp morning light. A pale form fluttered behind it and disappeared – Poppet, my wife, not yet Fluck's lover, getting dressed. Perhaps she would look out of the window and see us together. Perhaps make a choice. With a great deal of showy kindness, Fluck had put us in a room with a good view of the rockery. It was directly above his own room, which was on the ground floor.

'I'm so glad we had our little chat about your story,' said Fluck as we walked back, 'whatever it was called. You do realise, don't you, that stories are for inadequates. But don't let that put you off. Now, here is the rockery, rather famous in its day. How many flowers can you name?'

Breakfast was an unpleasant affair. Angel and I were understandably appetiteless after the excesses of the night before, and none of the girls ever bothered with food in the mornings, but Fluck bullied us into the kitchen regardless. He even went and woke Moyra who, when given a choice, rarely rose before lunchtime. She appeared at the breakfast table, dozier and more dumbfounded than ever, smoking already, squeezed into a slovenly pink nylon dressing-gown. The belt was knotted tightly around her waist. Her feet were bare and her toenails bore the scuffed remains of crimson nail varnish. For such instant arousals I am always grateful. But not even these intimations of Moyra's nudity could redeem the occasion. We sat in silence, watching Fluck eat and listening to him talk. The smell of fried eggs filled the room. Liquid strands of yolk festooned his stubble and occasionally dripped unnoticed onto his sleeves. Several times he dabbled his fingers in the marmalade jar and sucked them like a baby. 'While you were all sleeping,' he said, 'S. J. and I took a rain-check.'

'It looks like a lovely day,' said Poppet. Fluck stared at her.

'It is at least temperate,' he said. 'Not that I expect anything less than a blizzard to prevent you going down to the beach.' He chuckled dryly in the manner of someone quietly amused by the frivolousness of others. 'S. J. and I will join you later,' he continued, 'after we've got some work done. I think we could take an hour or so off later, eh, S. J.? Say at one o'clock. I presume you plan to picnic on the beach, so we'll bring the wine with us, it will allow the bottles to chill properly in the fridge. I find Chianti totally unpalatable if insufficiently chilled.' Frankly I did not see that it mattered, given the tiny quantities he drank, but he had always been fussy about wine. At university his battels bills were the largest in the college, though his reputation as a drinker was justifiably non-existent.

'OK with you, my dear?' he asked me. 'A couple of thousand words before luncheon?' I declined to answer this.

As it turned out he had no intention of staying at home to work. Half an hour after his original pronouncement, when the others were finally ready to leave for the beach and he was still sitting at the table eating, he suddenly 'changed his mind'.

'Do you know,' he said as they made for the door, 'I think I'll come with you after all.' Everyone stared at him. 'You've twisted my arm,' he added in the manner of a grand and much-hoped for announcement. But the real reason for his change of plans was apparent from the brief uproar he caused assembling his equipage of brushes, colours and papers. He simply craved attention. As he grabbed his artists' materials from cupboards and drawers he talked loudly to Moyra about the portrait he was going to paint of her. 'I have in mind a theme I think you will be interested in,' he said, and began to talk at length about the Great English Nude. Soon he was in full cry.

'Mmm,' said Moyra from time to time, 'mmm, I know exactly what you mean.'

I watched all this with vague disgust. Once Poppet caught my eye from the opposite side of the room and waved at me. Why did she wave, she was standing only a few yards away? She was being deliberately childlike and her wave was like a rudimentary copy of the real thing, as if she had just been taught how. Uncle Henry was taking her to the beach. Role play before roll play, if you will forgive the pun.

'*Au revoir!*' Fluck shouted to me as they left. 'Don't forget the wine and please be prompt.' They all waved and I smiled back, or rather, as they say, I showed my teeth.

I should have been delighted that I had not been left alone with Fluck; I should have put all thought of him from my mind, and curled up on the sofa with a cool drink and my book of *fin de siècle* perversities. I should certainly not have attempted to write a story. And yet, almost without reflection, I went up to my room, sat at the desk, and prepared to write. 'A Portrait of the Artist Enslaved by his Art.' Ridiculous. I laid out paper and notebooks, sharpened a pencil, and waited dutifully for inspiration to come roaring in through the window.

Nothing happened. The words wouldn't come. For the previous eleven months I had been churning out copy for magazines week in, week out, without ever missing a deadline, and now, in ideal conditions, I was suddenly struck dumb.

The house was very still and very quiet. Also slightly damp, despite the fine weather. It was impossible to work in such a house. The house, I could sense, was against me. I went downstairs and made a coffee – and thus, in desperation, began my wanderings round the empty house, idle, incurious explorations which took me quietly and cautiously from room to room, like a spy.

This is how it always begins, stalking down strange corridors on the off-chance of finding, in some hidden room, the secret of your own soul . . .

Of course I don't mean to suggest that I *snooped*, my wandering were far too aimless, but it is true that I sometimes found myself walking round on tiptoe even though there was no one in the house to hear me. I avoided creaking floorboards; by corners of corridors I waited and listened before going on. And though I did not snoop as such, it several times occurred to me that, quite without intention, I might find something I hadn't really been looking for, and that when I had found it, the purpose of my distracted rambling to and fro would become clear. Eventually, of course, as is the nature of these things, I *did* find it – to my inconsolable distress.

I had the whole morning to fill, so at first I confined my wanderings to the ground floor. Early on, I discovered the tiny lavatory under the stairs; I suddenly found myself sitting in it without purpose and without realising how I came to be there. It was, I think, the most peaceful room in the house. Certainly it was the only one without any of Fluck's pictures hanging in it. It was painted all over in bright blue which in patches had faded to the shade of a cool autumn sky. I discovered that if I leaned to either side of the toilet at an angle of about thirty degrees from the perpendicular, I could rest my forehead against the cool painted surface of the wall, and derive from this certain calming effects, so much so that I thought if I stayed in that position for long enough I might, by a kind of osmosis, extrude whatever in my head was causing my writer's block, and receive in exchange a calm and clear sense of purpose. But in the end I became restless and rose to go, instinctively pulling the chain of the toilet as I did so. The extreme loudness of clanking machinery and tumultuous waters was quite astounding.

From the lavatory my odyssey continued round the house, becoming ever more tedious. The boredom was such that I was now constrained to smoke a cigarette. This I got from a packet I found in Moyra's room. I must have popped in there for a few minutes. Then I found myself downstairs again, this time in the dining-room, where I lolled around, cigarette in hand, my mouth parched with smoke, stupefied with a sense of my own listlessness. I sat in Moyra's seat and imagined myself opposite her. I smiled sexily, but it was a stupid game and I soon wandered into the living-room where I occupied myself with the magazines and comics that littered the floor, the *National Geographic*, *The Spectator*, *Punch*, *Mind*, *Art Today*, *The Incredible Hulk*. I had not seen this last one before. WHAM! BIFFO! KER-THUNK! BLAP! The story seemed incredibly difficult to follow, interrupted, as it was, by almost constant outbreaks of gratuitous violence. When I had finished the comic I felt more depressed than ever. My sense that the house was odd and in some way hostile to me grew, blossomed, in fact, into paranoia. The whole ground floor had an odd smell, the furniture was uncomfortable, the comics felt damp. I couldn't possibly work in a house like that, and I imagined myself doomed to wander insubstantially through its deserted rooms for ever, day-dreaming, drinking coffee, smoking forbidden cigarettes. Again I had the impression that I was waiting for something nasty to happen.

These were my unvaried feelings, not just during that morning, but, generally speaking, for most of the first two days at Fluck's house. In fact I don't think I can readily distinguish between the first day and the second, for the same events belong to both. When I say I lolled around the living-room or sat in the lavatory, it hardly matters *when* I did this, I seemed to do it all the time. Such is the nature of boredom, blunting and muffling even crisp chronological facts. Only in the conservatory did I find a little comfort. I liked the terracotta plant pots that stood in a regimented row against the house wall, and I liked the way sunlight lit up the patches of rain-streaked dirt on the window panes, creating strange shapes out of them, caricatures of faces, blurred fingerprints of enormous hands. I liked sitting on the floor and looking up through the sap-spotted glass roof at the overhanging branches of an oak tree. But these were brief diversions, and even the bedrooms soon ceased to intrigue. The novelty of crumpled sheets, and opened drawers spilling over with underwear, and unusual devices in bags of toiletries, wore off all too rapidly.

But two rooms did continue to exercise my sense of curiosity: Fluck's bedroom and his attic studio. These alone, of all the rooms in the house, seemed to harbour real secrets. It is sad, I know, but, as I have said, I considered Fluck a genius, and as such, despite my efforts otherwise, he continued to interest me.

I did not know exactly what kind of secrets might be hidden

in his two rooms, but I vaguely imagined that they would offer a glimpse of the 'real' Fluck, whoever that was, a Fluck divested of his overwrought façade. Nudity is knowledge. Sooner than I expected both rooms would disclose secrets, more monstrous than any I had thought of, but I was not to know this yet. In fact I knew nothing because I could not bring myself to enter either of the two rooms. Some superstitiousness prevented me. Occasionally, I confess, I went so far as to mount the lowest rungs of the ladder that led to the attic, or else loitered nervously outside Fluck's bedroom door, but each time I could force myself no further. Interestingly, after such inconsequent brushes with mystery, I always went straight back to my room and redoubled my efforts to write. This was either to purge myself of furtive impulses or to alleviate my sense of failure. Needless to say, I did not write and nor was anything alleviated or purged, and I ended up as listless and disconsolate as before.

When, that first morning, I eventually glanced at my watch, it was gone two o'clock and I was already very late.

I did not immediately panic, such was my languor, but I soon perked up when I discovered that the wine was not, indeed had never been, in the fridge. This was clearly Fluck's fault, it was his wine, after all, but I knew even then that it would not appear so. I grabbed four bottles of lukewarm Chianti, stuffed them into a carrier bag and belted out of the house, clanking as I ran. In my fury I did not care if bottles broke, indeed I think I half wanted them to break – this would have been Fluck's fault as well, by extension, and serve him right. In the end, only one bottle did break, I heard it crack as I leapt over a small stile and saw wine trail from a hole in the bag. Cursing Fluck, I ran on.

'*Voici, le garçon est arrivé,*' he said icily when he saw me. '*Mon petit, tu es trop tard.*' Fuck you, I thought.

'Sorry,' I said, panting. 'Sorry, sorry.' I held up the dripping bag. 'I'm afraid a bottle may have cracked slightly on the way down.' I intended my tone to be bitter, but I was almost too breathless even to get the words out.

'Don't understand,' said Fluck bluntly. 'Speak properly.'

I repeated myself. Fluck sneered. 'As long as it wasn't *my* bottle that broke,' he said. 'But I expect it was yours, wasn't it?' He took the bag from me, peered into it, removed an unbroken

79

bottle, and, as I knew he would, tested its temperature with the pudgy palm of a hand.

'Been in the fridge long?' he enquired. 'Been *near* the fridge?' He was white with suppressed insults.

'Not *in* the fridge.'

'Remind me if I'm wrong . . .' he began, then abruptly stopped. Slowly he wiped his thin beard with a grubby hand. 'But then,' he said in an entirely different, sweeter voice, 'I expect you've been working tremendously hard, haven't you, closeted away with your muse, no time to think of such mundane things as tepid wine.' I fixed him with my own sneer. 'And you look so dejected and crestfallen,' he said, clucking sympathetically, 'I suppose we'll have to forgive you, poor thing.' He held out his arms in pastoral benediction, a bottle in one hand, the dripping bag in the other.

Thus he triumphed doubly, once in his gross and unjustified impertinence to me, and once again in his assumption of self-effacing forgiveness. This was characteristic of him, to have it both ways, and to lack all humility. It was hardly surprising the picnic was not a success.

'Don't worry about the wine,' said Poppet as we unpacked the hamper together. 'Four bottles was too many anyway. And' – she lowered her voice – 'Henry doesn't even drink at lunch-time, he told me.' I grunted. So, they had been talking. But I suppose it was nice of her to affect an interest in me. What she really wanted to talk about was her morning on the beach. Apparently Angel had stripped down to his imitation-leopard skin Y-fronts and waded into the sea up to his armpits. He did this for a bet. Subsequently he carried Moyra out to sea as well, and threatened to sink her, and she was hysterical with fear and sank her teeth deep into his neck. This aroused my interest, I admit, though later I saw the mark and was disappointed – it failed to live up to the splendour of my expectations.

After this we sat on the warm sand and I drank most of the tepid wine and the others did most of the talking. Fluck painted a little way off, sulking, but occasionally calling us to go and look at his picture. When we finally did, I was horrified to see how good it was. Also, it was nearly finished, he seemed to work with incredible speed.

'There are a few allusions in it,' said Fluck teasingly to me, 'of an art-historical nature.' Clearly his picture was a parody of Botticelli's 'Birth of Venus' and I promptly said so.

'Dear me,' said Fluck, 'how astonishingly astute of you. Is it really that obvious?'

Let me explain. In Botticelli's very famous picture Venus stands coyly on a scallop shell which floats on the waves near the shore. Her right hand gratifyingly fails to cover both breasts, but with her left hand she takes up the tresses of her long golden hair and modestly conceals her pudenda. On one side of her, dancing lightly on the wavelets, are the puff-cheeked zephyrs, who are blowing her to shore, and on the other side Spring, one of the daughters of Jupiter and Themis, greets her with a floral negligée. Venus is looking rather pensive, which is queer because although it is common enough to be *triste post coitum*, this is meant to be the *birth* of pleasure. But perhaps I am wrong. The painting has been subjected to much interpretation, and has suffered a great many learned and nonsensical theses, including the neo-platonism of Marsilio Ficino, tutor to the picture's original owner, and the fraudulent wit of ad-men promoting cosmetics and detergents. Others too have appropriated it for their own uses, and now Fluck was getting in on the act.

In Fluck's picture, Moyra was standing on the shoulders of someone half submerged in the water, presumably the bitten Angel. In one hand she held a cigarette, the other hand rested against her hip. She was fully clothed. She looked very happy.

'I'm thinking of calling it "The Mirth of Venus",' said Fluck, looking at me slyly. I looked back at him blankly to show I was not afraid of his humour. 'Not really,' he added. 'But I'm at a loss what to do about the background. I didn't bring any sponges with me.'

'Oh dear,' I said. I did not understand what he meant.

'You recall Vasari's comment?' he asked. I didn't, but nodded.

'Vasari thought Botticelli's figures were exquisite but he said the background was so crudely done Botticelli must have simply thrown a sponge at it.' Fluck roared with laughter and I smiled slightly.

'You do understand, S. J.?' I nodded again, coldly.

'It's funny,' said Moyra, who was standing with us. 'I just can't stop, well, laughing, when I look at it.' She laughed. 'But

I like it.' She gazed out to sea and then drifted away, lighting a cigarette as she went.

'Why clothed?' I asked. This, indeed, was my main objection to the painting. 'Surely this was your chance to do the Great English Nude you keep talking about.'

'But how churlish to steal the Great Florentine Nude to do it,' said Fluck. 'Perhaps later,' he added as I turned to follow Moyra. I didn't know what he meant by this at the time, so I paid no attention to his chuckling. It seemed to me Fluck had missed an opportunity.

After lunch I returned to the house, Fluck and Angel with me. The picture of Moyra was finished, sponges or no sponges, and Fluck was keen to press on with his series.

'I hope your writing's going as well as my painting,' he said as we walked. 'Done much?'

'A fair bit,' I said.

'Splendid, splendid. I don't know when I've painted as well as this. But I suppose that's the point of inspiration, eh, not knowing.'

Back at the house I actually managed to write a few paragraphs about something or other, but I was not particularly pleased with them, and they were a poor showing for a whole day's work. Also I was unable to stop myself smoking another cigarette, vainly pretending it was to keep me awake. The room was hot now, heavy sunlight fell in a great slanting wave through the window, which wouldn't for some reason open, and I began to feel drowsy. In desperation I attempted to divert myself by writing a limerick, but this failed to materialise. I was aware that somewhere in the house Fluck was having a great success with Angel's portrait. So, when I could no longer get any purchase with my teeth on my fingernails, I wandered downstairs. They were in the conservatory.

'When I've finished,' Fluck called over his shoulder, hearing me arrive, 'you can write an ode on him. But not before. I suspect that he couldn't bear so much art all at once.'

Fluck had set up his easel in the doorway and cleverly positioned Angel opposite him, sitting on a garden chair, with his head almost touching the sloping glass ceiling so that his hair, all aquamarine tufts and spikes, was clearly reflected in the bright dusty panes – his 'halo', of course. Angel was drinking beer from a can, looking bored.

'What chapter of your story are you on now?' asked Fluck, again without turning round.

'Oh, I'm not bothering with chapters,' I said. 'I'm just writing it all down, like Beckett.'

'Quite,' said Fluck. 'Still, you don't want to let your pen run away with you.'

I thought this odd, coming from someone who dashed off his paintings so quickly, and entirely without correction. To be frank, this rapidity of his filled me with envy. It was as if he were aware of an image pre-existing on the canvas which he had only to reveal. I never saw him do any preparatory work, nor abandon anything he had begun. And in all this he was self-consciously extrovert. At the easel he handled himself like a dandy, simpering and wise-cracking and eulogising over his own work in what he seemed to presume was a comic manner. 'You should see it,' he would cry to his sitter. 'It's really quite splendid. I haven't seen brushwork like this outside seventeenth-century Amsterdam. And what about this high-lighting, eh, a touch of genius if I'm not completely blind. And the composition, well, I amaze myself, not to mention the draughtsmanship . . .'

When he wasn't being self-congratulatory, he was ebulliently rude to his sitters. 'Double chin – in or out?' he barked at Angel, who swallowed beer over-quickly.

'Double chin?'

'Don't worry yourself,' cried Fluck. 'My decision really, shouldn't delegate. Which means,' he added *sotto voce* for my benefit, 'chins in.'

Concerning general manners, the resemblance to Whistler was hard to ignore, and Fluck had deliberately cultivated it. Physically of course they were very different, Fluck being approximately twice as large as the little American had been. In this was the irony of which Fluck was so infuriatingly unaware. He might mince and swagger, his pictures might be master-pieces of insouciance – his colours soft and exquisite, his draughtsmanship delicate to an almost oriental degree – but when he ponced backwards to take a squint at it, his arse still wobbled like a bean bag. I am not trying to be insulting to

83

Fluck, I have not the extremity of expression, I merely wish to draw attention to the discrepancy between Fluck's behaviour and his appearance, for which, of course, he himself was entirely responsible.

Nevertheless, let me describe Fluck's portrait of Angel. Fluck's pictures were all clues, even then. His house had turned me into a spy, remember. A little later and I would become a double-agent, all my friends turning to enemies.

The picture was as superlatively good as the portrait of Moyra, though very different. It approached the abstract. Angel's flattish round nose was the only fixed point of reference in a swirling circle of eyes, eyebrows, cheeks, mouths, and chins. This was a bold move on Fluck's part as Angel's expression is typically immobile. I assume that in portraying Angel's face as a whirling kaleidoscope of features Fluck was attempting a psychological realism, and although the style of the painting was ludicrously slick, he seemed, curse him, to have succeeded. He had created an impression of Angel as we knew him: wry, humorous, blatantly over-dressed. Fluck had made apparent the liveliness that Angel usually concealed behind his reticent manner. In this, Fluck was following Klee's dictum: 'The artist does not reproduce the visible: rather he makes things visible.'

Fluck's colour scheme was also interesting. Obviously ultra-marine figured largely in the abstract passages – these corresponded to Angel's hair and halo – but Fluck had mainly utilised the lighter end of his palette to produce a dazzling array of yellows and oranges. In effect it was like viewing Angel's face through the bright lit bottom of a glass of lager. The colours were not static, but shifted, sliding into each other, revealing every tint of the lagery amber from the most brilliant shades of buttercup and brass to the quieter and more elusive glimmers of gold and ochre and their specular echoes of sea-green and cobalt blue.

All this sickened me. I looked at the portrait with a certain irrepressible awe and recalled the brief bit of prose I had spent all day attempting to write – at least, the first sentence of it, which ran: 'Thigh, breast, hip, belly, bum; he played upon these parts as on a glockenspiel.' I did not think I had made a success of this. It had potential, but I had not sufficiently exploited it.

And suddenly, standing there, I was filled with a sense of my own inadequacy and of Fluck's beautiful talent – a strong emotion, an almost physical sensation, urgent and compelling like a tug on the testicles – and such was my conviction that Fluck was an artist of genius that I almost did a very regrettable thing. I could not help it, though I am embarrassed to recall it: even as Fluck flounced around me, falsettoing of his prodigious talents, I all but forgave him his impertinencies to me. I almost felt a kind of tenderness for him. Something I hadn't felt for a long time. I don't say I did *quite*, but almost. In retrospect of course, the emotion is bitterly ironic.

It would be easy to expurgate this little episode from my story, but I have decided to let it stand. It is important to tell the truth, this once, before I go, and part of that is to confess my weaknesses. Also, if Fluck was capable of such a direct appeal to my generosity, it throws light on his seduction of Poppet. Otherwise how can the fact that she let him fuck her so often be explained away?

There is, however, a rather interesting postscript to the incident I have just described. It concerns Angel's portrait. A few days later, after I knew about Poppet and Fluck, I saw the picture again. Fluck displayed it with a number of other portraits, and because they were together it was easy to see a generic likeness, i.e. that in the faces of all his sitters there was the same mobility and multiplicity of expression. Fluck seemed to have placed them all in an imaginary moment of extremity, at the precise instant when their features were dislocated by both joy and agony. And it suddenly occurred to me that this moment could only be the one of sexual climax. Orgasm, of course. It puzzles me that I didn't spot this straight away. Faces writhe and skip, astonished, overjoyed, overwhelmed, exploding out of themselves with eyes popping and jaws protruding, their noses scrunched up and their mouths amazed, their shocked fingers plugged into the sockets of their temples or creating static in their hair. For Fluck, the visible expression of love was not a subtle thing, it was extreme and contradictory, both laughing and screaming. Angel's portrait, among others, taught me this, and also, blast it, posed an unavoidable question: what did Fluck look like under the same joyful duress? Was he like his self-portrait, laughing and screaming at the same time? Was that the face Poppet saw each time she lay beneath him?

To be honest, I find it difficult to consider the point calmly, but it is imperative to know what happened, or rather *how* – the imagination being such a stickler for detail. There comes a time when certain efforts have to be made to ascertain the obvious. For instance, it is clear to me that a man of that size would exert a considerable degree of momentum on the situation. His fat belly, for a start, would have quite a swing to it, the sagging chest too, and the ponderous buttocks, all heaving and glistening (for it is hot work), slapping against her like a thick white wave. There would be variations, of course, but this must be the general idea. Yet what of his face? What did his mouth do, his eyes, nose, cheeks? And what did she think of it? Did she cry afterwards? Did she cling to him in those silent quaking moments after it was all over? Did they discuss it, I mean the thing that was over, holding hands, it wouldn't surprise me, reviewing moments and movements like pictures in a gallery? They could have told me if they had wanted to, if I had asked, what the faces meant; I might have been able (concealing my disgust, of course) to understand the twitch of features on the painted canvas, the true expression on Fluck's face that I could never decipher. All I want to do is understand it. That, and expunge it from my memory.

The morning of the second day dawned bright and summery, and I awoke with a splitting headache. I have missed out certain intervening events in the narrative, it is true, but I will come back to them later.

'Awoke', in fact, is hardly the right word for what I did that morning. I had not been properly asleep – for the second night running, damn that loathsome eiderdown. But I suppose there was a definite moment when I took in the fact that it was no longer night but a new day, wonderfully sunny, and at this moment, as I say, my head began to throb. I couldn't remember much about the evening before, but I could remember that I had been terribly drunk. Poppet, still fast asleep, turned roughly towards me and lay with her face next to mine. Outside birds were singing and the sunlight, falling across the bed through a chink in the grimy curtains, grew hot. I got up in search of aspirin, failed to find any, and sat in the living-room, waiting for the others to get up.

It was, as everyone decided later, a perfect day for another picnic. Not only that, but it seemed to be warm enough for sustained bathing. 'I hope no one neglected to bring their bathing costumes,' shouted Fluck. 'Today we brave the ocean!' A ragged cheer went up and my headache worsened. Fluck looked at me sternly.

'Dear boy,' he commanded me, 'chill the wine. Don't be late.' This, apparently, was my invitation to lunch. He didn't mention bathing costumes to me and it was evident that I was not invited to swim. I did not want to swim anyway.

And of course Fluck didn't swim either. He couldn't.

'Wouldn't your seascapes be better if you had actual experience of the water?' I would ask him later.

'When I want to paint a seascape,' he would reply scornfully, 'I shall take a nap and dream about one.'

Apparently, then, it was the organisation of the swimming party he enjoyed so much. It made me feel quite ill. He strode around in a silly plastic peaked cap and old baggy tracksuit, criticising costumes and ordering alterations and additions, and fiddling with other people's straps and waistbands. He was at his most ridiculous and improbable issuing commands in his false sailor's voice, and I was glad when he decided it was time to go.

I watched from the bedroom window as Fluck drilled them for the trip. 'Pilgrimage to the Island of Cythera' he called it, the loony, as if Jean-Antoine Watteau would have depicted such farce. By an effort of will, and hands over ears, I managed to shut out most of his squeaky exhortations and concentrate on the swimmers' appearance. Moyra first, why not? I noticed (inadequate word) that she was wearing a bikini of the minutest proportions. It was so small that by taking the top and bottom together you could not have made a decent sized dolly out of it. The top barely restrained her nipples, let alone her breasts, and the bottom did no more than cast a slight curved shadow, as if by accident, round her crotch and buttocks. Otherwise she was overpoweringly naked. The mere sight of her put all Fluck's theories about the Great English Nude to shame.

87

There could have been no greater contrast with her poorly-endowed twin sister. Myra was muffled into a full-length bathing costume which sagged in heavy folds round her shoulders, midriff and buttocks. Absence of buttocks. The colour of the costume was nondescript, perhaps olive green. She had, though, a bathing cap to match, which accentuated her sharp features and keen, inquisitive expression, and flattened her ears, making her look curiously like a whippet, poor girl. Angel, of course, was exuberantly attired. He wore Bermuda shorts, the front of which bore the legend 'Laugh now', and the back 'Laugh later'; a yellow airtex vest, long paisley socks held up by suspenders, and spongy-soled running shoes. The splash of jet-black hair on his chest that trickled through the holes in his vest was perhaps the only concession to realism, without which I should not have believed in him.

Delightfully, Fluck seemed irritated by Angel's attire. He considered it 'not subfusc'. 'What's that?' he demanded, pointing at Angel's hat. I have neglected to mention that Angel was wearing a battered, Al-Capone-type, Kiss-Me-Quick fedora.

'Picked it up cheap at Blackpool,' said Angel shortly. 'Second-hand. Off a mate. He said it didn't work.' Moyra giggled and her chest heaved, a moment of incredible suspense. 'It doesn't work,' Angel added in the same even voice. Fluck made no retort to this. He was fussing over Poppet again. I say 'again' because I have a distinct impression that this behaviour of his had become apparent some time earlier, replacing the coolness he had originally shown her. (A bluff?) At this point she still seemed indifferent to it. She was wearing her turquoise swimsuit.

After ten minutes or so they departed for the beach, Fluck of course leading the way. As they passed under my window, he looked up (had he known I was watching all along?) and gave me a peculiar gesture which I took to be some kind of salute and returned as best I could. Then he and the others were gone.

I sat at my desk and was unable to work. Fortunately this no longer distressed me. I suppose I was getting used to it.

Soon I left my room and went down to the kitchen. With a mug of coffee I came back upstairs and went into Moyra's room. It was nearest to mine, you see, and therefore the most convenient. Finding nothing of interest, I went briefly into her sister's. Then I went up to loiter on the lower rungs of the ladder to the attic; down again to the small blue lavatory; finally to the conservatory. There I sat on the floor and reflected on the events of the previous night which I have so far omitted from the narrative.

We were drunk. All except Fluck, whose sobriety did not in any case inhibit his embarrassing and childish behaviour. We were talking after dinner, and Angel had just gone to fetch another bottle of *vin ordinaire* from the pantry, when Fluck began to play his stupid games.

'S. J.!' he cried, rapping the table for attention. 'Correct me if I'm wrong but I don't think you've read us anything yet from your opuscule.'

'No,' I said, and turned back to Moyra, whom I was entertaining on the subject of fashion wear.

'But you must,' Fluck continued. 'We implore you. Besides you have contractual obligations to honour.' No one but Fluck was doing any imploring, but unfortunately the loudness of his voice somehow conveyed the impression of popular consensus. 'I'm tired,' I said eventually. 'I'm drunk.'

'Besides,' added Poppet, 'he's only had a day to write, and he hasn't done that much.' I suppose she thought she was being sweet. But her blunder gave Fluck the opportunity to take up the theme of my assumed unproductiveness.

'An absence of Muse?' he asked. '*Quelle horreur, mon brave.* You recall what Racine said about inspiration, or Victor Hugo, for that matter?'

'You two go off and talk together about art and literature,' Poppet said. 'We're far too stupid to understand.' Fluck expostulated blandiloquently at this, but nevertheless drew me down to his end of the table. I saw myself make the move in the mirror opposite. I appeared furtive and unsteady, quite unlike my normal self.

I now became drawn into a futile disagreement about the nature of inspiration, Fluck, despite previous intimations to the contrary, all but denying its existence while I crossly tried to uphold it, frequently interrupted by him, and eventually losing my way in my own shambling, slurred argument. All the time I drank as much as possible to inure myself to the Fluckian diatribe, but was largely unsuccessful. The talk turned to painting, and then inevitably to Fluck's own pictures. He made, I remember, light-hearted fun of an article of mine which had appeared in a magazine and was, vaguely, related to Fluck's work. It was the article in which I had omitted to mention his paintings. Suddenly Fluck leant across to the sideboard where he stored his smaller pictures, withdrew a rather grubby water-colour and placed it on the crockery-cluttered table.

'What do you think of that?' he asked shortly. 'Is it, for instance, inspired?'

As I have already said, all of Fluck's work is inspired, but I was now in the impossible position of having to prove the fact to the artist himself in the face of his own wilful denials. This, on his part, was false modesty so extreme as to be indistinguish-able from vanity. Nevertheless I did not want to be beaten. I looked at the picture.

It was a colourful landscape energetically rendered with Fluck's typical bravura, though the compositional elements were unusually brief. I guessed it was an unfinished piece Fluck had discarded. Cunning; he was making it as difficult as possible for me to praise the picture. Nevertheless I told him I thought it was splendid. He asked me why. Now I thought I had him. Extemporising in front of art is one of my few abilities. I can improvise with sufficient confidence to appear convincing, and I am not afraid to pirate any number of scarcely relevant authorities to support my suppositions, nor even to invent authorities if I have to.

To begin with, I quickly established the art-historical context of the picture by suggesting a number of possible precursors. The linearity of the work, I said, unusual in modern watercol-ours with the exception of Burra, has clear traditional anteced-ents, particularly in the work of the English Romantics, Palmer, Blake, John Sell Cotman, and the early Turner. The colouring however, unusually vivid, draws on non-English traditions, Mediterranean, viz. Dufy, or American, viz. Winslow Homer (thinking especially of his Florida pictures). Then I began an explication of the picture's specific merits. This was more difficult but there were three main points to be made: that the composition, while simple, was original and satisfying (Demuth's work could be usefully mentioned in this context); that the artist had been fully in control of his materials (the style was spare but suggestive); and that the picture had a revelatory purpose (like all Fluck's art), i.e. to reveal the extraordinary in the ordinary. All the time I talked Fluck was uncharacteristically silent. Merely to have shut him up seemed to me an incredible feat. The others too, I noticed with some pleasure, had broken off their conversations and were listening to me.

'You've certainly been swotting up, S. J.,' Fluck interrupted at last in his most patronising tone, 'but am I right in thinking you consider the picture good?' The question seemed irritatingly superfluous. His tone was irreverent. I told him the picture was good.

'You think it shows signs of . . .' here his expressions suffered inexplicable strain, but he recovered himself and continued '. . . maturity?' I told him I thought it did. Then Fluck slowly turned the painting over, and on the back of it, for everyone to see, were the words 'Pictur of The Trees Vincent Fluck 3C'. Underneath, in an adult hand, someone had written 'You can do better than this, Philip. Please use your real name on work you hand in.'

There was a moment's silence, out of decency as it were, and then Fluck spoke. He was near-hysterical, holding the pictur(e) aloft like a flag. 'My half-brother, Pip,' he explained. 'Seven years old, bless him. He hates school. He calls himself Vincent and is always getting into trouble.' He guffawed loudly. 'He'd be delighted to hear what you think of his picture.'

I suppose you will say that I walked right into this, with my eyes, as it were, tightly shut. I did not expect such childishness from Fluck – cruelty and snobbery, yes, but not childishness. And I was wrong, just as I was later to be wrong about his sexual drive. But there is no possibility that the picture was actually painted by Fluck's infant sibling; it was clearly by Fluck himself, who used it, perhaps painted it specifically, in order to trap me. He knew of course that the picture's very real qualities, being abstract in nature, would not be perceived by the others round the table. How simple then it was, given a certain viciousness on his part, to get me drunk, present me with a forged picture, allow me the rare opportunity to express my altogether intelligent views on it, and then pretend that the picture was not at all what it appeared to be.

All this was infuriating, but I might have borne it had Fluck's ridiculous laughter not proved so infectious. Soon they were all laughing at me, even Angel. 'Shot yourself in the foot,' he said, 'with a bazooka.' Fluck roared, and held up the picture for general attention. 'You maintain it is in the manner of the school of John Sell Cotman,' he said loudly, 'but I assure that the work is from Northanger Preparatory School.' Moyra and Myra tittered suddenly together, I heard them, though I did not look in their direction. Poppet leaned over and took my hand. 'I'm sorry, S. J.,' she said, 'it was a *lovely* speech, really.' But she caught sight of the childish autograph Fluck was displaying (the wax-crayoned letters were large and bright and greasy) and, dissolving into giggles, could say no more.

Of course I laughed with them, as best I could – I had no choice – but there was a bitter taste in my mouth no amount of *vin ordinaire* could obliterate. And though, after an interval, the evening proceeded with reasonable normality, every so often someone would catch my eye and begin to giggle and Fluck, ever observant, would recall, with an apposite remark, some humorous detail of my former discomfort. Round the table giggles and guffaws would be ineffectively suppressed, producing a medley of sneezes and snorts. I could not stand for this. I drank myself stupid, preferring oblivion to obloquy.

Consequently, after a certain point in the evening, I remember nothing. Perhaps I was ill. Certainly Poppet seemed to regard me with some distaste the following morning, as if she had had a hard job of it the night before. But we did not much speak to each other. The time for explanations and recriminations was not yet upon us.

I sat in the conservatory and thought these things. Then I returned to my room and sat at my desk and thought about the same things again. It seemed I couldn't escape them, and anyway what was the point of trying, I was incapable of work. It especially irked me to think that as I sat simmering in my room, outside Fluck was airily contemplating his second or even third picture of the day. By eleven o'clock he could have finished with Myra and already be on his first version of the eventual masterpiece of Poppet. He would be telling her smutty jokes and pulling silly faces. Quite soon I could bear it no longer. I descended to the kitchen, removed the semi-chilled wine from the fridge, and left the house.

It was even warmer outside, and there was no breeze. Seagulls, usually so voluble, drifted overhead, dazed with the heat. In the distance a tractor droned like a long snore. Sweating pitifully, I slithered down the steep path towards the beach.

When I arrived, the others showed no surprise to see me there so early. They were obsessed with their bathing, which had apparently become a test of nerve, the water being so much colder than the hot sunlight. Even Angel was being cautious. 'I've been in once,' he said, 'and I'm not the sex I was.'

From her supine position a few feet away, Moyra heard this and giggled, causing her whole glistening body to vibrate. She was covered from head to toe in tanning butter, and seemed already to be several shades darker than anyone else. When she saw me she gave what I took to be a friendly, lazy gesture. 'Can you get out of my light please?' she said. Her tone was, I think, cooler than she intended.

Poppet and Myra ran towards us, wet and shivering. When they reached us, they splashed Moyra and fell on their towels. I enquired about the temperature of the sea and was also splashed.

'You're early aren't you?' said Poppet to me. 'What's the time? Why aren't you writing?'

'Couldn't keep it up,' I lied. I hadn't got it up in the first place. Note that I didn't make the mistake, as many liars do, of saying the opposite of the truth. The nearer to the truth a lie is, the better.

'Where's Henry?' I asked. Henry was 'off painting' by himself.

'Come for a swim,' said Poppet.

'Can't. Haven't got my things.' This was the truth. I was beginning to feel quite hot in my nylon shirt and writer's baggy corduroys.

'Idiot, why not?' Ignoring her, I lowered my voice slightly.

'I want to talk to you,' I said.

'Not now, S. J., we're going for a swim. Angel's coming, aren't you, Angel?' Poppet jumped to her feet, grabbed a beach ball and threw it at Angel. A sprinkling of sand fell against my face.

'Poppet, please,' I followed her closely across the beach, treading on her lithe shadow.

93

'Never mind. Come and watch.' She ran ahead and I trotted after. What did I want to talk to her about so urgently? I have completely forgotten. Only the memory of my desire to talk remains. That, and the frustration of not talking.

She ran round me, lobbing and catching the stripy ball (oddly colourless in the bright sunlight) and the others rushed to join us, even Moyra, her body bouncing and shivering. Then, at a given moment they all plunged into the shallow foaming water, ducking and splashing. They left me to watch them from my position of safety on the dry sand, holding the beach ball, shielding my eyes against the sun, nursing my ungovernable, irrelevant sorrows.

As a non-swimmer (and non-giggler) it was not likely that I would share their sense of frivolity, and I did not. I felt weak and jangly and generally sorry for myself. But even allowing for such pained introspectiveness, the behaviour of the others was depressingly silly. As Fluck had foreseen, they regressed to a state of screaming infancy. I remember certain images now, like snapshots in a sequence: Moyra lifting a plump leg to kick fine spray over Angel, her left buttock exposed. Myra, thin in profile, filling her bathing cap with a small wave. Angel, already drenched, capsising Poppet in half an inch of swirling foam. Angel carrying Moyra out to sea. Moyra kicking and exposing most of both buttocks, but not, alas, biting. They whooped and waved. 'Come on. It's wonderful!'

Frankly, their shrill inanity distressed me. I was excluded, like the only sober person in a room full of drunks. Without saying anything, I turned and walked away. Poppet shouted after me, something about lunch, but I did not look back; quite suddenly I felt the need to be absolutely alone. Walking rapidly, I headed towards the group of rock pools that lay isolated in the middle of the beach, the first point of reference on my line of escape. I fixed my mind on them. Rounding them, passing out of sight on the other side, I headed towards the deepest corner of the beach where sand ran into shingle and shingle into dusty earth. I was at last free to think.

Yes, think. But of what? Fixing my eyes on the ground, I walked on across the sand. Eventually the sand gave way to shingle. I was very hot by now, so I removed my shirt and tied it round my waist like a schoolboy.

Beyond the shingle, I proceeded, naturally enough, up the coastal path which continued, on this side of the bay, the walk begun at Fluck's house. I had no particular destination in mind. I was not conscious of wanting to go anywhere. I did not guess that Fate was leading me to her awful lair. Almost before I knew it, I had climbed to the top of the cliff and was following the curve of the bay back out to sea.

The sun was now hotter than ever, and although a light breeze flickered at my face whenever I turned it towards the distant sea-hazy horizon, I was sweating almost continuously. Nevertheless, I was alone, and this I considered sufficient compensation. I was free, for instance, to stop and admire the impressive Caspar David Friedrich view from the headland, a vast glittering emptiness of sea and sky, lacking only the Byronic figure on the brink of the cliff, gazing out to sea, communing silently with Eternity. I did not, even then, pretend to myself that I filled that role. And in any case, since I discovered that Friedrich placed his figures with their backs to him simply because he was unable to paint faces, the image had lost some of its appeal for me.

I walked on. The further I went, the stickier I became. Freedom, solitude, began to pall slightly; I no longer thought of Caspar David Friedrich but of a callus on the big toe of my right foot which, in the heat, was causing me some pain. More unpleasant was the fear which occasionally flitted into my mind that in the middle of my slow hot progress over the tops of the cliffs, where everything seemed apparently laid out for my inspection, no squawking bathers to disturb and depress me, no oppressive rooms and obscure pictures, I should suddenly come across Fluck perched on the cliff edge, distorting the view. But he was nowhere to be seen.

When I reached the furthest point of the promontory I left the path and made my way through clumps of ferns and cow-parsley to the edge of the drop where I could look down on the beach I had left about an hour earlier. If I had wanted to locate Angel and the others I was disappointed; the beach was very distant. The only recognisable point of reference was the tiny cluster of rock pools, which, I could see for myself, was perfectly crescent-shaped, with the horns pointing obliquely out to sea. As I contemplated it, it occurred to me that I had missed lunch.

I think I was rather glad. Such little truancies give rise to a quite disproportionate sense of self-determination.

Round the other side of the bluff I noticed a sudden change in the landscape. The wild hedgerows and weed-choked meadows gave way to ploughed fields. A tractor was labouring up a slight incline towards me, followed by a wavering flock of gulls. Muffled engine noise was punctuated by their screeches. Beyond the tractor I could see farm buildings, barns, and granaries, and the beginnings of a tarmacadamed track. Towards these the path declined, becoming broader and more regular. The heat now achieved a special intensity. The ground ahead shimmered.

Twenty minutes later I passed the farm, followed the track that curved round and down towards the coast, and ten minutes after that I reached the coastal road.

It led me bleakly to a small and ugly harbour and a collection of grey stone houses, garages, and one shop. As far as I could see there was no pub and no church. As I reached it there was a change in the weather; a few clouds appeared overhead, and out of these appeared more gulls. They circled the harbour, calling disconsolately and occasionally diving to snatch up scraps of fish and mouldy crab from the quay. I stayed only to hurl a scattering of small pebbles at them and then walked on through the newly pressurised heat. The sky was rapidly bruising to an oppressive indigo, and a vast bank of cloud appeared over the horizon. Sweat ran into my eyes and made them smart.

A little way beyond the harbour, I left the road and, hoping to discover a breeze down by the shore, made my way across scrubby ground towards what I supposed at first to be a beach. It was not a beach but a large expanse of mud – two hundred yards of it, a stinking grey mess littered with the casual wreckage of the infrequent tides: cork-floats, chewed nets, boat boards, the occasional dead crab. It was utterly unlike the beach I'd left a couple of hours earlier, a lifeless *doppelgänger*, a shadow of mud cast by the other's golden sand and blue sky. It stank too, in the heat, and there were flies everywhere, droning and shimmering in the storm-thickening air. I liked everything about it. After my aimless wandering, it felt like a destination.

There was a long wooden gangplank extended like a shallow

pier over the mud flats, and I walked along it to the end, where I looked gleefully over the clotted, riveted, shit-coloured mud all around me. Somehow I felt in harmony with the foul place. I gazed at the mud, silently, as in awe. Gulls had left fork marks in its soft, bulging crust. I saw one appear from behind a crumpled plastic carrier, peck at the shy end of a coil of rope, then step fastidiously into a rotted row boat through a hole in its bottom. I didn't scare it away. Frankly it seemed rather wonderful to be there to see that gull, to have wandered off on my own, leaving the others to the picture-postcardism of sun and spume and lemming behaviour. It occurred to me that they would not know where I was. Perhaps, when they saw me leave they had stopped fooling around, needlessly bobbing and gurgling, and instead had stood flatly on the sea-bottom silently and wretchedly up to their waists in cold water, wondering where I was going. Perhaps. The thought gave me some pleasure.

And at that moment my imagination was suddenly excited and I had an idea for a story. I whipped out my notebook – naturally I always carry it with me – and began to make notes.

But do not get excited. These notes have not survived. Nor do I remember much about the story, only that it was a comedy, or rather fantasia, of sexual manners, in which the final scene takes place on a mud flat (literally on it) where the characters – ourselves: Fluck, Moyra, Myra, Angel, Poppet, and I – copulate in various permutations *without muddying ourselves*, thereby overcoming certain difficulties in our relationships and incidently performing a miracle contrary to the laws of physics. This sounds rather perfunctory to me now, perhaps I intended the narrative to be taken allegorically. But the point is that after two days of literary sterility, I began to write again. I remember the exquisite sense of release, the joy in my long-awaited inspiration, a real physical pleasure as I wrote furiously, bent double over my notebook, trying to keep pace with my train of thought. This lasted for about ten minutes. It was the lengthiest, most intense, and though I did not know it then, most futile bout of inspiration I have ever suffered.

Isn't it funny how things happen when you least expect them? I heaved a sigh and thought to myself that, after all, I was not to remain the constant butt of Fluck's jokes and sneers.

Now I intended to write something to shut him up; I felt myself perfectly capable of it; I was determined to have the last laugh. And so, when I turned to go, I had no doubt that I was going straight to him, to demand, immediately, his impossible approval.

Isn't this how it always begins, with the hubristic gleaming smile and hands raised aloft, mouth open to let rip with one's own name, a second before the trapdoor drops below one's feet?

As I ran back along the duck-boards, clutching my notebook to my chest like a precious gift, my shirt slipped from around my waist and slithered over the edge of the pathway to fall twelve inches into sticky mud. I skidded to a halt, too late. There the shirt lay, on its back in the mud, bent at one elbow as if casually propping itself up. For a second I was struck by the utter peacefulness of the thing as it lay relaxing on its soft bed – as peaceful, say, as the famous nude in Titian's 'Bacchanal of the Andrians' whose pose it recalled – then, quite gradually, it flattened out, and fell back with a squish of air against the sour dampness of the mud. The first stains began to appear, freckling the collar and cuffs, blotting the sleeves.

I don't know if we are meant to believe in auguries any more, symbols, omens, portents, but I felt a certain *frisson* in that moment which seemed to lift it out of the quotidian and invest it with meaning. I could easily have rescued my shirt – it was within reach – but I didn't. I let it die; it seemed to me both beautiful and apt.

I had scarcely stepped down from the duck-boards when I heard the first distant roll of thunder. By the time I had regained the harbour village, the first drops of rain had begun to fall heavily, staining the dusty pavement. Then the torpid atmosphere broke dramatically like smashed crockery as thunder cracked again overhead and the ground suddenly turned black. The street leapt darkly with water and I ran for a doorway, soaked already. This storm had evidently crept up on me unawares while I was busy with my story and my shirt. Looking back, I saw that both sky and sea were deep unbroken purple, into which the mud flat had disappeared. The main street was flooded, a black necklace of water swelling over the asphalt. I stood listening to the aggressive beat of rain on the slate roofs and gush of overflow from the eaves.

Fortunately, the storm was short-lived. After a quarter of an hour I stepped out into the softer rainfall and first glimmers of light beyond the clouds, and splashed my way up the street. Naturally I was by now rather regretting the careless divestiture of my shirt. I began to run to keep warm.

I have mentioned already that I am a keen runner. (Not *jogger*, please, my pace is superior.) Now, as I began to run, my precious notebook stuffed down my cords to keep it as dry as possible, I felt unexpectedly refreshed, invigorated by gusts of fresh clean air that carried the tang of salt off the sea. The storm had cleared the atmosphere. And I hadn't been running for long when the rain stopped completely and the sun reappeared, lighting up all the dazzling surfaces around me.

How can I describe my joyous mood? I felt like a jailbreaker fleeing his dungeon. A couple of miles up the coastal road, still running, I whimsically turned up a footpath I had never seen before, mounted a sandy incline, and at the top saw Fluck's house facing me. This orienteering fluke struck me as no way remarkable, rather it confirmed my sense of the world's bounty, of my own careless power. I thought that this was one of those days when I could do nothing wrong. It seemed somehow taken for granted that as I leapt easily towards the shining house, I would see, as I did see, a spectacular rainbow curving through clouds in the sun-and-shade tossed distance; a rainbow for me, my rainbow.

Perhaps it will seem strange that I didn't immediately seek out Fluck and put myself in a position where I might be asked about my writing – but good runners are fastidious about their exercise, and know that it is absolutely essential to stretch off after a run. I went into the garden while the rainbow still flickered in the sky, and positioning myself by the stone seat at the far end, finished off my run in the correct manner, stretching, swivelling, touching my toes (very nearly), straightening my spine, jogging on the spot. Then I sat down on the stone seat and gazed enraptured round the garden which, like the brightest Monet, sparkled impressionistically, with droplets of rainwater catching the sun and scattering its light mirrorwise across the flowers and shrubs. Once I heard voices from the front of the house, and shortly afterwards other signs of life appeared – an electric light switched on in an upstairs window, curtains flicked shut downstairs – but I ignored them. I was completely entranced. And even when I did leave my seat to saunter back down the garden, I still paused to examine the more beautiful of the flowers. The flowers at the back of the bed abutting the house were particularly spectacular, tall, tangled sheaves of red and gold, and in order to see these properly I waded right into the flowerbed, getting my trousers drenched in the process. I do not know what they were, those shaggy blooms that caught my eye so boldly, but if I had to give them a name, I would call them 'Fingers of Fate', for they beckoned me towards particular, instant disaster, and I seemed helpless to resist.

I did not perceive my happiness at that moment to be of the trivial kind that commonly proceeds some awful shock. No, I regarded the flowers in perfect contentment. The sun blazed. Water droplets sparkled. A fresh breeze stirred flowerheads at my feet. And looking up from my floricultural studies I found my nose next to Fluck's bedroom window, the curtains carelessly drawn, with a chink left between them; and peering through this chink I saw Fluck and Poppet, naked together on the bed. A small, sour constriction, perhaps my tongue, stopped my throat and prevented me from screaming in surprise. They were together on the bed, or at least not quite on it, nor off it either, but balanced along it and around it. The window pane was dirty and my view was not a good one, but they seemed to be mobile, two shadows blurring, melting, flickering. And at that moment, as I strained on tiptoe and pressed my face goldfishwise to the pane to verify the horror, I suffered a spasm in the back of my right leg and fell like a stone to the ground.

When I leapt to my feet again, only Fluck seemed to be in the room. I may have caught a glimpse of Poppet disappearing through the open door of a murky toilet *en suite*, but I wasn't sure. The next instant the door seemed to be shut. Fluck remained, sitting on the edge of the bed. He was entirely naked except for a limp coil of underpants round one ankle. His body was indescribably pale and fat and depressing. Weirdly, he was posed exactly like the girl in Munch's picture 'Puberty', with his pudgy hands folded shyly over his genitals, a quiet, modest, thoughtful nude. I saw no more. Perhaps I had steamed up the window. Choking soundlessly, I blundered backwards through the wet flowers, and fled down the garden.

The painting 'Puberty' (1895) by Edvard Munch deserves comment. My first thoughts after seeing Poppet and Fluck were of this picture, a great favourite of both Fluck's and mine at college. Munch, a Norwegian working in Paris, was one of the leading Symbolists, and had affinities also with the Decadents and Expressionists – he is well-represented in my book *Cold Caresses of the Sphinx* – but in this context his affinities are unimportant. 'Puberty' is a work of pure realism.

She sits upright on the edge of the bed and stares nervously at us. She is perhaps eleven or twelve years old. Her exposed breasts are shallow and undeveloped, but her hips have already begun to thicken. She covers as much of her belly, crotch, and thighs as she can with her long thin arms and raw hands crossed awkwardly between her knees. Her bare right foot tentatively covers her left. She would cry if she could, her wide eyes and grim smudge of a mouth indicate this, but she cannot. There is a feeling that she does not want to disturb the fragile equilibrium of her modest position.

She is thinking of her nakedness, of her alarmingly mutable body. Nudity is knowledge. I repeat myself – and others – but it is worth it. Nudity provokes certain discoveries. I refer partly, of course, to the casual acquisition of carnal, or at least corporal, knowledge, but I do not disregard that other kind – call it what you will, mental, spiritual, psychological knowledge – which is more profoundly possessed, and by which we understand the personality, the psyche, or even the *soul* of someone else. Munch's girl, for instance, is naked not only in physical fact but to the depths of what we might call exactly this, her soul, and her whole body betrays her; just look at those bony hands, the snub toes, her thin shoulders – every detail expresses her innermost thoughts more exactly and shockingly than if she were to speak to us and confess herself in familiar, halting sentences. And what part do we play in all this? We need only to observe her.

Observe, observe, never cease from observation. Poppet and

Fluck had observed each other, touched, had known each other's nudity. Above the sticky bed their souls had mingled, the shock of intimacy fusing them together. Yes, it happens like this, I know; it's human nature, wonderful thing. And there I was with my nose pressed to the window like a schoolkid outside a sweetshop.

I remembered Fluck's and my discussions of Munch's painting, and very apposite they seemed, for our shared views as for our disagreements. As I remembered, Fluck and I jointly acknowledged the importance of sexuality in the picture – this, we agreed, was paramount – but we differed in that I refined this down to a fear of sex – the girl was, after all, a mere eleven or twelve years old – and Fluck saw only its sadness. '*Post coitum omne animal triste,*' he insisted. At the time he was, unusually, unable to prove what he said, but now, years later when I had almost forgotten it, he was making his point in a totally irresistible way. Here it was in front of me. *Post coitum omne animal triste.* The death of Innocence. Thus Venus staggers home at dawn. Thus a fat man sits on a bed with his underpants round his ankles, hearing, sadly, the lavatory flushing in the toilet *en suite.* Fluck had been right about Munch's painting.

Was it seconds, minutes, or hours later that I found myself sitting on a low dry stone wall, staring at my hands? I seemed to have been retching and my throat hurt. In the bright sunshine, I felt queasy and faint. But I was no longer astonished. Rather (O my prophetic soul) I reviewed and re-reviewed what I had just seen with a sickening sense of *déjà vu.* It seemed in no way surprising to have found Fluck and Poppet together. It seemed almost logical and, in a narrative sense, quite proper. All those unheeded hints and forebodings of calamity, auguries, portents, omens. Now I knew why Fluck had wanted to paint Poppet so much (and *naked* too; he had actually used the word, he could not deny it). I realised what was really meant by his clownish criticisms of her bathing costume (tenderly meddling with her straps and buckles). But there were of course a thousand such things to remember, smiles, gestures, whispers; even the absences of smiles and gestures and whispers meant something else now. And what of their meetings that, over the last year, I had not witnessed? What of the letters and postcards

102

I had not bothered to read, but left for Poppet by her breakfast bowl of cereal? What of the telephone conversations I had been so keen to shut out, closing the study door or turning up the radio? He so fat and pale and ugly, and she so small and willing and compliant. 'I'll kill her,' I thought, 'the mad bitch.' But she was not so bad as him, not so complicated or shocking. And what I thought of then, as I sat there (or was I still lying twisted on the garden path?), were Fluck's put-downs, the bad-teeth smiles, that snobby voice, and most of all the sight of him through the wet windowpane, sitting naked and triumphant on the edge of his bed, a blank expression on his face and one pale pudgy hand resting bluntly on his spent cock. Nudity is knowledge. From that moment on I knew I was dealing with a monster.

Let's see. I could have punched a hole through the window, jumped into the room, and killed them both as they lay entwined on the bed. Or I could have done the punching and breaking in, and then killed Fluck only. Alternatively, I might have rushed round into the house the front way and broken down the bedroom door. Or, by way of contrast, I might have quietly tried the door, found it open and, sauntering in, confronted them in an attitude of icy fury. There were numerous possibilities. Total or selective slaughter was, I admit, a favourite, but there was a variety of less frenzied responses that allowed the criminals their cringing reaction to being caught in the act. Poppet would squeak, and run for the bathroom, or abase herself at my feet. Perhaps she would be frozen with terror, only her mouth would be able to move, slowly, '. . . please, S. J.'. If she left the room, I would deal with Fluck alone. Strangle him with his underpants. Suffocate him with the duvet. Or deal a single savage punch to the jaw, ripping his head from his body. With Fluck dead, I would leave the room as coldly as I had entered, Poppet sobbing and stumbling penitentially after me.

No, none of the above. Instead it was I who sobbed and stumbled from the scene. I left Fluck and her *in flagrante delicto*. I don't think I caused even as much as an *interruptus*. I Hamleted on it, to coin a phrase, but unlike Hamlet I was to have no

103

second chance; having done nothing once, nothing was to be my speciality.

Life, unlike literature, has a habit of mistiming its climaxes. Here, for instance, the high point of the tragedy occurs midway through our little holiday with several days of it still left to endure, days which drag on, like Molloy on his crutches through the undergrowth, to their unremarkable conclusion. Of all the numerous possible versions of our particular story, most of which I foresuffered, we somehow ended up with the most ludicrous and trite.

Back in the house, in my room, I reviewed my contingency plans again, though in my excitable state I was more or less incapable of dispassionate consideration. And so occupied was I by the detailed imaginings of lurid revenge that I hardly noticed myself continuing the routine of exercises I had begun in the garden. This in itself seemed to have a calming effect, and gradually, as I stretched and jogged and massaged my feet, I regained a tentative hold on reality. I went, as usual, for a shower. Soon I was wondering whether the whole thing hadn't been a momentary illusion. Henry Fluck, the man with the incredible porpoise body, making love to my wife? I began to compile a list of innocent explanations. I suppose I was tired. The shower buzzed in its cubicle, and I sat apart, on the tiled floor, thinking.

But my sufferings, my humiliations, were not yet over. When I left the shower room I found Poppet and Fluck standing intimately together in the hall. I was tiptoeing squeamishly over the chilly parquet, a small cloud of steam clinging to me, a towel knotted insecurely round my waist, when I saw them ten yards ahead of me. They were talking in whispers by the bedroom door, his big form and her small form blocking my way. Evidently they had not heard me coming. I had a horror of surprising them (and then watching them guiltily jerk apart, sharing the same foolish smirk), so I coughed. No reaction. I loudly cleared my throat – but they were oblivious to my presence. Eventually I reached them and, to my amazement, they continued to ignore me and I was forced to negotiate a narrow passage round them in order to gain access to my room.

'Hullo, S. J.,' murmured Fluck as I squeezed past him. I may have opened my mouth to reply ('Out of my way, you fat cunt') but Fluck was already re-engrossed in conversation with Poppet. I heard them both begin to giggle as I entered the bedroom and closed the door behind me. This is how it all begins, I thought to myself; this is how your nightmare of the end of the world gets under way, with a sneer and a giggle. I am not melodramatic by nature, but it seemed to me that the situation warranted a degree of hysteria. A kind of instant invisibility seemed to have been bestowed on me, as if my tormenters, now finding me dispensable to their purposes, no longer chose to acknowledge me. I had become what I had always feared most to be, an insubstantial furtive thing, a gollum, a Childe Roland to the Dark Tower come, fit only for the jokes and knocks and knee-jerks of Fate.

Of course I couldn't be expected to adjust to this straight away. I had to have a cigarette just to stop my hands trembling. I coughed at the first drag and hastily threw the cigarette away.

Poppet came into the room while I was struggling with my underpants, and began to dress for dinner.

'Open the window,' she said, sniffing cigarette smoke.

'It doesn't open,' I said shortly.

'Then I'd rather you didn't smoke.' She smiled suddenly. 'Please.' Still smiling, she edged up to me, made a face, and standing on tiptoe kissed me on the forehead.

'Thank you,' she said sweetly. 'Good boy.' She continued, 'You're looking a bit queasy, you know. I thought you were trying to cut down. How many have you smoked today?'

'I called you, by the way,' she went on, as she slipped out of her bathing costume.

'What?'

'I called you on the beach. When you walked off, cross boy.' She put her hands on her hips and looked at herself in the mirror.

'Didn't hear you.' I expected to be quizzed, but she was too impatient to tell me what she had been doing.

'After you went, I had my picture painted. Half-painted, I mean.' She was keeping it simple, like the best lies. 'We came back here,' she said. 'And I expected to find you here, but you weren't here, were you? Oh dear, his room is *so* dingy, I thought I would die, but he is *so* nice, and funny, S. J., he told jokes the whole time, I did enjoy it, and I didn't think I would at all.' She yawned contentedly. 'I think I'm enjoying the whole holiday. Are you enjoying it?'

'When we arrived,' she went on, 'I thought he was rather unfriendly, off-hand somehow. Not with you, with me, I think he thinks I never let you out on holiday. But he was so sweet today. It's lovely to see him happy, poor man.'

I wished to empty myself, to merely observe what was unmistakably in front of my eyes. Naked, she stepped delicately towards the wardrobe like a movie star or a well-bred mare, the gluteal muscles faintly rippling in her narrow buttocks. This observation redeemed nothing.

'He wanted to paint me nude,' she said, and giggled. Not being able to speak, I made a faltering attempt to raise my eyebrows. I had not quite drained myself of all emotion, I found. 'For the sake of Immortal Art,' she added, imitating one of Fluck's voices, the detestable squeaky one. I nodded stiffly. 'Funny boy.' She hastily pulled on cotton knickers, which sagged behind. I had not been paying attention. What had happened to the pair she had just taken off? Had she been wearing knickers? No, I remembered; she had been wearing her swimsuit. My eyes roved wildly to locate it, and failed. Never mind. Later. Examine the evidence later.

'Do you know what else he said?' asked Poppet. But from then on I trusted only my eyes, observed only – her moving mouth, her swinging bob of hair, the smooth sheen on her skin as she clad herself slowly in cool summery things. She disdained make-up, I noticed, but she did not need it. Love had made her up. Her eyes sparkled as she looked in the mirror, and all the time she talked, apparently not caring whether I was listening or not. What she said, I have no idea.

Eventually, after half an hour or so, pure purgatory, she was ready and looking quite stunningly beautiful, having dressed with the close attention that befits amatory celebration or anticipation, or both. By her side, in uniform-grey trousers and jacket (looking, she said, like a postman), I appeared depressingly down-at-heel.

'But a lovely postman,' she said softly, narrowing her eyes to lascivious slits. 'Lovely, scruffy postman.' She slipped one hand inside my jacket and laid the other against my hip. Her face was suddenly very close to mine, her breath against my face, and I noted with disgust that her bright lipstick was smudged at the corner of her mouth.

There was a confused shouting outside, Fluckian in character, and she immediately broke away from me.

'Coming!' she called. Then, looking back towards me, whispered archly, movie-star-wise, 'You look adorable. So roguish. Pale and poetic. I'd like to caress you all over.' She took a step towards me. 'Oh, I forgot,' she said, smiling, 'how is your story going? No, wait' – Fluck was bellowing outside the door – 'tell me at dinner.' She opened the door and stepped into the hall. Fluck had disappeared. Together we descended for dinner, as into the proverbial pit.

'The Caress' is a very famous picture by the Belgian Symbolist Fernand Khnopff, leader of an avant-garde group known as Les XX, launched in the naughty nineties – and, surprisingly, the nineties were very naughty in Belgium. His picture, which Poppet's comment had suddenly brought to mind, is charged with the most gorgeous atmosphere of perversity. A semi-naked young man with decorated nipples leans against the side of a dusty platform on which squats his lover, a sphinx with the body of a leopard and the head of a woman (modelled on the artist's sister incidentally). Her tabby haunches are raised off the ground, and she is nuzzling him, one soft deadly paw caressing his belly. Various unrelated details assert themselves. In one hand the young man holds a slender staff with a baubled head in the shape of a large, blue-winged insect. Behind the sphinx, visible over the sinuous curve of her yellow-and-black spotted tail, stand two thin blue obelisks, like decorated telegraph poles. To one side of these, at some ambiguous distance from the mismatched lovers, stands a crumbling plastered wall on which is inscribed a string of faded, indecipherable symbols. I had realised a long time earlier that without these details the picture would not be half so weird. In fact, the semi-naked young man and his bizarre lover, divested of all this intriguing marginalia, might have seemed rather ordinary. It struck me that there was a lesson to be learned from this, viz., that the mere fact of Poppet's infidelity was not in itself sufficient to convey the horror of what had happened. Such a fact soon became familiar. Already I had doubted what I had seen through the foggy

107

windowpane. Plainly, it was the perverse peripheral details that would keep the image sharp, her smudged lipstick, her damp, discarded swimsuit, Fluck's genial roar, his smug grin. This was a desperate knowledge, but real.

By the time Poppet and I reached the dining-room I had regained some sort of self-possession. We were handed our gin and tonics, we lounged around with the others. Everything remained exactly the same, and yet everything had changed. Fluck talked maniacally as usual; Angel quipped as dryly; Myra sniffed and twitched; Moyra gazed vacantly into her cigarette smoke; and Poppet and I were as unremarkably conversational as we had been before. Chair legs squealed across the polished floor, glasses were emptied and refilled, plates were scraped by cutlery as fish, salad, cheeses, came and went. I raced to get drunk. Nothing unusual in any of that. And yet, at the same time, everything was utterly different because all the meanings had altered. Whenever Poppet smiled at Fluck's jokes – which she did not much more frequently than before, on account of the need for secrecy, no doubt – the movement of her lips suggested other possibilities, a kiss, a nibble, a suck. Whenever Fluck, conversational despot, swept a fat hand round the table to emphasise a point, ending up with his fingers (soft, white, manipulative digits) hanging for a moment in front of Poppet's face, this gesture also enclosed another which carried his hand across her cheek and throat and under her small, unperturbed breasts. This gesture, that smile, everything they did, was in a code that I had cracked and could not unlearn. I was forced to watch secret messages being tremulously transmitted through the smoky after-dinner glow. Fluck was tirelessly inventive in these communications, and nothing escaped me. When, at the end of the meal, after pillaging the well-stocked cheese board, he glanced at me with twinkly amusement, I followed his gaze and saw that he had left behind a block of cheddar in the act of mounting a half-unwrapped wedge of cambazola.

The worst thing was that my own behaviour was also coded. Twice I noticed my hand shaking as I poured wine into Poppet's glass; once I blew smoke in Fluck's direction, and the blue cloud swelled angrily towards him. It occurred to me that perhaps Fluck could read my code as well as I could read his, and I lived in fear of a moment at which our naked eyes might meet in stunned recognition. I preferred the baiting games we played. They suited the spy I was.

Eventually the secret we shared infected our conversation as well as our gestures.

'Smoking rather a lot, aren't we?' Fluck enquired as I lit up between entrée and dessert. I said nothing, and he laughed.

'Our chain-smoking writer,' he said, 'crouched in your garret with your inefficient primus and one kipper a day. A bad case of writer's cramp.' The garret was Chatterton, the kipper was Edmund Gosse. Fluck thought I did not know. As he laughed I saw his eyes flick towards Poppet. Chatterton died young and Gosse suffered fame without talent. Fluck was staking his claims.

I suppose I can't have been drunk during dinner after all. Perhaps there was a lack of drink, perhaps my body was impervious to alcohol's bitter comfort. Either way I remained sober enough to perceive all of Fluck's little jibes. Poppet and he were playing a subtle duet just below the surface of the ordinary conversation, variations on a theme I had heard for the first time only hours earlier but was already learning to recognise in its many disguises.

Poppet complained eagerly to him of sunburn. 'I sunbathed for ten minutes,' she said, '*ten minutes*, no more, and now I can't even sit down properly. It wasn't even that hot.'

Fluck left the room and reappeared shortly afterwards with a bottle of calamine lotion. 'Here,' he shouted tossing the bottle to me with a stupid nonchalance that nearly took my eye out. 'Calamine for your burnt spouse.' Calamine doesn't take the heat out of passion, I thought. Silently I handed the bottle over to Poppet. 'Aren't you going to rub it in?' she asked in a playful tone. Fluck immediately put his hands up to his face. 'I won't look,' he squeaked. 'Go ahead. Don't mind me. I can't see a thing.'

This ridiculous performance, and others like it, at least taught me a degree of necessary self-control. As we came to the end of dessert, and Fluck wiped custard from his bowl with two fat fingers, he regarded me with a cocked eye and said in a perfectly calm voice, 'I saw you this afternoon, S. J., capering round the garden like a young faun. You didn't think anyone could see you, did you, but you can't hide from me, oh no, my spies are everywhere, the very walls of the house have eyes, ha ha. And what a treat for me, eh. All those memories it brought back. I realised that in some respects you really haven't changed at all. S. J., you're still as fit and lean as you ever were, and just as boyish – it warmed my heart, it really did, to see you trying to touch your toes. You can almost do it, can't you, but not quite. You don't keep your back quite straight. Such a pity.

'But I nevertheless congratulate you,' Fluck went on. 'You appear radiant with good health by comparison with these idle creatures' – he gestured – 'who lie on the beach drinking cocktails all afternoon. Naturally I don't exclude myself. O sloth!' he scolded rhetorically, 'O decadence! *O tempora! O mores!* You know Cicero, of course, stupid man, a complete idiot though not bad as an orator. Not unlike Mussolini in that respect, though the two are seldom compared.'

'What nonsense!' exclaimed Poppet, who knew nothing of either Cicero or Mussolini. 'What do you mean?' How eagerly, how proprietorially she busied herself with her lover's uninteresting opinions. Also I was furious to hear Fluck talk of *his* spying on *me*. Did he know I had seen him in his bedroom? It would not have surprised me.

Some time after dinner, Angel suggested we play squash, and I accepted with relief. I wanted to escape the house and I desperately needed some sort of distraction.

'But where,' I asked, 'do we play?'

'Henry has the key to a court,' said Angel.

The idea that Fluck might be a member of a squash club struck me as indefinably disgusting. But I was jumping to conclusions. Northanger Preparatory, Fluck's old school, just down the road, possessed a boys'-sized squash court, and by long-standing agreement Fluck's family had use of it out of term time. 'We Flucks have had the key for generations,' Fluck said. 'It's almost a family heirloom. And like all heirlooms, utterly worthless.'

While Fluck went to fetch the key (large and rusty like the traditional keys of dungeons and treasure chests) Angel and I packed our kit. Down in the living-room five minutes later, I exchanged a few desultory words with Poppet as I waited to go.

'Shall we all come and watch you?' she asked, stifling a yawn.

'Don't feel you have to,' I replied. Moyra got up and switched on the television, and Poppet sipped her drink, her gaze sliding towards the flickering screen.

'Not if you don't want to,' I said again.

'I'm rather tired,' she said. She meant sated, of course. 'Where's the remote control thingy?'

'There isn't one,' said Myra from behind a magazine. 'Or rather, there was, but Henry broke it. Trust Henry to do that.' She sniffed with laughter.

'Wait a moment,' said Poppet. 'Oh, it's only football. Try the other channel.'

'I'm going,' I said. 'I expect you'll all be in bed by the time I get back.'

'I expect so,' said Poppet absently. 'Oh, S. J.,' called Moyra as I left, 'if you go to the pub, be a sweetie and get me some cigarettes will you?'

I sighed. Some people will treat me like a pack-mule.

I waited for Angel in the car for quarter of an hour. Twilight formed a double windscreen between me and the world outside, the trees and hedgerows, the gravel drive, the sky, the rising moon. Outside, peaceful; inside, frantic. Eventually Angel arrived. 'Sorry,' he said. 'Couldn't find my kit.'

We drove in silence down country lanes chilled by shadow. Twice we got lost, but eventually we found the school, a depressing collection of Victorian brick chalets and crumbling prefabs standing off the road in a few acres of playing fields. Following the asphalt drive beyond the buildings and past a concreted playground marked out for soccer and tennis, we came to a squash court. It was a ruin. Ivy covered the entire wall facing us, and several roof tiles were missing. The door, a splintering hulk, was fitted with an enormous rusted padlock. 'There's absolutely no way we are ever going to get in here,' I said angrily to Angel as he turned the key smoothly in the lock and let us in. Small things like this tend to enrage me.

Silently we ascended the small balcony, and surveyed the court. It was the most dilapidated court I had ever seen. The floor was grey concrete (usually, I should explain, it is wooden) and was completely without markings. In several places plaster had fallen off the walls, leaving a scattering of debris on the floor; elsewhere damp had incubated a bloom of maroon fungus, and in the front corners of the court larger vegetation flourished, dandelions, dock leaves, chickweed . . .

'Right,' I said through clenched teeth.

After we had changed and forced an entry onto the court, I realised the second awful thing about it: it was barely three-quarters the size of a normal court. I had been told this, of course, but had forgotten. It seemed to have been built not for squash but for solitary confinement.

Neither Angel nor I found it easy to come to terms with our dwarfish surroundings. During the knock-up we were perpetually surprised by the speed of the returning ball, and fooled again and again by its erratic bounce. Worse was the sense of constriction. It was difficult to take more than two strides without running up against a wall. I realised that although I had anticipated a sweaty catharsis of aching muscles and bursting lungs and healthy physical pain, I was to experience merely another ironic downturn along the descending spiral of my fate.

Of course, I lost. I never lose to Angel; he is basically talentless. But on that runt of a court I lost to him emphatically.

Yet it was not my defeat that distressed me, but the manner in which the game assumed its place in my more general predicament. I was trapped; the squash court was my prison cell – no, let me be more precise, not my cell, my *torture chamber*, yes, that's it. And Angel, more than a mere jailer, was my unwitting torturer. I can see him now, running ahead of me, wearing a red mohair jumper, brief blue-and-yellow zigzag swimming trunks and green baseball boots. The slightest movement caused his trunks to ride up his buttocks. I can see that now, too, a painful detail for someone so finely attuned to details as myself. Details, in fact, tortured me. They *were* the torture.

But don't think I refer merely to the rallies – the forehand drives and backhand boasts, the lobs and dropshots and lengths – no, I have forgotten all that. As Angel and I played out our scrappy game, I found myself distracted by the streaks of rubber left by the ball along the walls; scorch-marks which slowly assumed, under my horrified gaze, the rudiments of certain features: squinting eyes, puffy cheeks, camel lips. Whole faces were coming into focus like photographs developing in the hypo fluid. Everywhere I looked I saw Fluck's face, both sad

112

and smug, reminding me of an image I could never forget, the bulky nude posed on the dishevelled bed, every inch of him post-coital, from the penile sag to the *triste* expression on his face. I slipped unobtrusively from despair to desperation.

The end was, thankfully, premature, and came when, almost blinding myself with the butt of my racket handle as I botched a backhand volley, I dropped my racket altogether and tripped over it, seeing Jasper John stars and Bridget Riley spots and eventually a solid, colourless Mark Rothko blur that covered the whole court, as I crashed to the floor and lay prone. Angel fussed over me, trying to discover the exact nature of my injury. As there was no injury he was eventually forced to give up. 'Terrible,' he said. 'Fucking disaster. No point in playing on a court like this.' He was chatty because he was embarrassed. I congratulated him on his victory, dismissing his modest protests. I was well-beaten – the loser, the genuine article.

There were no showers attached to the court so we decided to go straight to the pub. It was Angel's idea but I was more than willing. However, as we drove back past the school playground and buildings, now inky silhouettes against the cool drab uniform-grey of the sky, a rather infuriating thing happened.

'The others might be there by now,' said Angel.

'What?'

'The pub. Poppet and Henry might be there by now. They said they might go to the pub after their walk.'

'What walk?' My voice was not at its smoothest and Angel looked at me.

'Along the coastal path,' he said. 'Didn't they tell you?'

'They seemed rather tired when I spoke to them,' I said. 'And I can't imagine Moyra going for a walk anyway. She never walks anywhere if she can help it.'

'No,' said Angel. 'Moyra wasn't going.'

'I see. What about Myra?'

'Not her either.'

'I see.'

'Just Henry and Poppet.' Angel obviously felt that this was sufficient comment. 'So we might see them in the pub,' he concluded.

We didn't, as I could well understand. It was a beautiful

evening; how delightful it would be for them to steal such moments together, rolling bare-arse-deep in foxgloves and cow-parsley, making as much noise as they wanted to without fear of being overheard. Although, let me not forget, it was equally possible that they would be silent; I could see them walking quietly, hand in paw in the moonlight, not needing to say anything, newly adolescent.

All the way to the wrong pub I nursed my nausea, and Angel drove in silence. Physical exercise had failed me. But I had more faith in the efficacy of booze.

From the outside, the pub, a large converted farmhouse, appeared quaintly rustic, and inside it was a heaving sprawl of jukeboxes, pool tables, and video games. A brightly lit sign announced Happy Hour, 4.30 p.m. to 5.30 p.m. every week day; non-stop disco was compulsory on Tuesdays and Thursdays. Angel bought the first round and, after a quick look round for the elusive Fluck and his lay, we retired to the least noisy corner.

'Perhaps they're in another pub,' shouted Angel.

I had to be careful what I said to Angel. He is just the type of person to whom I might have suddenly blurted everything out. But luckily I was in my first flush of bitter self-containment. And besides it occurred to me that as he had let slip the information about Fluck and Poppet's little outing that evening, he might let slip something else, if worked on inventively. It was not, however, always easy to talk. Partly because I occasionally choked on my barely contained fury, partly because of the music which thundered around us. During Angel's frequent trips to the bar I sat with my hands over my ears.

Nevertheless, our conversation got easier the more we drank. We had been drinking for about an hour when the talk turned (I turned it) to Fluck.

'Wouldn't catch old Henry playing squash, eh?' I shouted jovially, interrupting Angel who was asking something about our forthcoming holiday in Majorca. 'Too busy painting his opuscules,' I shouted. Angel looked puzzled. 'The maestro's works,' I added loudly. 'His masterpieces.'

'Which?' shouted Angel.

'All of them. His picture of you,' I shouted back.

114

'Rubbish,' said Angel. I didn't hear him say this exactly, but I saw his mouth move.

'Don't you like it?' I shouted. Angel shrugged his shoulders, took a deep swig of beer.

'Bit of a bore,' he said. 'Don't think much of Henry's pictures. He asked me once what I thought and I told him I didn't think much of them. He thought that was the greatest joke, he clapped me on the back and shouted "splendid, splendid" like he does.'

'He's a bit mad, Henry is, isn't he?' I shouted.

'Can be,' Angel said.

'Well, he won't get the girls, will he, if he spends all his time cooped up in his studio,' I shouted.

'Don't think he's interested,' said Angel.

'No point in being interested,' I shouted (through clenched teeth), 'him being mad.'

'Not interested in girls at all,' said Angel, and rose to get another round. 'Doesn't like girls,' he said, as he moved away.

This, you can imagine, intrigued me. And it struck me – I could not deny it – that Angel's opinion was perfectly reasonable. Fluck's attitude to sex was ostensibly, even flamboyantly, unserious. But Angel was unaware of Fluck's real cunning. He did not have such insights as I had. More than ever I was impressed with the way Fluck had arranged things, and more than ever I was terrified as to the final consequences.

Angel returned with the beers. Before he had a chance to sit down, such was my eagerness, I began to talk again of Fluck.

'He's always going on about art, isn't he?' I shouted, to begin again at the beginning.

'So are you,' said Angel. This stumped me for a moment.

'Yes, but he doesn't do anything else,' I shouted eventually. Angel said nothing. 'I can't think of anything else he does, can you?' I shouted after another minute or so.

'You should know,' he said, 'you lived with him for three years.'

'Halcyon days,' I said acidly.

'Did you?' said Angel, deaf and drunk. 'That's right, you're the only one he talks to. And the only one he listens to as well.'

'What do you mean?' I shouted indignantly, emotion rather getting the better of me.

115

'You're always talking together about art,' he said. 'Whenever I talk to him it's always "S. J. says this" and "S. J. says that". Poor chap has no real friends except you.'

Despite the large quantity of beer I had drunk, I felt horribly sober.

'Fuck him!' I shouted.

Angel retreated to the bar again and I sat immobile behind my empty glass, Fluck's 'only real friend'? It was difficult to know whether to laugh or weep. I thought of him sitting dishevelled and naked on the edge of his bed, Poppet just disappearing for a douche, and I sat very still behind my froth-webbed glass, my own hands pressed knuckle to knuckle in my lap.

We arrived back at the house around 12.30 a.m. We had been lost, or else we had been slow getting the car started, or else we had failed to start the car at all and had been obliged to walk. I forget exactly what had happened. In fact I have no memory of the journey whatsoever, nothing at all after leaving the pub, until we actually reached the house. Perhaps I had sobered up a little by then. I went into the kitchen to get myself another drink. Angel had gone to bed. Perhaps it was even later than 12.30. Country pubs tend to stay open into the small hours.

In the kitchen there occurred a small skirmish with a cupboard full of bottles in which I remained the passive party. Something may have smashed. I forget. Eventually, however, I found some whisky and made my way into the living-room. Moyra was there, sprawled on the sofa.

'Oh hi,' she said, a note of faint surprise in her slow drawl. 'You've just got back?'

I nodded, reluctant to struggle for speech. Moyra looked at me a little wide-eyed. 'Where have you been?' she said. With great effort I managed to tell her.

'So you've been to the pub,' she said. 'Did you get my cigarettes?' I didn't think I had.

She was stretched out somewhat in the attitude of Titian's famous Venus. The television was on, with the volume turned right down. A magazine rested on the arm of the sofa, but it had not been opened. I was puzzled as to what she had been doing. Again with great effort I asked her if she had been

116

watching the television. She gaped at me. I repeated my question, making a mental check of all its parts before speaking them out loud. Now she understood.

'No,' Moyra shook her head. 'There's nothing on.'

Let me say here that I don't understand Moyra. I have never understood her. She is beautiful and stupid, but though stupid, she was at the university with us; and though beautiful, she has never, while I have known her, had a boyfriend. I looked at her as she lay on the sofa, groping blindly over the edge of it for her few remaining cigarettes. Even this was rather beautiful. Mustering all my concentration, I embarked on a longish question to her about the others.

'In bed,' she said, yawning. 'Most of them.' There was a long pause and then she changed her mind. 'Henry and Poppet went out,' she said. 'I don't know if they've come back yet. The pub stays open after hours. I think they know Henry there.' With a little yip of delight she accidentally discovered her cigarettes and immediately lit up. Then, as if she read my thoughts, she said suddenly, 'Maybe they've got lost on the way back.'

Without thinking I began to moan, but miraculously turned it into an ironic laugh.

'No, really,' said Moyra seriously. 'After a few drinks, you know, they could . . .' Her voice trailed away. 'It's very dark out there,' she said finally.

Of course it was. It was about one o'clock in the morning. I reached a decision and staggered to my feet.

'You're not going to look for them?' Moyra asked horrified.

I uttered the same ironic laugh as before. 'Bed,' I said briefly.

'Night night,' said Moyra, 'sleep tight.' I lurched away out of the living-room, found the staircase, and began, clumsily, to climb the stairs. I was not going outside to look for Fluck and Poppet, but nor was I going to bed. Slowly I climbed, taking care to make as little noise as possible. I passed our bedroom door and continued upwards. Once I tripped over a ruck in the carpet and nearly smashed my nose in, but I kept going, and eventually I reached the foot of the ladder that led into Fluck's attic studio. While Fluck was out with Poppet (I ground my teeth), I would take a look round the inner sanctum of his art, search for clues, for evidence: condoms, billets-doux, scented

117

underwear. His studio had exerted a fearful fascination over me since I arrived. Now fury had overcome fear.

The ladder was steep and unstable and I made several noisy false starts before I reached the trap door in the ceiling. Opening this was even more difficult, but after a protracted and hectic battle I got the better of it and swung it upwards and over. Luckily Fluck had left the light on, which was a great help to me as I negotiated the final few steps and made my entrance, swaying and puffing. I find that drink tends to impair both strength and agility. It was even an effort to close the trap door behind me. But I was determined not to arouse any suspicions if I could avoid it, and at last, sweating inordinately by now, I eased the heavy door down onto its frame, with only the slightest woody thump.

'Hullo,' said Fluck.

The sound of his voice was the most appalling shock imaginable and I think I may have screamed out loud when I heard it. My first definite memory after that is of staring in horror at him from my crumpled position on a soiled and stained old sofa.

Fluck was sitting on a small stool in the middle of the room. His back was towards me, his head seemed to be in his hands. In front of him was an easel with a large canvas propped on it. Even at that distance I could see that the rudimentary marks on it formed the beginning of his portrait of Poppet; her head and neck. I looked round the room for her but she seemed not to be there.

Fluck eventually turned round and put a finger to his lips. 'Shh,' he said, 'nearly finished.' He began to dab his face with a large greasy floral handkerchief. He had evidently been weeping, the bloody fool, not from remorse though, I knew that. Perhaps from joy, or fear. He need not have been frightened. He had startled me out of all aggression.

'It greatly surprises me that you detected the sofa under all that rubbish,' he said after a little while, recovering himself. 'It's usually hidden from view.' I was covered in rags and newspapers, tubes of paint, brushes, sponges, debris which my sudden agitation had brought down on me. I suppose I appeared slightly ridiculous. Soon Fluck was giggling again. As I slowly extricated myself, he picked up his brush and palette, still laughing, and began to attend to his canvas. He became instantly preoccupied. He wore a dingy red dressing-gown, like some down-at-heel yeti, a faded Fauve.

Though I understood less and less how and why he had such talent, alas, talent he had. There he was, obviously painting from memory without the slightest hesitation, with the most outrageous facility, and before the picture was completed I knew it was good. It occurred to me that in a curious way Fluck was painting my future. He had only just started, of course, but it wouldn't take him long, and when he had finished, I would be trapped in his version of things, like a figure in Hieronymus Bosch's terrifying triptych, frozen in the same torment in the same hellish picture for ever and ever.

'Come and have a look,' said Fluck without turning round. 'Don't be bashful. I didn't intend to scare you off. Now, who do you think this is?' He beamed at me over his shoulder, and continued painting. I seriously felt I was going to weep. My turn, I thought.

'Come on,' said Fluck. 'Three guesses. *Come on*, you do know her – oops, there's the gender for you, what a giveaway.'

It was one of Fluck's more realistic pictures and he knew I couldn't fail to guess the subject. Some details were already clear: the hair, bobbed at the back, curling round her left ear, a fine sweep of ochre; the imperfect knit of her tiny eyebrows; her chin, a pale oval highlight, which rose when she smiled and broke quivering when she wept. Fluck had there, already, in that half-completed face, whole smiles and frowns and lusts. All she had given him. And when the picture was finished, when her lovely naked body was hooked onto that head and throat, it would reflect him too. His Great English Nude. 'I paint with my penis,' Renoir once said. Fluck might have done.

'Name begins with P,' said Fluck, tauntingly. 'First syllable rhymes with strop.' I stood close behind him and watched him paint. I looked down at him, at the greasy top of his head. Now might I do it pat, while the bloat king fiddles with his brushes. But no, there was nothing to be done, nothing.

'It's Poppet,' I said quietly.

This drew a round of lazy applause from Fluck. 'Congratulations,' he drawled. 'I thought perhaps I had forgotten what she looked like and painted another person altogether.' He cocked

119

his head on one side to examine his own picture. 'Nice piece, isn't it?' he said ambiguously.

There was nothing for me to do but go. I turned.

'Don't go,' said Fluck. 'Have a drink.' He indicated a bottle or two on top of an old sideboard. 'I keep it there for guests,' he said. 'I never drink when I'm working. I don't need it when I work. It's only when I stop working that I need it.' He sounded pitiful, but he never drank anyway, so he was putting it on.

'Do stay,' he suddenly pleaded, half-shouting. 'Why don't we have a little chat. Like old times. You remember the old times, don't you? It's not very cosy in here, I know, but I've some paintings I'd like your opinion on. Wait, I'll get them.' He was rummaging now in a pile of rubbish, muttering. I backed off mistrustfully. 'One gets such little opportunity to talk to friends,' he began again in the tones of Eliot's painted lady, 'and I would like to know, truly – ' Fluck getting louder here; I had retreated some way off ' – what you think of these, it's so long since we talked, such a terrible long time since you packed me off to New York . . . and everything else . . . Please stay, just a few minutes. One gets so lonely.'

He said a great deal more as I fumbled my way to the trap door, but I do not remember exactly what. My general impression was of petulance. A crude attempt to baffle and unsettle me. I struggled once more with the heavy trap door, and Fluck rose from his stool and hobbled towards me, whining of his pictures and his loneliness and his need for conversation, and an odd thing happened which I think I was not meant to see. Halfway across the narrow room, he seemed to stumble and, producing an astonished expression of pain, clutched suddenly at his groin and staggered sideways against a sideboard. I was on my way down the ladder at this point, and just had time to glimpse this before disappearing below the level of the floor. But the sight of it froze me and I halted, uncertain whether to go back or go on.

Fluck seemed to assume I had gone. He made no attempt to follow me. I stayed where I was, crouched on the ladder. After a minute or so, I heard him groan and say something under his breath, but although I peered up through the open trap door, my view was limited, and I could not make him out. I waited, listening. Almost immediately there was another sound, a rattling, as of buckles, and a thwacking noise like released elastic. Then something heavy was thrown across the room, landing amongst the debris on the sofa. I distinctly heard Fluck say 'Bingo', and then all was silent. I tiptoed down the ladder.

I wish now I had seen the object that was thrown, but it appeared only as a blur passing over the trap door mouth. I became convinced, however, (and I expended a great deal of thought on this) that the object was a truss. It would at least account for Fluck's chronic difficulties moving around, which I remembered from our early morning walk. But it considerably complicated the scenario I had witnessed through his bedroom window. What horrific and unnatural ingenuity was required for him to make love to Poppet with a truss? Forgive me, but I trembled with vindictive rage at the mere thought of it.

The following day I did not get up until after lunch. I was ill and had been so periodically throughout the night. Poppet was naturally disgusted with me and at some point during the night had moved onto the floor, taking most of the (hideous) eiderdown with her. I was too miserable to complain. After her breakfast, she came up to see me.

'You're stupid,' she said, standing over me, a dark outline in the dim, curtained room. 'You drank too much last night. It's ridiculous.' I groaned at the thought of what I had drunk. 'Here's two aspirin. Now you won't be able to do any writing today, and you'll miss our walk in the country, and it's a lovely day. It really is ridiculous, S. J.'

Then she softened; my suffering was evidently very conspicuous. 'Poor boy,' she said. 'I know. Now you'll be bad-tempered all day. Try to get some sleep. We'll be back later this afternoon.' Bending to kiss me, she thought better of it, perhaps caught a whiff of me, and instead touched me gently on the nose with the tip of one forefinger. 'Be good,' she said, opening the door. 'Everyone sends their . . .' She searched for the appropriate word, gave up, and was gone.

I lay in bed, exhausted and distraught, listening to the bloody birds outside and the occasional voice rising from downstairs as everyone else prepared to leave the house. I heard Fluck most frequently, of course, usually bossing the others.

'Don't tell me what's wrong,' I heard him say, 'I know exactly what's wrong. *Delirium tremens.*'

'It's just a headache,' Angel said. Poor Angel, it sounded as if he was getting a scolding.

I slipped in and out of sleep for a while after this. Next I remember hearing them actually set off on their walk. Snippets of conversation came up to me from below my window.

'Do you really think so?' Myra was saying. 'I would have thought it unlikely.'

Poppet was disagreeing with her. 'I'm sure,' she said. 'I have to be.'

'The point I'm making is . . .' Myra went on, but I could not make out what the point actually was.

'No,' said Poppet. 'Really, it will be fine in Majorca, you'll see. Think of those lazy blue skies and sunshine and spring flowers and everthing . . .'

They were talking about the weather – that was my last, wry thought before I fell asleep. My dreams were full of laughter, falsetto giggling and base belly-laughs and, once, the sight of Fluck crouched on the floor like a giant brooding hen on its egg.

Towards three o'clock in the afternoon I rose and cautiously went downstairs for a cup of black coffee. There was no one about. Carrying my undrinkable medicine, I tottered in and out of various rooms, not knowing how to begin the day. I badly needed occupation to ease my pain. I did not consider writing. All the rooms I entered were uncongenial except for the downstairs lavatory, which was dark and cool and uncluttered. I sat there for a while, with my forehead resting against the cold, blue wall, almost at peace. But all the same I was eventually driven out. The pain in my head and belly commanded perpetual motion. For a while I sat in the garden, squinting at Fluck's bedroom window which, the day being hot and sunny, flashed with effulgence of reflected light.

There I tried my hand at a small poem, to begin, 'O Gut thou art sick', but I was devoid of inspiration. I had not really attempted to write poetry since my juvenile experiments at college; indeed, it is a peculiar fact that once my book, *Prohibited Caresses*, was printed I lost all my lyrical impulse. Of course, this had nothing to do with the fact that the book was unsuccessful; I had expected that, and I would not have had it printed in the first place if Fluck had not persuaded me otherwise and given me a contribution towards printing costs. He paid for it all, in fact, and very generous it made him feel too, though the result was effectively to kill my poetry, as I have said. I don't wish to appear ungrateful – at the time I was naively overjoyed by his offer – but once the book actually existed, he tended rather to treat it as his own personal property, hawking copies of it round the colleges, reading various pieces to his tutors during tutorials, even going so far as to arrange a number of readings for me, which, I am relieved to say, I did not take up. The book received only one notice, an anonymous one-liner in the college satirical broadsheet, *Loo News*: 'Poems to share with a friend. Not enough copies for one to a cubicle.' Shortly after that I destroyed all the copies of the book that remained unsold, which was all of them except five. Fluck was astounded at this. 'I can't believe it,' he kept saying. 'You're on their side.' Though I tried and tried I could never make him understand that his pretentious and irresponsible publicity for the book had been the cause of it all, though I suspected he never forgave me for the attempts I made. This bad feeling between us lasted far longer than it should have done. Eventually it formed the basis for our final arguments.

I went indoors, brain stewing, and sat in corners, plotting elaborate suicides (it had occurred to me even then) and eloquent last notes, and finally my pain faded a little and I was able to return to bed.

I suppose after this I really did fall asleep, because the next thing I remember is being woken by Poppet. Immediately I knew I was much better.

'This is a record,' she was saying playfully. 'Have you been asleep all this time?' I nodded. 'Do you know what time it is now?' I shook my head. 'Seven-thirty, *in the evening*. You've been asleep for – ' she began to count on her fingers, then gave up ' – ages. You've missed dinner. We had a Niçoise salad which Henry called his *pièce de résistance*. He said you wouldn't want any. How do you feel, by the way?'

'Terrible,' I told her.

'Here's two aspirin. Are you well enough to come for a walk?'

'No.'

'Please?' I looked at her questioningly and she said quickly,

'Myra and Angel are going to see a film, but I'd rather not, and Henry asked me to go for a walk with him. Actually – ' she lowered her voice, ' – I don't really want to go, he's been a bit odd today. So please come.'

I thought immediately that Fluck must have told her about the previous night. Perhaps she was remorseful. I shook my head. 'No thanks.'

'Please.'

'I'm still ill,' I said finally. 'You go.'

This was a test, of sorts. She got to her feet – apparently she had been kneeling – and moved away from the bed, looking thoughtful, 'S. J. . . .' she began.

'Or I may go back to sleep,' I said brusquely, fearing she might blurt out a confession when I wasn't ready for it. Besides, she hadn't yet had time to suffer the appropriate remorse for her sins. Poppet nodded, but went on, 'Apart from a hangover, is everything all right?' She had a worried face which she reserved for just such questions and which she produced now – although I suspected it meant less than it seemed to.

'Of course,' I said roughly.

'Then I suppose I'll go for a walk anyway,' she said with a sigh. 'See you later.'

I watched her go in great turmoil. Half of me wanted to cry out for her to come back, stay with me, weep together, and the other half of me sneered terribly at the very notion of this. I did nothing of course, which was worst of all.

But my turmoil continued, even after she had gone. Although I had already begun to harden my heart against her, my feelings were irrepressible, distinct and contradictory: sadness, fury, tenderness, amazement, bitterness and regret. I even suffered the last convulsions of unwanted hope. To spite the both of us I had pushed her off to ramble round the countryside with Fluck. The twilight would soon be gathering in the spaces between the trees; the lanes would turn to mauve to indigo to charcoal grey; moonlight would catch the mirror-side of fields of grass; and there would be no better evening, with the soft, cool breeze, and the hooting of night-birds, and the murmur of the nearby sea, to lower your lover to the ground, and wrestle with his truss.

I sprang out of bed, dressed untidily, and went downstairs.

In the kitchen I got myself a can of lager and a cigarette and wandered disconsolately into the living room to watch television. There to my surprise I found Moyra.

'Oh hi,' she said from the sofa. 'You're up, then.'

I had forgotten about Moyra, and I expect she had rather forgotten about me, but I was glad to find her there anyway.

'How do you feel?' she asked, frowning sympathetically and pulling herself into a sitting position as if for a serious conversation. I said cautiously that I wasn't as poorly as I had been, and she immediately reclined again. 'The others have gone to see a film,' she said. 'That horror one.'

I commented on how strange it was to keep meeting her in the living-room when everyone else was out.

'Mmm, it *is* strange,' she said slowly, frowning again, 'really weird.' She thought deeply, then added, 'I have a headache.'

I couldn't help noticing the clothes she was wearing. Her sweater, a drab Fairisle, was very tight indeed. Her grey woollen skirt was even tighter, clinging faithfully to the curves of her buttocks. She was also wearing thick stockings and a pair of battered old slippers, and her hair was in a mess, slovenly and lovely. There was a moment when I saw myself wrestling with Moyra's clothes, wrestling them off her, I mean, with my hands or teeth, in some bizarre sexual romp. After half an hour or so this moment passed. Our conversation did not sparkle, and apparently there was 'nothing on' television. After a time I found myself actually wishing the others would return.

'Has he painted your picture yet?' Moyra asked after a while.

'What?'

'Henry's painting everyone's picture.'

'Not mine.'

Moyra looked puzzled. 'Oh I think so,' she said, 'he said so, I think.'

'What did he say exactly?'

'Something about . . . your picture. I *think* so . . . when he painted mine, he said something about . . .'

'I see,' I said.

Despite her extreme uncertainty, it occurred to me then that I might learn something of Fluck from Moyra as I had from Angel. I should have thought of this before: information is the spy's *raison d'être*. To begin with I began to talk about Fluck's

125

pictures. It was difficult to know to what level Moyra would be able to rise; she did not respond when I said that the paradoxical achievement of abstract art had been to make deconstruction as important as construction (with its inevitable logical conclusion, the implications of which are clear), but she grew almost enthusiastic when I mentioned in passing the more naturalistic picture of her that Fluck had painted.

'Do you want to see it?' she asked.

'Your portrait?' My tone was innocent, but my heart was beating in my throat.

'It's in the bedroom.' She rose and I followed her ripe legs and swinging buttocks up the steep staircase.

Her room was a mess, as I was sure it would be. Or rather as I knew it to be in fact, having spent some considerable time in it over the previous two days. Overflowing ashtrays were balanced on piles of dog-eared magazines (did she go nowhere without magazines?) and clusters of empty coffee mugs crowded a small gate-legged table and the seat of a bedside chair. The carpet, a luxuriant russet shag pile, was visible only infrequently between piles of clothes, and on top of the dressing-table there was a huge mound of make-up and toiletries. The smell of the room was a curious mixture of stale tobacco and lavender.

'Sit down,' said Moyra, rummaging in the wardrobe, although I doubted there could be very much left inside it. I moved a bundle of assorted T-shirts sideways and eased myself onto the floor. 'Vodka,' said Moyra with a peculiar echo, her head bent inside the wardrobe.

'What?'

'Do you like vodka?' She emerged from the wardrobe with a bottle of Smirnoff. 'Henry doesn't keep vodka; it's really weird, he just won't,' she said. 'I bought this.' She rinsed out two mugs and poured me a generous measure. 'I'm afraid there's nothing to go in it,' she said, smiling.

I smiled back. 'Never mind,' I said. Although I hate vodka I held out the hope that as everything was different now, irrevocably changed, as you know, perhaps vodka would be different too, nicer. It wasn't. After a while, however, this ceased to matter.

126

Once settled on the edge of the bed, Moyra began to chain-smoke in earnest. She made no attempt to locate Fluck's picture. She seemed to have forgotten about it. What was she after? It was her bedroom she had led me to, after all. I began to watch her carefully. Observation was a habit I was trying to cultivate. Ignoring me, looking elsewhere altogether, Moyra lit another cigarette. Her movements, I noticed, were surprisingly exact, crafted almost, like moments in the final scene of a sentimental film when the hero cautiously gains the heroine's confidence and they ride the elevator together to her penthouse flat, silently expectant, his gestures polite, to usher or protect, her face already smudged by soft-focus. And so Moyra slowly up-ended the cigarette packet and the cigarette floated out onto the palm of her hand, and, with deceptive carelessness, she put this cigarette in the precise corner of her red mouth, the lower lip being permanently at half-pout to support it, and then she brushed back a fallen curl of hair and briefly examined her fingernails – cumulative distractions necessary to suspense – and then, tension mounting as in the best performance art, she calmly lit up, shook the match to extinguish it, and inhaled deeply; though this wasn't, yet, the moment of climax, for she held the spent match delicately away from her before dropping it onto the carpet, and then, finally, after holding down a lungful of smoke, a dreamy expression on her face – the delayed climax approaching now, what blissful torture – she opened her lovely mouth and half-closed her eyes, and exhaled a delicious, blue, satisfied swirl of smoke.

All this is not, as it may seem, a mere digression. It is an exercise in dispassionate observation. Note the details – details, details, details, there is no end to them . . . As a student of art and literature, and life, I am aware that, for better or worse, the main thrust of any story is to be found in its incidentals. They *are* the story.

Moyra and I talked tentatively of various inconsequential things until I could stand it no longer and began to peer conspicuously round the room for a sight of the picture. Moyra giggled abruptly, producing a dimple. 'You're looking for the picture, aren't you?' she said. 'I'd forgotten. Wait.' On all fours, her tight skirt disclosing the intimate outlines of her buttocks and thighs (no knickers? I moistened my dry mouth with

127

horrible vodka), she groped under the bed and eventually tugged out the painting.

'There.' She laid it on the bed, rather pleased with herself. 'He gave it to me. To keep.' I nodded. 'Do you want another drink?' I absently nodded again.

I had not seen the finished version before. Fluck had evidently made a few interesting late alterations, but essentially the painting remained what it had been before: a parody of Botticelli's 'The Birth of Venus'.

'Do you know about Sandro Botticelli?' I asked Moyra. She looked blank. 'The picture is a parody of a famous painting by a fifteenth-century painter.'

'Oh, I know that,' said Moyra. 'A parody, yes. Henry told me that.'

'I see,' I said. 'More to the point, it's a very good parody.'

'Yes, he told me that too,' said Moyra.

And so I fell eagerly to appraising the work in detail. ('It's pretty, isn't it?' said Moyra in the background.)

'The Mirth of Venus' Fluck had called it, and indeed it displayed a great sense of fun; I noticed immediately two details I hadn't seen before: the Sony Walkman that Venus was wearing, and her gaudy swimsuit. Both nice touches. They suited Venus's confident stance above the waves, poising as if her miraculous elevation was merely a publicity stunt. She was not naked, as I have already regretted, but, as if in compensation, she was smiling the wonderful Moyra smile, a full-lipped, dozy, sexy smile disclosing a glimpse of the inside of her mouth which was clean and pink like a cat's.

In Botticelli's original, Venus coyly hides her pudenda with the tresses of her hair. In Fluck's parody Venus's cigarette gives rise to a wreath of smoke which rises to the level of her shoulders to form a decorative motif, obscuring nothing but a patch of rudimentary sky. This, I thought, was also a clever touch.

'Here's your vodka,' said Moyra. 'You hadn't finished the first one, so you've got quite a lot to drink now.'

Botticelli's style is an exquisite one, combining a delicate linearity with cool, acidic colours. His paintings belong to the Early Italian Renaissance (Florentine version) when it was still possible for artists to display the true spirit of rediscovery of the classical arts, later lost in the grandiose schemes of High Renaissance virtuosi like Michelangelo, Leonardo, Raphael, Lotto, Pordenone, Sebastiano, and the rest. Botticelli's pale figures, quiet and dignified, slightly aloof, relate to that glimpsed earlier era, and are more akin to, say, marbles by the great fifth-century sculptors Polyclitus, Phidias, Myron, than to paintings by Botticelli's contemporaries. Their paleness was much noted, indeed they famously excited Walter Pater's morbidity. But there is nothing of this paleness or morbidity in Fluck's painting. His Venus is the post-sexual revolution, contraceptive-liberated, casually consumerist, contemporary girl: Moyra, Venus, the perpetual adolescent bursting from her swimsuit with girlish giggles. Perhaps this is why Fluck had to clothe her, so that there would be something for her to burst free from. The thought of this appealed to me.

My thoughts were interrupted by Moyra giving a low growl as she exhaled smoke and bent forward over the picture, self-consciously holding her cigarette behind her.

'Do you like it?' I asked.

'I like this bit,' she said. She bent even nearer to the picture, peering myopically. The poor girl was evidently half-blind. She bent over till her face was within inches of the painting, and her left breast touched the canvas with its soft woolly tip. I watched her progress keenly. She swayed forward and both breasts engaged forcefully but uncritically with the central part of the picture, coincidentally obliterating their pictorial doubles. Tit for tit.

'I like it all,' she said finally, then giggled. 'I think I just like that kind of thing,' she said. 'The sea and sunshine and everything. I don't know much about painting. Not like you.' She looked round for an ashtray, then suddenly turned back to face me. 'I feel ever so funny,' she said. 'It must be the vodka.'

'Have a bit more,' I said, holding up the bottle, 'it'll clear your head.' We both laughed a lot at that.

Sea and sunshine, yes. In Botticelli's picture there is no sun. It is, according to Pater, a sunless dawn, a cool, calm clarity of sea and sky, and Venus rises, as she does every morning, to face another long hard day of love. No wonder the pensive expression and general lack of enthusiasm. But in Fluck's parody, Venus stands in a blaze of noon; dazzling highlights

129

brighten her hair and waves catch fire as they roll towards the shore. Botticelli's sea is goldfish-bowl-grey and tiny wavelets, denoted in a kind of painterly shorthand, merely ruffle the surface in decoration. Fluck's sea, on the other hand, swells and dips and splashes Venus with spindrift. It is boyish and mischievous, it seems to heave and leer. It is, incidentally, closer to the original Greek myth in which a sudden intromission of testosterone into the sea, caused by the castration of Uranus, actually engenders the goddess – Aphrodite, meaning 'foam-born'. 'Do you know the very interesting myth behind the painting?' I asked Moyra, who was returning from the loo.

It was not interesting to Moyra. She reclined on the bed, a blue and grey cloud of smoke drifting perpetually above her. Vodka fumes seemed to reverberate round the room.

'Note the ice cream cones on the beach,' I said, indicating as appropriate with a forefinger. Moyra blinked and stared bug-eyed at the canvas. 'There,' I said firmly. 'On the beach. Ice cream cones.'

'They're not ice cream cones,' she said slowly, her nose touching the moist canvas, pursing her lips in concentration.

'In Botticelli's picture,' I went on regardless, 'Venus is strewn with pink roses by the allegorical figures of the Zephyrs.'

'Mmm, lovely.'

'In this, you are presented with ice cream cones. In the original myth, Aphrodite is also attended by doves and sparrows. In this . . .'

'Why?' asked Moyra.

'Traditional symbols of love and lust,' I said.

'Ice cream cones?' Moyra looked dumbfounded.

'Doves and sparrows,' I said briskly.

She tittered. 'Silly me,' she said. 'But why then,' she insisted, 'the ice cream cones?'

They were symbolic phalluses, of course – with their rigid stems and creamy heads you could hardly mistake them for anything else. Moyra looked at me enquiringly.

'It's a joke,' I said evasively, 'a joke allusion to the birth of the ice cream industry in Italy in the fifteenth century. Botticelli's brother-in-law was one of the first major investors.' I was modestly pleased with this slight departure from the truth, but Moyra smiled broadly.

'Really,' she said gaily. 'What balls, S. J.' Scornfully delighted, she poured me more vodka, and also offered me a cigarette – a sign of some intimacy.

'It's all part of the parody,' I said, grinning too, feeding her more smiles. As casually as I dared, I tossed the cigarette into the air, and by a tremendous fluke caught it first time in my mouth. Moyra, who had her back to me, looking at the picture, continued to talk.

'It's really weird, isn't it, to do a parody like that,' she said, her head on one side. 'But the thing is, what I want to know is, why did Henry paint me in Poppet's swimsuit?' She giggled.

I laughed too, nodding, encouraging her, the vodka sweetening the joke, and then I realised what she had said and stopped.

She was perfectly right of course. Moyra had no swimsuit as such, just a tiny bikini. And, as I looked again at the picture, I abruptly remembered what Poppet's swimsuit looked like, a turquoise thing with a wet-look satin finish; it had a matching belt, and a cutaway crotch which necessitated painful shaving at the start of each summer. And there it was in the picture, Poppet's pretty little costume stretched to accommodate Moyra. It became clear to me then what Fluck had done; he had painted not Moyra but a Moyraesque version of Poppet, with all the sex of their relationship superabundant and the whole scene simmering with his testosterone, agitating the sea Venus walked on, everything fertile and fuckable. It was, in a sense, a version of the Glorious Scenario I had witnessed through his bedroom window. Yes, this was his message to me. And thus, in the gallery of my mind, 'The Mirth of Venus' took its place immediately next to the triste Norwegian nude of Fluck alone with his underpants, and together they formed an edifying, horrifying diptych. This was how he had wanted her, yes, of course, one of the ways at least, buoyant on an incoming tide, with almost airborne Mae West breasts, hair haloing her face, smiling, willing, newly-formed from the foam of the sea.

Moyra was talking in the background, asking me if I was all right. Apparently I had nearly fallen over.

'Do be careful, S. J.,' she said, 'you nearly dropped the bottle.'

Not dropped it, no. I had been about to throw it at the painting. To be truthful, I should not have drunk all the vodka she offered me, not on an empty stomach. Manfully I struggled to regain control of myself. I rose from my knees and unclenched my fists. The shock I had received was enormous, but I was dedicated to the discovery of the exact nature of Fluck and Poppet's affair, and would not be intimidated by my conniving imagination. 'I hurt my ankle yesterday playing squash,' I said, 'I expect I'll be a little wobbly for a few days.' I winced, as if in pain, at which Moyra showed very little surprise, and we continued to talk.

Naturally I was curious to know what it had been like for Moyra to be painted by Fluck. This, in a sense, was the key; a missing link in the chain; one of the last pieces in the jigsaw. She reclined on the bed and trailed an indolent hand through the smoke-tinctured air as if to express something she couldn't put into words. She was, in fact, often put to this recourse.

'*You* know,' she said, and giggled. She was plainly drunk by now, but began to sketch in a few of the major themes. Much of the story I was forced to piece together for myself.

'He finished the picture in the studio,' said Moyra. I imagined bitterly how Fluck had followed her up, his piggy eyes fixed on her swaying, suspended rump, his mind already bent on subtle transmutations only I would understand. Moyra declined to stand on the sofa, despite Fluck's cajoling ('Too dirty, Henry, really horrid'), so she was stood on a battered old pouffe. He talked to her at first in a shrill cockney accent, a favourite of his, and most of what he said was unintelligible. He asked her not to smoke and she refused ('I can't not smoke, Henry, I'd die'). He agreed, on condition that she would talk to him to keep him amused, which was probably a joke on Fluck's part, but Moyra did her best all the same.

'Then he just, well, disappeared,' said Moyra. 'Behind the easel,' she explained. 'And I couldn't see him at all. Just hear his voice. It was *very* weird.' As far as Moyra was concerned, that had been it. She sat there smoking and occasionally saying something she hoped would amuse Fluck, and she didn't see him again, apart from rare moments when he peeped out at her round the side of the easel, until it was all over and he stood up to pontificate: 'It is finished. *C'est fini*. Another masterpiece from the brush . . .', etc.

Clearly this was not good enough. Not nearly enough detail.

I prompted her again about Fluck's conversation, and after some urging on my part she admitted that Fluck had occasionally mentioned the names of painters she had not heard of, telling her rather sensational details about their lives and works. 'To keep himself amused, I think,' she said, unusually astute. 'He promised to show me some of their pictures.' She thought particularly that she was going to be shown paintings by three artists, a man, Clint, and two women, Suzanne and Sheila, all of whose surnames she had forgotten. 'Yes, yes,' I said. I thought of Klimt's famous picture 'The Kiss', and a number of drolly titled works by Egon Schiele, 'Reclining Girl', 'Nude Girl with Crossed Arms', 'Nude with Mauve Stockings'.

'And once,' said Moyra suddenly, laughing, and attempting to stand, 'he shouted out "Bingo", just like that. It was *so* funny. Really, I nearly *choked*, I think he must have finished the painting or something.' Hearing this I became very depressed. 'Oh dear, I *am* sorry,' Moyra said, breathless with giggling. 'All that vodka I've drunk. I shall have to go to the loo. Oh dear.'

While she was gone I had another look at the picture. It was all too easy to see, and vividly, Fluck painting Moyra in his attic.

He sits on his little three-legged stool with brushes in one hand and a messy palette in the other, and grins to himself. He grins because he has had a good idea for the picture, but also because, although he is going to paint Moyra face on, and has told her so several times, she is plainly determined to show him instead her wonderful profile, and consequently stands facing the sofa at the end of the room. Typical of Fluck to take advantage of the fact that Moyra can't see him by peeping out from behind the easel and licking his lips at her in a jocular fashion. Not that it would matter if she did see him, it's only a joke, funny old Fluck. And it doesn't matter that she has taken up the wrong position either because he's painting her not from life but from memory, the memory of a fantasy he had, about someone else, or rather, *with* someone else.

He paints brusquely with a heavily loaded brush. The hand holding the palette rests on an ample hip, but is occasionally raised and he is talking to Moyra, feverishly, of love: love in life, love in art; he is making things up, but it doesn't matter.

His mobile face folds and unfolds like something a pastry cook is hopelessly trying to reform.

'But what of Delacroix, my dear?' he shouts, having already told Moyra about the sexual habits of Caravaggio, Klimt, Schiele, Modigliani, and most bizarre of all, Gwen John. 'The loves of Delacroix occupy the lengthiest and most entertaining chapter in Vasari's immortal book *Sexual Lives of the Artists* – with the possible exception of Grandma Moses.' Fluck is enjoying himself immensely. He can tell Moyra anything and she giggles like a schoolgirl.

'Don't let that profile drop now,' he calls out to her sternly, peeping round the easel to watch her swallow painfully and revive her pose. 'Keep it up!' He lets out a moist chuckle. 'Tit up,' he says to himself, painting even more furiously.

'Delacroix!' he shouts suddenly. 'In French the name means "of the crotch", something of a giveaway, don't you think? But as if that wasn't enough, he kept a diary as well. Silly man, he shouldn't have done that. Now everyone knows!' Fluck twirls a brush and cheerfully sloshes viridian green onto the canvas.

'And in his diary,' Fluck continues, 'he made certain marks on certain days. Do you follow me? Some days, in fact most days, he made several certain marks. Are you with me? He spent so much time making certain marks in his diary, I'm surprised he managed to do anything to make a mark about. Do you see what I'm driving at? His appetites were apparently . . .' pause for effect '. . . insatiable! What a man! Man? I rather think I mean beast. One can only resort to that vile deity Priapus for precedent.' Fluck is in his element by now, is roaring along. But variety is his hallmark.

'My dear,' he calls more softly than usual, 'imagine what it was like for his models. Delacroix was especially fond of his models, you see. To be blunt, he seemed not to be able to resist them. The time he spent actually painting them was little more than foreplay. Nor were any of them able to escape his attentions, he was so splendidly indiscriminate. How they must have trembled, eh, Moyra, as they entered his studio, knowing the fate that was in store for them. And it didn't matter whether they were primped out in their satins and velvet drapes or simply plonked stark-naked on an old orange crate. In a manner

134

of speaking – ' he giggles here ' – they were crated and fated, or fêted and fated. Do you follow?'

Poor Moyra, a little flustered, throttles a confused giggle and tries to recapture the purity of her profile. Frankly she does not understand who Fluck is talking about. She doubts whether she has ever met them. Fluck paints passionately onto the central section of the canvas, brows knit, eyes narrow, the tip of his tongue slinking out wolfishly over his drooping lower lip, and then he suddenly snorts with laughter.

'But now then, Moyra, what do you think *they* thought of it? The models, I mean. That's the crux, as it were *La Croix*, of the matter, isn't it? What do you think? Never mind – your opinion is rather unimportant – the fact is, *they loved it*. It is stated unequivocally in Vasari.' Fluck peeks out from behind his easel and again smacks his lips in an insulting manner. Moyra is smoking nervously.

'They were queueing up outside his studio,' Fluck bawls, 'waiting for his summons. High society women, marquises, countesses, princesses, *toutes les belles du grand monde*, were offering themselves up to be painted as flower-sellers or chambermaids or, even better the slaughtered concubines of Sardanapalus's harem. Delacroix, you see, had become necessary to their reputations.'

The painting's nearly finished now, but it occurs to Fluck that the beach at which Aphrodite is to alight is a little dull. He has a brilliant idea and immediately attacks the canvas with redoubled energy. Ice cream cones appear. Moyra's profile is drooping and she is fidgeting lazily with her pack of cigarettes. Although Fluck has not been painting for long, and although his conversation could not be said to lack elements of a certain crude humour, she is already bored. It is wearying work keeping up a profile. But Fluck (I can tell it from his face) has not yet finished his little fable; he is preparing to stage a dramatic finale.

'Moyra!' he shouts loudly, startling the poor girl again. 'Moyra, *my dear*, who have we left out of our reasoning? Delacroix, of course, you're quite right. Let us consider him. Imagine: he's forty-five years old, he's been making certain marks in his diary, sometimes several certain marks a day, for twenty-five exhausting years. And still they're queueing up along the Rue Notre-Dame-de-Lorette waiting for his studio to open its doors. Moyra, my god, *mon dieu*, think of poor Delacroix waking up each new day with a blank page in his diary waiting to be filled with marks; think of him bleakly considering the consequences of a reputation made too early and too splendidly. Let us consider carefully who is the victim in this particular story. I think you will agree that it is not so clear as we originally supposed. What might the moral of our little story be?' Fluck's voice has slowed right down by now. The painting is finished. He is merely being mischievous when he leans round the easel and shouts, 'But chin up, my dear, while you're considering!'

It is time. *Monsieur le peintre* struggles briefly with elastic and aluminium buckles, and then he is free. 'Bingo!' he shouts, rising in sudden freedom and relief to address Moyra over the top of her picture – though not really Moyra, of course; he is addressing the other one for whom Moyra is a surrogate, and he himself is not so much Fluck as Delacroix, the dirty dog. It is time, but how can he begin to say what he really means? He wags a finger at Moyra who has allowed her profile to lapse so badly.

'We are all victims, my dear,' he says sonorously, stepping out from behind his most recent masterpiece, 'all victims in this mortal, uncomfortable, wearying world.'

And he is naked, utterly nude, without the slightest shred or thread of decent clothing, and he trips forwards nimbly like the famous dancing hippopotamus towards Moyra, whom he thinks of as Poppet, who is too astonished to smoke or giggle or even pout at the sight of him rising like thick scum to the surface of his fantasy . . .

'Do you know, they're not back yet,' said Moyra, returning yet again from the loo.

'Perhaps they've gone for a drink,' I said automatically.

'Not this late, surely?'

'The country pubs stay open after hours,' I told her bitterly. 'And they all know Henry.' I continued meanwhile to gaze morbidly at the painting. How everything seemed always to have been arranged in advance by Fluck, the Master Planner! He created anecdotes about himself for other people to relate to me, he painted pictures he knew I would see and understand, he inhabited my memories, changing them in emphasis and meaning each time I recalled them. He told fables with morals both obscure and intimidating. And was it even possible that he had stage-managed his seduction of Poppet simply so that I could witness it? Was it for me that he had posed himself, fat and naked and ugly, on the shaded bed, a dismal nude in the tradition of Munch (but perhaps in the style of Rembrandt, seen through the stained, rain-streaked window as through accumulated layers of dirty varnish)? As I watched, did he know that I watched, and did he hide his exultation? Was he the voyeur and was I the victim? Nudity is knowledge, but *what* knowledge I no longer knew. I began to suspect, and, suspecting, was held spellbound by the nightmarish thought that he was wilfully leading me, my hand in his paw, through a maze of his own Daedalian making, gently admonishing me as we went, and chuckling to himself as we approached some terrible, unavoidable destination.

After we had smoked some more cigarettes and finished off our drinks (there was, I think, at this point, no more vodka left) Moyra, with a rather odd expression on her face, offered me a coffee. I was amused to notice how like a student she was in her habits: she had an electric kettle in the room, and a small carton of milk on the window-sill outside. I watched her move languidly about, collecting coffee mugs. She gave me another odd look, a sidelong, lazy glance, as she bent to plug in the kettle. I was standing up, near to her, and I noticed how uncertain and jangly my own movements were; my hands were trembling; certainly I had drunk more than I thought. So too had Moyra. As she rose, she nearly overbalanced, and I lurched forward to stop her from falling. The wool of her sweater was warm and soft, and through it I could feel the warmth and softness of her body. I felt the mobile nub of flesh covering her ribs, and as she slipped back against me, my hand accidentally slid under her armpit. A sharp scent of cheap lavender broke through the cloud of nicotine and enlivened the moment. We laughed, of course, and struggled to extricate ourselves.

The kettle eventually boiled, and I helped Moyra with the coffee. Her hands moved slowly, lifting the kettle, taking up the teaspoon and wiping it mechanically on her woollen sleeve. Curiously, she seemed to be decelerating all the time. Soon, I thought, she would come to a dead stop. I noticed also that she avoided looking at me, picking up her coffee in both hands and turning slightly to one side, staring into the steaming mug. She was suddenly and unaccountably shy. I seemed to be standing right next to her; I smelled the lavender again, and I couldn't help admiring how soft and tight her sweater was, nor how somnolently her chest rose and subsided as she breathed. The perfume hypnotised me, that and the sight of the nape of her neck as I leant forwards, seeing her hot, pale, downy skin between curls of disorderly hair.

I am deeply embarrassed by the memory of what happened next. The fact is that as I stooped towards her, Moyra suddenly spun round to see what I was doing and, grinning now (oh god, my awful empty grinning), I slid my hands firmly under her buttocks and pulled her towards me. There was a moment of horrid suspense, and then, from her, sudden laughter. She was laughing even before she spilt out of my grip, and the transformation of her face, so close to mine, was extraordinary and terrifying. One instant it was frozen and the next convulsed with giggles. 'I'm sorry,' I heard her say, in a cracked whisper. 'It's my fault. I just can't . . . just can't stop.' And she buried her face in a tissue. Fortuitously, at that moment my drunkenness overwhelmed me, and I staggered backwards against a convenient sideboard, to take no further part in the farcical affair.

Following this, all was confusion. I half remember doors being opened, the sight of my own lurching shoes, the sound of voices. Then my bed rushed up to meet me; the enveloping darkness bounced once, quivered, and was finally still, covering me.

That night I dreamt that out of the darkness the room was suddenly filled with a great crashing light and a clamour of voices arose, all talking about me, vague accusations, mumbled threats which I could not quite make out. And then I was suddenly woken by strange cries, 'I didn't do it! I didn't do it!' which apparently I had made. Then the room was indeed filled with light – sunlight – and outside the window operatic birds were belting out the dawn chorus. I was not at all comforted to discover that it was 6.30 a.m., and not the visionary middle of the night, nor to find by the bed a note from Poppet which began 'I cannot sleep with you if . . .' and which I did not read to the end. She had left me the eiderdown. Just for that I could have hated her. By the bed someone had thoughtfully placed a washing-up bowl which I immediately used. Then I fell asleep.

When I woke up again, it was some time in the afternoon. There didn't seem to be anyone about; certainly there was no Poppet dispensing aspirin and a mild moralistic scolding. I had a feeling that the time for such mildness was over. My head ached, a twin concentration of pain behind the eyes. My whole body felt cramped and dirty. There was, not surprisingly, an unpleasant taste in my mouth. Yet all this was pathetically minor compared to the pain of my emotional state. Nothing I might now attempt could possibly do justice to it. I thought first of Fluck, which threw me into a terrible rage, and then I thought of Poppet, with a different but even more furious rage; and then finally I thought of myself, and the rage which accompanied this effort was the most blinding and brilliant of all.

Through a chink in the curtains I could see that the weather was fine, and I guessed that the others would be on the beach. This would explain, perhaps, why no one had visited me. Certainly Fluck would otherwise have found it difficult resisting the desire to play the nurse. I could imagine him 'keeping me company', perching owlishly on the edge of my bed, insisting that I share his memories, and invoking the mythical 'good old days' we had the misfortune to share. He would remind me of the rounds of parties in poky rooms where we had first met Poppet, and he would disingenuously recall my unfavourable first impression of her. Did I still remember how she laughed when, to impress a small group of lack-lustre party-goers, I had attempted a short one-man dramatic interpretation of *Macbeth*? Did I remember my peeved opinion that she was 'totally innocent of aesthetic standards'? Wasn't it true that we didn't hit it off at first? Nor at last? How Fluck, wheezing next to me, would giggle over these reminiscences – and I, inevitably, would reflect that in a sense we had come meanly full circle, with Fluck again sitting shabbily on the edge of my bed as he used to do at college, preventing me from going to sleep even though it was 3 a.m. And he had long ago finished his drawing of me; continuing to talk, and continually shuffling further onto the bed. '*Do* move over, S. J., I'm almost over the edge. I don't understand at all why your knees have to take up so much room.' Yes, I remembered those days perfectly. They were hell.

The house was silent with a malevolent silence. Even in my room I felt betrayed, with Poppet's dresses and underwear littering the floor, her lipsticks and eyeliners and blushers, put on at night for Fluck, crowding the table. I got up and padded down to Fluck's study. There I selected several books from the shelves and carried them back to my room. In bed again, I began to flip through them, trying to contain my nausea and keep my thoughts from the distressing reconstitution of memories and dreams. I was just beginning to think that I had never, in my life, felt more alone or more in pain or more desperate for relief, when there was a knock on the door, and without waiting for an answer, Myra scuttled in. She did not represent the kind of relief I had in mind. She squinted at me through the dim light, sniffed the air, and said, 'I've brought you a drink.' She was carrying a mug which I shuddered to recognise from the night before. It had alka seltzer in it, and smelt pungently of stale vodka.

'I'll leave it by the bed if you don't want it now,' she said, her nervous face twitching like a rodent's, 'but you have to drink it, all right?' I made a mumbling noise intended to express reluctance.

'Good,' she said briskly, pulling up a chair to the bedside. 'How are you?'

I have already mentioned the rather anxious nature of the relationship between Myra and me. A common memory unfortunately divides us. I sensed, correctly, that her appearance at my bedside would not guarantee my comfort.

'Poppet doesn't know I'm here,' she began, 'but as her best friend I have to talk to you frankly, S. J. I don't think she's very happy.' I stared at her with all the malevolence I could muster.

'Three nights on the trot,' she went on, 'you've been drunk.'

She was wrong; last night was the fourth. 'And on the subsequent mornings I have been ill,' I replied with an effort. Scolding from Poppet is something I take very well, but I was not prepared to indulge Myra.

'You have,' she agreed, mouth pursed, 'and that hasn't

helped, has it? And what a waste, really, for you as well. Look, it's such a beautiful day. Shall I draw the curtains for you?'

I shook my head, and repeated that I was ill. She shot across the room, and drew back the curtains.

'You don't look very well,' she observed. 'Pasty.' Her voice was bright, but edgy. She sat, crossed her legs, attempted a smile, and began to cough. 'It smells in here,' she observed. 'I'll open the window.'

'Doesn't open,' I said.

'You could do with some fresh air,' she insisted.

What I needed was an oxygen tent. I bit my lip. It was clear that Myra was settling in to stay, and I doubted whether our conversation would maintain the delightful air of inconsequence with which it had begun. I was right.

'Poppet's not looking well either,' she said.

'Too many late nights,' I muttered.

She seemed about to make a retort to this, but apparently changed her mind. She stared towards the window. 'She spent last night on my floor,' she said eventually. I didn't reply. I don't think I believed her. 'On my floor,' she repeated ominously.

We looked at each other warily, neither of us really knowing how far we would go down our respective paths of righteous-ness and surliness. I was prepared, I must say, to go quite far – but circumstances, as always, were against me. Myra turned from me, made a small noise of surprise, and suddenly rising, bolted over to the desk at the far side of the room. 'What's this?' she cried, holding up an empty half-bottle of Scotch. 'S. J., have you drunk all this?' I had. It was a little something I had borrowed from Fluck's larder to help me through my days alone in his house.

'Of course not,' I said. 'Do you think I'm an alcoholic?' My tone was defiant because I knew the other bottle was under the bed where she was unlikely to find it.

'Why, S. J.?' she asked, stepping primly towards me with the empty bottle held up between forefinger and thumb. 'Why? You never used to drink so much; not this much. What are you doing to yourself?' She sat down on the edge of the chair and leaned towards me, nostrils flaring. 'I talked to Poppet last night. She wouldn't tell me very much, you know how tough

141

and independent she is, but I don't think she can handle this much longer, I really don't. And I told her so. If I'd had my own way, I'd have come to see you straight away, but she wouldn't hear of it.' She narrowed her eyes. 'Not that there would've been much point anyway, judging by the state of you today.' I rolled my eyes to the ceiling, but she seemed not to notice.

'Moyra blames herself, of course,' she went on. 'Just like her to do that. She's not very well today either,' she added. No one, apparently, was well today. 'Do you realise you drank nearly a whole bottle of vodka between you?' I remembered only that the vodka had run out much too soon. Myra regarded me with a strange, wistful expression. 'You don't even like vodka, S. J.,' she said sadly.

This amazed me. 'How do you know?' I shouted, outraged at her glib assertion of the truth.

'Don't you remember the summer ball you took me to?' she asked softly. 'You know, where we had our argument. Remember those free vodka cocktails they served? It was part of a promotion; at dawn they simply handed out the leftover bottles. Don't you remember any of it? Well, I suppose it's hardly surprising; I've never seen vodka have such a bad effect on someone, I thought you were going to kill me.' She gave a dry laugh. 'Oh, don't look at me so balefully, S. J., it's all in the past. You know I don't bear grudges.'

I was sure this was a lie, but couldn't immediately refute it. Myra went on. 'Not like Henry,' she said, sniffing. 'Poor Henry, living in the past. That's another thing; your drinking is really upsetting Henry. Surely you've noticed that. Didn't you hear him shouting yesterday?'

'No,' I said firmly. 'I was asleep.'

'He went berserk. Kept asking everyone if we thought you should see a psychiatrist.' I spluttered at this.

'I know,' said Myra, 'I know what he's like. It must be very difficult for you, being his best friend. But you can't not feel sorry for him, can you? Not after what he's been through, first with his mother, and then his father leaving, and then that awful trip to New York.'

'Yes, yes,' I said, 'quite awful.'

'Well it was,' said Myra sharply, gauging my tone too

accurately for comfort. 'He hardly ever stops talking about it. However, it isn't Henry I've come to discuss.' Here she rose and began to pace up and down the room, and I realised at once that she was entering a more terrible phase of disapprobation. 'It's Poppet,' she said hotly, 'your wife.'

I choked a little at this, naturally, and to my alarm, Myra abruptly stopped speaking. I was afraid I had betrayed something of my true feelings to her, but this was not the reason for her sudden silence. No, she had been brought up short by the sight of the blunt snout of my second bottle of whisky poking out from beneath the pink eiderdown. She snatched it up and took a fierce grip of it as if about to hurl it at me. Her face was colourless and her voice, I knew from experience, would be an evil mixture of pity and sarcasm. I recognised the moment of judgement. There was nothing else for it; I began to cry.

Softly at first, of course; later in explosive sobs. I wept for myself who had been dreadfully abused and was lost among enemies, but as I wept I confessed to Myra an almost endless list of barely redeemable failings of mine connected with my job and my writing and my marriage. These were the excuses for my 'wildly anti-social behaviour' – a charge I was quick to bring against myself. I was out for her sympathy, though it was hard work getting it. She remained aloof when I spoke of my money problems, recurrent illnesses and the pressures of my job, and she was sceptical when I ran through a long list of imaginary personal problems – depressions, neuroses, lack of self-control, childishness, vindictiveness, and so on. In the end, however, my tears won the day (for who can bear to see a grown man cry?) together with the fact that after every weepy outburst I returned to the theme of my great love for my wife. It was quite a performance.

Perhaps all this sounds a little glib, but anyone who dissembles desperation to such a degree runs the risk of becoming desperate for real. By the time I had won Myra round, I was weeping real tears, and hating her for having demanded so much. I endured all in the hope she would eventually leave me to my preferable solitary disquiet.

'I won't deny it's been difficult for you,' she conceded at last. 'All I ask is that you think of Poppet. Now drink your alka seltzer down,' she said pushing home her advantage. 'Go on, it'll do you good.' I drank it meekly, knowing myself to be nauseated beyond remedy. But even then, though her mood had changed, Myra showed no inclination to leave. She perched at an uneasy angle on the bedside chair and told me about the lovely picnic I was missing. Apparently she had returned from the beach early for her spare pair of glasses (astonishing black-rimmed contraption), having smashed her other pair playing volleyball.

'Actually,' she confided, 'Henry broke them. They fell off in the middle of a rally and he got confused and stamped on them. Sometimes he does the wildest things,' she added. I ventured that Fluck – Henry – was an artist and as such had licence to behave in a Bohemian fashion. It was now an instinct of mine to probe for information in this way.

'He likes to think so, I know that,' said Myra with a wave of her bony hand, 'but he's only playing at it.' Evidently she indulged him in this peccadillo. 'He's terribly fond of us, especially you. But,' she became serious, 'he doesn't have many friends. It makes me very sad because he can be so hospitable and kind-hearted. And fun.'

I began to feel more in control of the conversation now, and ventured diffidently that the lack of recognition of Fluck's talents made him impatient at times. I did not mention, though I thought of it, the gross impatience of his sexual desires.

'Oh, he can't paint,' said Myra dismissively. 'That's part of the problem, isn't it? He has no theme, no personal style. Painting is a game for him; in fact, his whole life is a game. I don't believe he'll ever make a serious painter. He doesn't even need the money, unless his father manages to spend it all before he dies.'

She then began a tedious documentary on Fluck's family background, much of which I had already heard from Poppet, not to mention the many versions spun to me by Fluck himself. His family, Myra argued, had given him money but nothing else. Fluck's affluent father, the villain in her account – 'a horrid little philanderer' she called him – had never shown the slightest interest in his sons, nor in his wife – who, it appeared, was given to seeing visions, usually of a biblical character. When Fluck was still quite small, she fell under the more or less permanent delusion that she was Susanna, eponymous heroine of the Apocryphal book of the Old Testament, doomed to be perpetually surprised by the Elders. Consequently she was often to be seen loitering naked in the garden of Fluck's house, waiting, I suppose, to be surprised, and once, perhaps in frustration at not being surprised, she had attempted to board a bus in the same state. This was one of the first traumas in the young Fluck's life. Soon after that she went abroad (she was French by birth) and there divided her time between the home of her aged parents and, with increasing frequency, a private clinic for the mentally ill. Her husband visited her only twice. After the first visit she made a suicide attempt, and after the second she found herself pregnant with his second son. I had not known these details and found them moderately entertaining. Also, as Myra's diatribe drew to a close, I began to entertain hopes that she might leave. But these were ill-founded.

'You're looking a little better,' she said, with a narrow smile. I was in fact beginning to feel worse. 'What are you reading?' She gestured towards the books scattered on the bed. 'Can I see?'

Most were already opened at certain pages. The book on Titian at the double-page illustration of the 'Venus of Urbino'; the book on Goya at the 'Naked Maja'; on Velasquez, at the 'Rokeby Venus'; on Boucher at 'Mademoiselle Murphy'. I was also studying Ingres' 'La Grande Odalisque', Correggio's 'Danaë', Baldung's 'Death and the Maiden', Delacroix's 'Mademoiselle Rose', and Manet's 'Olympia'. In one book, entitled *An Encyclopedia of Twentieth-Century Erotic Art*, I had marked several pages on which appeared Modigliani's 'Seated Nude', Bonnard's 'Nude Against the Light', Dufy's 'Nude Lying on a Couch', Delvaux's 'La Voie Publique', and Wesselmann's 'Great American Nude No. 57'. There were other books too, displaying illustrations of a similar nature.

I was researching the possibilities left to Fluck, trying to imagine how he would proceed with his picture of Poppet. Forewarned is forearmed.

Myra dragged the book on Goya towards her. I murmured that perhaps it wouldn't interest her. 'Nonsense,' she said briskly. 'Let me see.' Her nostrils flared as if she meant business.

Goya's 'Naked Maja' is a rather stunning painting, even if the

Maja is (in my opinion) slightly unanatomical. I refer to the balloon-like buoyancy of her breasts, which seem to be drifting up towards her chin. About the sister painting, incidentally, the 'Clothed Maja', I have no such reservations. It is both more correct and more erotic. One is naturally encouraged to imagine undressing the woman, and I have had, I confess, dampish dreams about the clothed Maja, whose 'clothing' consists merely of a loose-fitting suit of transparent gauze drawn together at the waist by a scarlet sash. Repeatedly, in my oneiric escapades, I have had this sash between my eager teeth.

Myra ignored both Majas, and rapidly flipped through the rest of the book. 'Too gloomy for me,' she said. 'I'll get you another alka seltzer in a minute.'

In a way Fluck reminds me of Goya. There is a touch of evil about them both. They share the same virtuosity of painterly style, the same antisocial and off-putting personality, the same physical unattractiveness. Nor can I forget the affair with the Duchess of Alba. Goya is remembered now for his talent, the duchess of Alba for her beauty. No one remembers the Duke of Alba. I pondered on this. While I pondered, Myra had turned up an illustration of the famous 'Third of May' execution, Goya's melodramatic contribution to national fervour during the Napoleonic occupation of the Iberian Peninsula. 'This,' she said, poring over it enthusiastically, 'I call really gloomy.'

I studied the 'Third of May' for a while, then flipped forward a few pages. A series of studies for the famous execution which I had not seen before caught my attention. One was especially interesting. It was unlike the *magnum opus* in all respects except that it depicted an execution. Where the final version was dark, this was bright; where the former was bloody and histrionic, this was pleasant and cheerful. I examined it carefully.

In front of a low red brick wall a man stands nonchalantly, his hands on his hips. He wears a flowing white shirt and black breeches. Not a politician or soldier, but a poet, obviously. Beyond the wall, in the middle distance, there is a low green hill, and beyond that, on higher, more distant ground, it is possible to make out the rudimentary schemata of buildings, rapid details of walls, windows, and roofs. A path runs from the wall in the foreground to this village on the hill, and from various vantage points along the path it would be just about possible to see, over to the left, a glimpse of ocean sparkling beyond the green fields. It is a warm day and the sun is shining. In other circumstances the disarrayed poet might have strolled away up the path to enjoy these scenic diversions, but at present he has to face a firing squad, which is banked neatly in two rows over to the right, waiting for the command to fire. Curiously, these soldiers fail to intrude on the picture's essential peacefulness. Despite their bristling weaponry they are no more than an abstract block of colour (gaberdine green) adumbrated as airily as the houses on the distant hill. No shot has yet been fired; everything stands calmly still. Overhead the clouds are immobile and the sky is a permanent blue. Birdsong can be heard from behind the wall. A butterfly swings past; a bee drones. The sounds of seaswell and gulls can be faintly heard from the distant coast. It is, to sum up, an intimate languid scene, and marred only by the expression on the face of the underdressed poet, who happens to be screaming with terror. Yes, for all his cool poise, leaning casually forward with one foot as in a remembered ballroom, he gapes incontinently at the thought of the ripped-up corpse he is about to become. He is indeed in a tricky position. There is no way of escape. His eyes protrude, his mouth crumples stupidly, his chin dithers like a tearful child's.

This was the strange wonder of the picture, it seemed to me, the source of its terrible beauty. It was the beauty of irony: that one man howls for his life while Life goes on peacefully around him – and as that thought came into my head I felt a shudder of recognition. It was the kind of painting that Fluck would have painted of me.

Looking up from the book, I saw how the sunlight insinuated itself through the glowing parted curtains of my room and I felt peculiar. The eiderdown on my bed was suddenly hot and oppressive. I was aware of Myra leaning towards me and saying something sharply, but could only gobble a few nothings back at her. It wasn't pain but a sort of neuro-muscular tingle spreading through my body, atavistic hairs rising on the back of my neck, the palms of my hands sweating; and in this queer state of immanence I had then my Vision, my first and only proper vision, seeing before me, not in the book but in the dim mid-air of the room, a man screaming in soft sunshine, his features cracked open and mercilessly bathed in golden light, while cotton-wool clouds, butterflies, bees, the susurrating ocean, together obscenely blessed his sudden and violent death, and this man, I noticed then, had my face and my fate.

'Glass,' I forced the word out. 'Glass of.' The submerged bile of my hangover rose and I retched into my cupped hands. Myra seemed to have disappeared and with my hands wet I cried aloud, blindly, 'Is there no end to my misery?' These are the exact words I shouted.

Myra rushed back into the room to find me shivering. 'Into this!' she cried repeatedly, holding a washing-up bowl I recognised. 'Into this, S. J.!'

It was my first Vision, as I say. It is natural that I should have been disorientated by it, and I think my behaviour can be excused on grounds of inexperience. Also the excessive quantities of alka seltzer Myra forced me to consume after my upset had further unsettled me. Of course I regretted it later, she may have hurt herself dragging the bedside table down on top of her like that, but at the time I felt that there was literally no other option, and I flung her violently away from me. As she disentangled herself from chunky mahogany and rose, I could tell that she was on the verge of tears. We stared at each other in astonishment. Then she spun smartly round, and I shouted after her in fury, 'Don't slam the door!', and the door was slammed behind her.

As it is the purpose of this story to tell the truth and not attempt to place anyone in a good or bad light, I should add that within an hour of our unlucky little incident, I apologised to Myra and she said, very decently as she thought, that she wouldn't tell anyone what had happened. I had to do this because that evening was the evening of Fluck's great party and we were all required to be happy and enjoy ourselves and perhaps talk to each other.

'I was only trying to help,' said Myra, blinking vigorously behind ugly spectacles, her mouth peevish.

'Forgive me,' I replied, 'I was ill and irascible. Thank you,' I said. 'I won't forget it.'

But neither, more importantly, would I forget my Vision. The

148

thing about visions is that people do not think they are real; I mean real as in flesh-and-blood-real. But they are. Be warned. Those moments when my flesh first began to creep, and my blood sing in my ears, and my hands shake, I will remember for as long as I live, though that won't be long now. I remember this: the image of myself ravelling together in a hot flurry, like a geyser of steam and water. And I remember this: the sudden sense of recognition as if faced with an obvious but oblique truth which once learnt would irrevocably change my life, placing it on a different, perhaps higher level. This last consideration is important. Why did I have a vision? What was its purpose? I believe I was at the farthest edge of Suffering, and was given the vision to indicate to me this, my dodgy and desperate position. It is also, of course, the nature of visions to change people's lives; I am acquainted with this fact – it happens, I remember, especially often in the Bible. But did it change *my* life? I wonder: its immediate effect on me was roughly that of a vomitory, but then I never expected extreme psychic experience to be a gentle thing; even in the 'modern' period visions have attracted the kind of stressed ravings we associate with Dostoevsky, Ruskin, Robert Lowell, Modigliani, and the like. But yes, let me stick my neck out, my Vision brought me certain insights. And, yes, I will say that it changed my life too.

To be brief, my Vision presented me with a symbolical revelation of my exact position within the fate Fluck had arranged for me, it prepared me for eventualities, and, as is also in the nature of visions, it gave me certain commands.

Some hours later I was in our room exercising when Poppet came in carrying several tightly scrolled sheaves of paper. Incidentally, do not think that because I was exercising I felt better, but the effects of bad temper, jealousy, and guilt had galvanised me into action, however aimless and painful. Anything to try and stop thinking, although I could not stop.

'What are they?' I asked from my prone position on the carpet, indicating the papers. She did not seem to hear me.

'Are you feeling better now?' she murmured after a while.

'Yes,' I said.

It was not in fact the first time Poppet and I had talked that day. About two hours earlier, not long after Myra had beaten her ungainly retreat, Poppet had come tiptoeing into my room and shut the door softly behind her.

'Are you awake?' she asked, without looking round. The question was fatuous; I was sitting up reading a book. I had borrowed a biography of Goya from Fluck's library and was swotting up the section on the Napoleonic invasion of 1808. She crept over to me and sat on the edge of the bed. 'I think we need a serious talk,' she said.

For an exhilarating moment I thought she was about to confess her affair with Fluck, but instead she asked me how much I had drunk the night before. On this basis we could have nothing to say to each other, though she stayed for some time asking questions. Presumably she was motivated by guilt. I tried not to think too much about her feelings, they only led me to Fluck, and I had been doing my best to avoid him.

'Henry asked after you,' she said.

Yes, I thought, thus the bully enquires of his victim how it feels, the fist in the cheek, the boot in the small of the back. But as yet I was unready for, or perhaps incapable of, rage. I still wanted Poppet to make a confession of her own free will, and for the time being I played along with her, trading superficialities: I told her I loved her; she forgave me my drunkenness; I swore that my apparent unhappiness was a temporary illusion. Then we embraced, and Poppet wept, and after I declined to make love ('I am ill; not up to it') she left me to 'get better' in peace.

I pondered all this while I lay on the floor doing my exercises. These exercises, recommended by the Canadian Airforce, are wonderfully strenuous. When I had recovered from the sit-ups I was doing, I repeated, in strangled tones, my original question to Poppet.

'Henry's sketches of me,' she said, 'I'm to study them; why I don't know. He asked me. He's mad.' With a loud sigh she let herself fall comically backwards onto the bed, her bare, tanned legs left dangling over the edge. This is a familiar trick of hers. Her answer to my question was obviously disingenuous, but what else should I expect? Without getting up, but turning my head to my extreme left I discovered to my surprise that I could see up the right leg of her safari shorts as far as the crisp black line of pubic hair nestling between groin and khaki cotton. She was not wearing knickers. Details, details, they blind, do they not, like red-hot needles.

I rose, and retreated to the far side of the room to continue my exercises. Poppet sat up and watched me, and I was seized with embarrassment. She was a stranger to me now, no longer the familiar girl who for eleven months of cohabitation had watched me as I blithely took my daily exercise. Acutely self-conscious, I lay on my back and with a laborious contrivance of effortlessness lifted both my feet six inches off the ground (squeezing my eyes shut to try and relieve the pain of the knotting abdominals) and held the pose for five seconds. Then moved my feet apart, and held it. Then back together again . . .

When I opened my eyes, my feet still suspended off the ground, Poppet was standing with her back to me, trying to open the wardrobe door. It was stiff and she tugged at it several times before it jolted open with a woody squeal. Counting out my seconds slowly all the time, I watched her pick out a bright crimson blouse with enormous decorated collar and cuffs and take it off the hanger, which immediately tumbled from her hands, falling against the foot of the bed. Putting on the blouse, she left the hanger lying on the floor where it had fallen, its dull metallic gleam remaining visible to me as I lay there, my agony impelling me to continue with my exercise, despite everything. Then, with my eyes closed, taking no chances with distractions, mouth dry, head throbbing, I counted on: 'One, two, three, four, five. One, two, three . . .' When I reopened my eyes, Poppet was naked again and the red blouse dishevelled on the bed. She was on the point of stepping into a pair of gold-and-black-striped flared trousers. Apparently she was not intending to put knickers on for Fluck's party. I came suddenly to the limit of abdominal control, snorted twice, and dropped my feet. Sunlight slid upwards off her buttocks as she bent forward and lifted her leg, a bright ripple of warmth along her spine like liquid poured the wrong way.

'Are you going to have a shower soon?' I heard her ask.

'Ten minutes,' I panted. 'You go first.' But I heard her rummaging in the wardrobe again, more coat hangers falling softly to the floor. Frankly I doubted that she would shower at all, she was already half-dressed, but supposed that if she did

151

it would give her another chance to remember her underwear. For some reason the thought of her dressed otherwise distressed me, though this distress, of course, I carefully concealed.

Jogging up and down on the spot now, both arms dangling loosely at my sides, I watched her try on three different blouses in quick succession, all lurid and styleless. Her expression, concentrated in the lower lip, was absorbed and critical, and I remember with a terrible clarity the tip of her tongue appearing moistly whenever she struggled with a recalcitrant button. Her shoulders were the colour of syrup, the smooth golden skin bisected by shallow white stripes made by the straps of her bikini top. I had not realised she was so tanned. It is possible I had not seen her shoulders naked since the tan was begun. I was pale, unnaturally pale as I always am. I *felt* pale.

'The white blouse,' I said in staccato fashion through pants. 'Shows off. Your tan. Best.'

My headache was getting worse and I would soon have to stop exercising altogether. Nevertheless, I now dropped lightly to the floor and did thirty rapid press-ups. Then I collapsed onto my side, catching my breath in painful sobs. The air in my lungs seemed suddenly to have solidified. Poppet, naked again, porcelain-delicate, was sitting on the bed with her legs crossed, filing her nails. A small bright hair grip prevented her fringe falling forward. Her small breasts sagged. Details, details, details . . .

'Shower now?' she said, briefly looking up. 'Wet boy with red face.' Why did she say this? Why the constant recourse to our cosy private language when the intimacy it depended on was defunct?

While I waited for the water to run warm in the tiny shower cubicle wedged into a corner of the bathroom, I carefully examined myself in the mirror for signs of lunacy. Apparently, you see, I thought I was going mad. I remember staring myself in the eye and attempting to recite an apposite passsage from the end of the second act of *King Lear*, but, to my disgust, all I could bring to mind was the negligible observation, 'The King is in high rage.' I said this out loud, watching my lips move, hearing the flat noise I made. It lacked ferocity, in my opinion. I lacked ferocity. My only reaction, the only sign of life, as I spoke and stared into the mirror, was a mild surprise in perceiving that I still existed. My eyes were dull and weak, chin stubbly, hair matted as if I had spent all day lying in bed, which I had. What of rage and resolution? I am tame, sir, as it is said somewhere and as I said to myself; slowly I am losing my looks, the pretty bits of me are fleeing, and soon, like a piece of Fluck's threadbare furniture, I shall become a part of this ugly house, and of my uglier memories, neither of which I shall ever be able to leave.

With the shower running I sat on the tiled floor, naked, cross-legged like one of those third-century buddahs fashioned of stone or schist. I did not want to shower after all. I wanted, I think, to die, but instead I thought constantly of Poppet as I had just seen her, stepping into her trousers. Her arched back was dappled with shadow, darker and deeper where it narrowed into the cleft of her buttocks, the gluteus sulcus; one leg was slowly lifted causing the shadow to ripple like water. In my memory I could not see her face. The dreaminess of her general movements suggested that her thoughts were elsewhere, but they did not, must not, concern me. Only the changing outline of her body held my attention, its eurhythmic grace something to admire in the same way that a painting by, say, Vermeer is admired, with a kind of wistfulness and an almost thrilling sense of regret.

Eventually my thoughts exhausted me. I dabbed at myself inefficiently with the sweaty T-shirt I had discarded, turned off the shower, and left the bathroom.

When I returned to our room, Poppet was still naked, lying on the bed, reading a book. One of her big toes was wiggling gently as her eyes scanned the pages. She appeared contented, her mouth settled into a half-smile like a sleeping child's. No child's, of course, but the adult sharer of Fluck's monstrosities. I had to keep that in mind. As I quietly closed the door behind me and padded across the carpet, I could hear her regular breathing, and the dry rustle of the pages of her book. Watching her all the time, I talced myself, applied deodorant to my armpits, and began to dress.

'Good shower?' murmured Poppet. Softly I murmured assent.

After a few minutes Poppet shut her book, let out a sigh, and

153

sprang off the bed. 'Soap,' she sang out, 'flannel, scrubbing brush, shower cap.' She was using a peremptory tone of voice we sometimes considered humorous.

'Soap's in the shower,' I said, and continued dressing.

'Flannel?' I shrugged. 'Pass me the wash bag,' she said. Still half-undressed, I rummaged in the bag and pulled out a bottle of depilatory gel. Poppet immediately took the bag from me.

'See if the cap's in the suitcase,' she said, as if her wish were still my command.

It is an inexplicable fact that I have never really got used to walking around naked. Not that I was entirely naked then, but I was certainly less than fully clothed, in fact wearing only my shirt and socks. As I knelt to drag the suitcase out from under the bed, I felt my shirt tails flapping and fiddling against my groin like soft hands, and there seemed to be a tickling breeze that titillated my thighs as far down as the profunda femoris. Nevertheless, biting my lip a little, I managed to extricate myself from my shameless on-all-fours, arse-upwards position, and got to my feet, clutching the suitcase. Unsupported, my genitals jostled in and out of sight beneath my shirt, another unfamiliar sensation. Strangest of all, despite my determination to remain aloof, I began to feel less than fully detached and inconsequential. Hastily I searched the suitcase.

'Not here,' I said, slamming the lid shut.

'Must be here somewhere,' said Poppet. 'You did pack it, didn't you? I asked you to pack it?'

'You didn't,' I said.

'I did,' Poppet cried. 'The blue shower cap, I asked you. The *blue* one.'

I dimly remembered. 'You certainly didn't,' I said hotly.

Poppet marched across the room towards the chest of drawers. Nakedness posed *her* no problems. As both Fluck and I knew. She stood on tiptoe, her arms bent awkwardly at the elbows to reach deep into the back of the top drawer. Her calf muscles were clenched, her buttocks lifted upwards in a delicate arc. As she groped blindly through the woolly entrails of socks and knickers, I happened to see her in perfect profile leaning against the opened drawer, her whitish breasts squashed slightly at the tips where they touched the coarse-grained wood. It was not my fault that I happened to glimpse her in just this pose. (Nudity should be knowledge, but Poppet's nakedness made her appear stranger than ever.) Neither was I responsible for the unfamiliar sensations of groping shirt tails and the sniggering breath of air round my thighs which I have mentioned before. I must say, however, that when I was halfway across the room towards Poppet I became aware that the pendulum of my genitals had ceased to swing quite as before. To be brief, I suffered an erection. I do not remember feelings of embarrassment at the time, only slight emotional confusion and a certain difficulty in walking. Eventually, thus discomfited, I came stiffly to a halt behind Poppet. I did not want to alarm her. Frankly I doubt that she was aware of me at all, for at that moment she bent blithely to open the middle drawer, and again sunlight dappled up her spine, and sudden shadow plumped out her buttocks. It was then that, on impulse, I crouched silently and slavishly behind her, anticipating, I suppose, some uncharacteristic joy – but putting myself, as regards balance, in a completely untenable position, from which after only a few moments I crashed helplessly backwards. She turned on hearing the yelp I could not suppress and regarded me as I lay obscenely crumpled on the floor.

'Where the bloody hell is it?' she said, all patience gone. 'I asked you to pack it. Did you pack it? You didn't, did you?' And she flung on her dressing-gown, grabbed the wash bag, and swept out of the room. A minute or two later I heard the distant, drenching hum of the shower through the walls.

The guests began to arrive at about eight o'clock. Waiting for them, we, Fluck's 'inner circle' as he put it, were lolling around watching an American war movie on the tiny monochrome TV. (Colour television wasn't good enough for Fluck. 'I prefer to invent my own colours,' he was fond of saying.)

Everything was organised for the party. Food and drink were ready in the kitchen, enough to debauch a multitude; the furniture in all downstairs rooms had been pushed back against the walls; the stereo was primed with party tapes; little dishes mounded with cashews and tortilla chips adorned the mantelpieces and coffee-tables. I noticed also that Fluck had rearranged his paintings on the walls, replacing some, adding others, and, oddly, supplying them all with titles and dates printed in gothic scripts on little white cards he had blue-tacked to the frames.

'A *bijou* piss up,' Fluck had smugly dubbed the occasion beforehand. 'Even as we fall unconscious to the floor, we shall effect all the embodiments of the bourgeois manner.' I remember how I scowled; I would fall to the floor in my own crude manner and not otherwise. And anyway, alcohol was to spectacularly impair Fluck's own snobbish poise; by the end of the party he would be as meanly and vulgarly downward-dropping as the rest of us. He claimed, and just prior to the arrival of the first guests was still claiming, that he had sent out 'a hundred or so' invitations, this statement accompanied by a careless gesture of the hand. 'Most of them to old school chums. Sickening, isn't it, how we stick together?' On the contrary, I was charmed to observe how few school chums stuck to Fluck. Only a handful of them turned up, the friends of friends of Fluck, as it were, not one of them able to boast firsthand acquaintance with their host. Fluck ignored them as best he could, though this was difficult, the gathering being so small. Thus the party was a failure from the very beginning – but I am getting ahead of myself.

Before the guests, or non-guests arrived, Poppet led me into the kitchen, summarily indicated two cocktail shakers, a recipe book, three dozen triangular cocktail glasses, and a vast array of colourful liqueurs and mixers, and informed me that I was to be in charge of mixing the cocktails. I was incredulous.

'What do I know about cocktails?' I asked.

'Read the book,' she said. I remonstrated violently, to no effect. She stepped back into the living-room with an air of unconcern, and I followed. 'Why should I spend all evening being butler to everyone else?' I demanded.

'I'll help,' Moyra put in from her lazy position on the sofa. Her large, dark eyes rested on me for a moment, then slowly returned to the vapid flickering of the TV. I stared at her furiously. I had cured myself of desire for Moyra.

'Good,' said Poppet. 'It's just for half an hour or so, until the liqueurs run out. That's all.' Her smile was sweet and encouraging.

'I'll be in the kitchen doing the food,' added Myra, 'so I can give you a hand if you get really busy.' I looked helplessly at Angel.

'Coats and hats and social niceties,' he said, tapping his chest. 'That's me.' Moyra giggled, the beautiful fat bitch, and I left the room.

Down the hall Poppet caught up with me. Her smile had vanished. 'Stop it,' she hissed. 'Can't you stop thinking about yourself for five minutes?' I asked her what she meant. 'Just don't spoil it,' she added irrelevantly.

Coldly I turned my back on her and mounted the stairs to the first landing. I did not particularly want to go upstairs, but in turning from Poppet, I somehow found myself pointed in that direction, and could hardly turn again. The house itself conspired against me, as I had already noticed. Through a window on the landing I could see that the lower sky had clouded over. Above the clouds, dusk gradually descended. It was already rather dark. As I watched, a ray of light flashed weakly in the gloomy middle distance, went out, then flickered again. A minute later I heard a car engine whining. 'Here they are,' I said bitterly out loud, to no one. But at that moment, with the knowledge that the waiting was now almost over – not just the waiting of the past few hours but the indeterminate, unresolved shiftlessness of the whole week – there came over me a feeling not totally unlike relief.

The kitchen, when I returned to it, was perfectly quiet. How well I remember the scene, the silent, biding ranks of accoutrements gleaming under neon; the stacks of plates; the piles of cutlery; the rows of glasses neatly arranged according to size and shape, all with the identical bluish sheen. Along the deep window-sill, bottles of wine, fruit juice, squash, spirits and mixers were ranged according to colour, from red to violet across the spectrum. Below, on either side of the sink, the food was displayed in similar abundance. Sausage rolls, canapés and quiches, onion rings and meringue puffs were to the left of the sink, and to the right, a meat loaf, a ham, cubes of cheese and pineapple, and a perfectly square sponge cake. On the opposite side of the kitchen were bowls of fruit, dishes of cheese straws, a chocolate mousse, a massive lasagne, and, on a silver platter, in pride of place, a splendidly humpbacked roast chicken. The girls had been quite busy. My cocktail equipment was divided between the two shelves of a large tea trolley, by which I stood, fiddling with glasses and bottles, and silently deriding the extravagance of the provisions, waiting out the last moments.

At the impatient third knock on the front door, someone in the living-room shouted 'They're here!' and there were rapid footsteps in the hall. As barman, not footman, I had remained indifferent to all the knocks, preferring to bide my time in the quiet kitchen as long as possible, though, ironically, any peace I might have enjoyed was soon destroyed . . . In a moment of incaution, I crunched a strange spicy sugar puff from a half-empty bag of snacks. It was indescribably poisonous. Brief panic ensued. I could find nothing in all that orderly kitchen to spit it into: two bowls of trifle, one oblong, one oval, were wedged inviolably into the sink, and I could not reach the window past the colour-coordinated phalanx of bottles. There was no bin. I rushed roaring round in the kitchen like a wasp in a jam-jar, occasionally sweeping sausage-rolls or glasses to the floor – but in the end, I simply had to swallow the thing down. I came suddenly to a dead stop by the cocktail trolley. The whole kitchen seemed to give a grimace. I could not escape the feelings that I was being led, via the most ludicrous little mishaps, to my fate.

Sounds, muted, from the hall indicated that the house was now occupied by party-goers, and, as I listened, I gulped down a measure of Scotch, the familiar rawness of which somewhat obliterated the heat of the rogue snack. A moment later the first guests found their way into the kitchen, and I began to make, incompetently, cocktails.

Fluck's party, as I have said, was not a crowded affair. It was jaded and inconsequential, with intermittent moments of frenetic jollity, apparently designed by some to bring the proceedings to life – a hopeless intention. The five guests who constituted the massed throng of Fluck's faithful school chums all arrived early. They had come to get drunk – to my irritation, as I was forced to make cocktails more or less continuously, with little apparent effect on their desire for more.

The names of these five I have forgotten. Mercifully I will soon forget everything about them, but for the time being I am obliged to recall certain details of their ridiculous costumes and something too of their behaviour and conversation, at least in the early stages of the party before both they and I slipped gratefully into drunkenness and out of memory. There were two girls, rather similar in appearance, evidently either sisters or close friends, though I do not remember discovering which. They were already tipsy when they arrived, emitting the same nervous bray of laughter when addressed. Both had painted a Ziggy Stardust lightning streak across their faces, a jagged rainbow from forehead to chin. They wore tight tank-tops, Oxford bags, and sensible shoes 'for dancing', although as far as I remember they hardly ever danced. Certainly they did not dance with me.

With them, or perhaps arriving just after them, was a short, dark-haired man dressed as Mussolini in Italian para-military uniform. He was also wearing a red nose. Apparently he had been told that the party was fancy dress. 'And are you Mussolini or Coco the clown?' I asked him. 'Julie Andrews,' he replied wittily. But I later caught him making short-armed fascist salutes and pulling strange faces that made his jaw look larger than it was. Obviously he considered himself something of a wag, but the only special powers he seemed to possess were those of flippancy; he displayed a crude and constant need to elicit laughter and amazement from those around him and, in short, was obscurely popular. Moyra, for one, gagged with laughter at everything he said.

The remaining two guests arrived at the same time, although they hadn't travelled together. One was dressed as if for a formal dinner in a drab dark suit, and made it plain that he had not been invited. It is possible he had heard about the party from the star-dusted girls whom he seemed to know. The other guest, thinking that the theme of the party was Bad Taste, had come disguised as a pregnant nun. This was the youngest brother of one of Fluck's real school-friends who had predictably declined the invitation, but sent his sibling in his place. About sixteen years old, with his sallow ascetic features at first composed in an expression of appropriate piety, I assumed him to be of a demure disposition. But he was inclined to be wild when drunk. Luckily he was physically too slight to cause much damage, though this was not through want of trying.

And what of Fluck, while all his guests were arriving? Fluck was conspicuous by his absence. I got the story from Poppet whom I plaintively accosted when she came into the kitchen to help carry out the food.

'Painting,' she said coolly, 'in the studio.' Her portrait, of course. 'Leave him alone, will you?' Poppet said.

'But why isn't he here?' I persisted.

'Look,' she banged down a tray of sausage rolls and turned to face me, 'he's not feeling very well either.' Suppressing a sudden glow of satisfaction, I enquired, in what I hoped were the tones of sympathy and concern, as to the nature of his illness.

'He's upset,' Poppet went on, 'about the party. Well, imagine.' She gestured angrily. Apparently things were even worse than they seemed. One of the many invited guests not to have turned up was an old friend (speaking approximately) who worked in a commercial art gallery in London. Fluck had hoped to impress him; hence the careful reorganisation of his pictures along the walls – hence the whole carefully stage-managed party.

'After all his work,' said Poppet bitterly, 'it makes me . . .' She winced and faltered. 'Poor Henry.' Her face was white, and she fixed me with a look of malevolence I found surprising. 'I knew something like this would happen,' she said. 'I knew it from the day we arrived. And you don't help, do you? I've had enough of it, S. J.' She almost shouted this last sentence, then turned briskly and left the kitchen, carrying the sausage rolls at a sharp angle. Soon, I knew, she would be comforting her fat, distressed lover. With sausage rolls? Perhaps without. To be frank, I doubted the truth of Fluck's story. He was a wealthy man negligent of commercial success, and besides he possessed exactly the kind of talent unappealing, if not positively inimical, to fashion-mongers. What Fluck wanted, if his vanity permitted him so much unsatisfied ambition, was critical acclaim, or preferably notoriety, which had the attraction of offering him superiority on his own truculent terms. In my opinion, Fluck's party was for kicks. Had he really invited more than a hundred people? Did he ever expect the invitations to be seriously entertained? More likely, he had concocted the evening's grotes-querie on the merest of whims, in order to sit at the centre of it all and regard each balls-up with an arrogant eye, like an amused intellectual following the vagaries of a soap opera. But I could hardly have expected Poppet to see this.

The party faltered forward. Had we but realised it, we were only a couple of disciples short of a rather suggestive number, but this fact went unnoticed. Other, larger absences pressed upon us.

'Oh god, isn't it *weird*?' said Moyra. 'All this food and drink and no one here.' She was dressed half-heartedly in tight flared denims and inadequate boob tube. She was not looking her best. 'I mean, what on earth are we going to do with it all?'

'I told Henry this would happen,' said Myra from her side of the kitchen. 'Would he listen?' Gaunt and awkward, she bent over pizza and quiche, delving rapidly with a slicer. 'Half of this will go to waste.'

'Oh I *know*,' Moyra cooed impulsively, turning to her sister. 'What can we *do*?'

There was a brief silence which made clear our intention to do nothing, and then suddenly – in so much as she did anything suddenly – Moyra gave me one of her vague, puzzled, brilliant smiles. Baffled, I returned a wry, resigned gesture meant to imply that I entirely agreed with anything her smile could possibly have signified. I was very much aware, of course, of our recent misunderstanding, but strangely, Moyra's manner towards me hadn't altered at all. It was as if nothing had happened between us; as if I had dreamt the whole episode.

Some time after this, we all went into the living-room. The atmosphere here was oppressive on account of there being so few people. On the stereo the first volume of Elton John's Greatest Hits was winding laboriously to a close. Two muted conversations were in progress: Mussolini was entertaining the Ziggy Stardust girls with an anecdote involving his Fiesta GTI; and Moyra was listening to the man in the boring suit, who abruptly stopped talking as I entered. Perhaps he smiled. Or perhaps it was I who smiled. I did not want to obtrude; I had come, I think, merely to observe the ripening of a certain relationship. But she was not there, and neither – still – was he. So, I deduced without satisfaction, she had gone to his studio after all to minister to his immediate cravings. At the thought of this I became slightly emotional and with one of those awful things, a pang, I directed my mind upwards, to Fluck's studio.

I remembered the studio well from my visit – the dim squalor of it. The skylight was furred over with what I imagine were the accreted exudations of the dingy artist himself, a kind of sooty sweat, a biological stain keeping out the daylight. A naked bulb glimmered somewhere in the gloom, no more, and the shadows, ugly and unrelenting, flickered along the whole length of the attic room. In the centre of the uncarpeted floor stood an easel. In front of the easel was a stool: beyond it a chair. On the stool sat Fluck. The chair was empty. Around this little island of order all else was anarchy, old furniture heaped with crushed tubes of oils, battered tins of turpentine, bundles of old brushes, sponges, boxes of chalks and pastels, aerosol cans of fixative, sized and unsized canvases, coffee mugs, chipped plates covered with crumbs and thumb-smears of wet paint, Brillo-pads, tumblers, empty cans of Coke, magazines, books, half-empty tins of baked beans, racks of powder paints, sawdust, rags, sandpaper. Yes, I remember it all. There is so much mess that the old sofa, armchair, gate-leg table and whirring fridge that support it all cannot be seen.

Not so much perching on his tiny three-legged stool as enveloping it like a hen on an egg, Fluck's big form, thus centrally positioned, gives off a warm, tangy, camel-house odour that fills the room. In the stagnant air of the attic, his smell seems to create its own currents, swirling and drifting unpredictably.

It is to this room, to this stinking presence, that Poppet had gone so slavishly. No doubt she climbed the final ladder with a practised fluency, pushing aside the hatch (no warning knock required), heaving it up and replacing it softly behind her. Fluck wouldn't have bothered to turn round; he is a single-minded worker, difficult to distract. So she sees first the bland, monumental expanse of back and rump. And as she looks, he shifts slightly in reaching the upper right-hand corner of the canvas, and this movement reveals for an instant the bowed rim of his diminutive stool, before, with a hydraulic hiss of breath, he settles back to mix more rainbows on his palette. By now she knows his manner, his secret proclivities, and his favourite sensations. She does not need to speak, only to begin everything as usual, to pick her way through the jumble towards him, being very delicate and deliberate like a young nurse

162

approaching an ailing, irascible old man. When she reaches Fluck, she stops behind him and stretches out a hand, and he for some reason grunts before she actually touches him – and (for some other reason) I see her in perfect profile, entirely naked and white as a freshly-sized canvas, her breasts pale and snub, her buttocks a delicate arc as she bends somehow sadly and passionately towards him, a neat lock of hair hanging across her face and her mouth bent as if to speak or kiss – and, unnoticed, I fall backwards again and again as they kiss or speak or . . .

I did not actually fall, of course. I refer to my playful and painful train of thought as I stood in the living-room. Empty glass in hand with my mouth liplessly shut as for my death-mask, and my eyes, I imagine, vacuously wide, probably I was considered to be a little reticent in conversation. All this time, too, I had not neglected to drink as much as possible with, I cannot deny it, certain effects, the majority of which are widely known. I expect I was swaying slightly; mildly hallucinating; the usual.

Back in the kitchen again, I recovered some sense of purpose and mixed a Margarita for the highly-strung pregnant nun, who had already divested himself of his mock-vestal modesty and asked me now in a slurred voice when exactly everyone else would be arriving. His eyes were hungry for god knows what, the poor delinquent. I replied briefly that I did not know and, rubbing the rim of his glass with lime juice, dipped it deeply in salt. He departed with his drink, visibly dissatisfied. Toasting his retreating back with a sour expression of my own, I finished the other Margarita in a single gulp. It wasn't long after this that, in a typically frustrating way, the liqueurs ran out. Resourcefully, I switched to lager and, freed from the cocktail trolley, drifted out of the kitchen.

I was sitting on the bottom step of the stairs, drinking from a can of Tennent's when Fluck and Poppet finally came down to join the party. At last.

'Ha!' boomed a voice from above me, as from the storm clouds of nightmare. 'Makest thou this shame thy pastime?' The voice was not that of the sorrowful Fluck of Poppet's compassionate imaginings, it rang with the stridency of a man used to grand theatrical effects. I squeezed to one side of the

163

stairs as he passed by with a toss of the hand. What tales that hand could have told me, under torture. Halfway to the kitchen, Fluck spun round in a wobble and shouted 'Ha!' again. 'Makest thou no more cocktails, thou naughty boy?' he shouted. '*King Lear*, Act II, Scene 4, *you know*, of course you do. Kent in the stocks, enter Lear, the Fool, and a Gentleman. What's he that hath so much thy place mistook to set thee here?'

'Cornwall,' I said finally, 'and Regan.'

'It is both he and she,' Fluck cried delightedly, 'your son and daughter. Wonderful! How well you remember.' He wagged a finger at me, spun round once more and disappeared into the living-room.

Poppet remained behind, like a residue. 'Come here,' she said coldly.

Insolence, I guessed, would as yet do me no good, so I rose unsteadily and followed her into the kitchen.

'Why were you out there on the stairs?' she asked, face set, manner brief.

I tried to explain about the cocktails running out.

'What's this?' she asked. 'And this?' In one hand she held a full bottle of Curaçao and in the other a bottle of dark rum. On the serving trolley in front of her were bottles of crème de menthe and Angostura bitters. 'Well?'

In order to choose my words carefully I stared at these bottles for some time before answering. 'Obviously there are some leftovers,' I said at last.

'You're drunk,' said Poppet with feeling. As if to make a pointed contrast, she went over to the sink and poured herself a glass of water.

'Listen to me,' I said suddenly, surprising myself. 'I want to talk to you.' Poppet shook her head.

'No,' she said softly. 'I can't talk to you.' As she left the kitchen I called after her 'This party's awful.' But it didn't bring her back. She was drawn to him, as once she had been drawn to me. With a flap of her flares she disappeared into the living-room.

Almost at once Mussolini bore down on me from the direction of the downstairs lavatory.

'Ah, barman,' he said with horrible chirpiness, lifting his empty glass so that it caught a glint from the electric light, 'same

164

again, whatever it was, a Red Russian.' He seemed unaware of the irony of a Mussolini ordering a Red Russian.

'Black,' I said. 'Or white perhaps.'

'Are you sure? I would have thought black was *completely* the wrong colour. Who's ever heard of a Russian negro?'

'Cocktails are off,' I said savagely. 'Unless you can find something left on the trolley. Help yourself.'

'Bloody great!' he said happily, grabbing the grenadine which had been standing unnoticed on the worktop next to the cooker. 'Watch this!'

I didn't. I turned my back on him and helped myself to more lager from the fridge. Two cans, wet and cold against the palms of my hands, icy against my forehead, sobering against the groin.

Was it then, or was it later, collecting yet more lager after yet another disconsolate sojourn in the living-room, that I rose from the fridge at just the right time to see Poppet and Fluck flit past the kitchen door on their way upstairs? Naturally I followed them, pursued myself, I remember, by the soft whimperings of a Donny Osmond number drifting through the opened living-room door. But I was afraid, I suppose, of rounding a corner and finding them in front of me, gaily copulating on the carpet. I did not follow them for long. Round corners and up stairs, their voices and footsteps receded, occasionally throwing out the bright sound of a laugh, which, in between my breathless sobs, I heard. I felt very tired now, tired of betrayal, tired of vigilance. I stumbled away to my own room along the dark corridor.

And I remembered again, despite my best intentions, something that had happened years before, when Fluck and I were not unlike friends. I refer to the night when Poppet and I first came to an understanding. Fluck and I were giving a party in our college rooms. We had hired a machine to provide swirling pools of coloured light. I remembered the awful heat of those lights as everyone danced in a hot dense mass to the clean clear decibels from the stereo. Poppet and Fluck and I were dancing together, in an awkward *ménage à trois*, rather drunk and excessively polite, a sure sign of worse to follow. We continually jostled and bumped for space against other dancers. Whenever I pretended not to be looking, Fluck took hold of Poppet's hand or performed some other surreptitiousness of supposed intimacy to which Poppet invariably responded with a neutral giggle . . . So the party went on, and we repeated ourselves in endlessly subtle ways, I silent and rapt, Fluck never stinting to make a spectacle of himself, until eventually, as I knew we would, in a different room both calmer and darker, Poppet and I made predictable love. I remember the coolness of the room and the piles of coats and jackets on the bed (it was Fluck's bedroom, used that night as a cloakroom) and Poppet's unusual agility, which took me by surprise. In the room next door we heard the muffled whirr of disco and felt the vibrations of monotonous dance. Although I cannot look back now without bitterness and irony, I suspect that at the time I was happy.

Then something rather awkward happened. As Poppet and I lay motionless together among scattered bundles of clothes, the door squeaked open, a face slowly filling the upper gap, and Fluck's eyes met mine.

It was a bad moment, and we all made it worse by doing nothing to terminate it, doing, in fact, nothing at all, absolutely nothing – a difficult accomplishment under the circumstances and in itself a grotesque over-reaction – until the door slowly shut again and Fluck's face disappeared. And as the bedroom door gave a final click, Poppet burst into tears and said to me, 'Now he knows. He'll never forgive me.' But she had not grasped the situation. It was me Fluck would never forgive. After all, it wasn't that she had stolen me from Fluck, but that I had stolen her from him.

This memory visited me in the darkness of my room into which I had fled to escape exactly such memories, and so I soon returned downstairs. Apparently I had finished my cans of lager by then, so I made my way first to the kitchen, and from there, newly laden, to the living-room again. Nothing had changed, unless the music had, which seems likely. Everyone was standing around, sipping drinks, occasionally tapping their feet, making an effort. The Ziggy Stardust girls had begun to sway slightly in time to the music and were working up to a dance like timid bathers easing themselves into cold water. At the far end of the room, Fluck was shouting to the man dressed as an accountant as he drew attention to one of his pictures on the wall. Poppet stood next to him, demure, satisfied, within reach. She had not seen me enter, so I propped myself against the near wall and watched her unobserved. As I watched I drank, seriously now, first from the can in my left hand, then from the one in my right, with unflinching regularity. The picture I had of myself as I did this was of passion constrained; a cold gaze, a hard silence, a bottled-up stillness of my arms and legs. I doubt whether this was noticed much. Poppet, for one, never looked my way. But, at some point, Angel ambled over to talk to me, bringing Moyra and Myra with him and unintentionally putting a virtual end to my surveillance, damn his friendliness.

'Do you think anyone else will come?' asked Moyra.

'I think he's been bloody lucky to get this many,' I said in a slur.

'I think this is it, don't you?' Angel said, looking round. We were aimlessly ticking over, like watches without hands.

Then, once again, the voice:

'S. J., a word!' Angel and Moyra parted and he came to face me, breathing heavily. 'It is time,' he said portentously, 'to begin.'

'Already?' I asked, not knowing what he was talking about.

'Indubitably,' he replied richly, 'time for you and time for me.'

'Time yet for a hundred indecisions,' I reminded him, hopefully.

'Ah no,' he said, 'no, no, no. It is time now. For you to read us what you have written. Your, what shall I call them, lucubrations.' He beamed despotically, like a sultan who has clapped his hands and awaits dancing girls, but what with the drink and everything, I did not yet know what all this nonsense was about.

'A deal's a deal, dear boy,' said Fluck. 'Signed in blood, more or less. You remember: spit on our hands and cross our hearts and fervently hope to perish. You do remember, I know you do. And I've kept my side of the bargain, oh yes.' He swept a fat hand round the walls of the room, indicating, I realised, his pictures. '*Voilà!* The portraits. Before your very eyes, there they are, count 'em up.' He waved more wildly. 'And now you *must* read what you've written. Fair's fair.'

167

Now I remembered, a horrible sensation, and opened my mouth to say I did not remember.

'Otherwise,' Fluck interrupted, 'you will be pilloried. Ostracised,' he continued gleefully, 'from polite society.' He leered as he said it.

At this moment, as if things could not be worse, the music from the stereo faded away and left Fluck booming in silence. I felt the grip of Fate tightening around my testicles.

'So what shall we do with him?' Fluck asked at large. 'What awful punishment fits this heinous crime?' No one knew what he was talking about, but it didn't stop them.

'Forfeits!' shouted someone in the background. 'Cold shower!' shouted someone else. 'Fuckin' splitter!' shouted the pregnant nun inconsequentially. I smiled and politely declined these offers. There was a pause and then Fluck said, 'Have you actually written anything?'

'Yes,' I said.

'And may we ask what it is?'

'It's a comedy,' I said bitterly, on the spur of the moment.

'Excellent!' shouted Fluck. 'Read it to us, there's a good chap, and give us all a laugh.' By now everyone was looking at us, puzzled but nevertheless eager, like witnesses of a schoolboy fight.

'I mean comedy in its formal generic sense,' I said, 'like Shakespeare's. The vindication of rightful order. Basically,' I added desperately in the sudden silence, 'something with a happy ending.' (I meant happy for the hero. The villain has his hands cut off or eyes plucked out.)

'Ah, happiness,' Fluck intoned, smiling broadly. 'Do you remember what Flaubert said about happiness?'

'Yes, of course,' I said. Naturally I lied. I had rather counted on Fluck telling me about Flaubert's happiness.

There followed a very long unbroken pause during which everyone in the room seemed to be looking at me. It seemed to me that my humiliation had reached a kind of maximum, a zenith.

'Not in the exact words,' I said after a while, to the floor.

Fluck clucked disapprovingly, producing a ridiculous noise like a duck filtering weed through its beak. Then he made a short showy speech in French. 'Ah,' I said when he had finished, mimicking deep comprehension and giving a miserable smile, *'bien sûr.'*

Fluck roared with laughter and looked around at the others. 'For those of you without the Gallic tongue, I offer a simple translation,' he said. 'Flaubert, incidentally, was a French writer of sentimental romances. Correct me if I'm wrong, S. J.' I stayed quiet. Fluck cleared his throat, then said, 'I've seen what they call happiness at close quarters. To wish to possess it is a dangerous mania.' A stunned silence greeted this, quickly dispelled by a belly laugh from Fluck. 'Dangerous mania!' he barked. 'Happiness! Isn't that delightful?' Mussolini, apparently feeling Fluck's eyes upon him, smiled briskly and said 'bloody good'. But this did not seem to be the desired response, and Fluck was just gathering himself, filling his lungs for some outsized sneer, some whopping snub, when, incredibly, the stereo started up again, very loud. Poppet had put another record on.

Come on, come on, Gary Glitter sang thickly. *Come on, come on, come on, come on, come on.* 'Do you remember this?' Poppet shouted from the other end of the room. Several people were dancing already. *Come on, come on, come on, come on, come on, come on, come on.* The music speeded up and Angel, Moyra, and Myra rushed forward. Soon they were obscured by other bouncing bodies, and the chant was taken up by all. 'Come on, come on, come on, come on, come on, come on.' The party had begun.

And so, momentarily, I was left standing in a corner with Fluck. As we stared at each other, he hardly seemed to see me, his eyes were dull and small, and he looked tired, his face heavier in repose, the premature grey streaks in his hair visible. I said nothing. And I almost failed to notice, his movement was so uncharacteristically modest, when, for no reason, he slowly lifted a hand and limply indicated his pictures where they quivered on the walls that vibrated now with the thumping of dancing feet. Still he said nothing. When he turned away from me I noticed that he walked unsteadily, and I wondered if he was drunk.

By now, with Gary Glitter's voice vibrating in our ears, the living-room had become the scene of frivolity. Ten people, several staggering on platform shoes, leapt wildly in a central

169

flurry, and Fluck – who seemed rapidly to have recovered his spirits – stalked round them, taking photographs.

'Don't hold it!' he shouted as he stalked. 'Don't smile! There's no birdie to watch! Forget that I'm here, I want you to be absolutely natural.' The dancers grinned and posed grotesquely as they twirled, but this did not deter him. There was a popping of flash bulbs. A Night at the Circus, I thought, if ever there was one. A Bacchanal by Toulouse-Lautrec. I drank and watched. When I remembered, I drank from the can in my left hand first and then from the can in my right hand, but I did not often remember any more. Some discipline seemed to be lacking. And the more I drank the less disciplined I became. Time passed slowly. After about an hour or so and several trips to the kitchen, I lost my self-containment altogether and danced with the others, with a grim frenzy, though still, I should add, keeping a close eye on Poppet and Fluck.

'Bravo!' someone shouted as I danced, but my lips were tightly shut, and I did not reply. The sounds of T Rex, Slade, Mud, The Sweet, Geordie, the Bay City Rollers, propelled us stomping and prancing round the room.

Eventually a record finished and no one replaced it. We drifted to the sides of the room, or sat down. I noticed again how wobbly Fluck was on his feet and moments later observed him swigging colourless liquid from a fancy pint mug – perhaps gin or vodka. Once, in fact, Poppet tried to restrain him, but he shrugged her off mid-gulp and began to laugh. O the freshness and the humour of love. I could almost weep, but not yet. Bite my tongue off first and gouge out my eyes. Then weep. Horrible thought. What a masochist I have become.

As I sat watching all this, something passed across my line of vision, retraced its steps, and finally stood still in front of me, blackening my view. It was the pregnant nun. His wimple had come adrift, forming a ragged coil round his neck like the halter of a Burgher of Calais, and his black habit was mysteriously rent up one side. His pregnancy had drifted across the other hip. When I looked him in the face I noticed that he was the colour of a Bath Oliver and very moist.

'Games now,' he said with unprovoked violence.

'Go away,' I said, peering round him to where Poppet and Fluck had been standing. But some other imbecile immediately shouted, 'A game! A game!' and soon everyone else had taken up the cry.

Fluck, of course, took charge. I mainly watched, and occasionally I was the score master. But my scoring at this time of the evening was not of the best and the pregnant nun, I remember, particularly felt cheated. Perhaps he was, the little shit.

Most of the games were tedious failures. For example, Fluck devised a game called Noah's Ark in which the names of various creatures were written on strips of paper, a pair of names for each creature, and then the strips of paper were folded up, shuffled, and distributed, one per person. You became the creature whose name you had unwittingly chosen, and your sole objective was then to discover your creaturely partner by making noises appropriate to your species. I imagine it is a dull game at the best of times, but Fluck had ruined it by drawing up an impossibly eclectic list of names. If I remember correctly there were two iguanas, two moths, two gophers, two dung-beetles, and three shrimps. I was a moth, I think. Amidst the ensuing phonetic confusion and laughter, I sat slumped on the sofa, one hand raised in the air, shouting loudly, 'Moth! Moth!' But it was all over almost before it had started, being one of those games that takes twice as long to explain as it does to play.

'You're drunk,' hissed Poppet as she stood behind me listening to my criticisms of Fluck's games. 'You're making a fool of yourself.'

It was a classic understatement, but before I could remonstrate she had glided away to join Fluck at the stereo. I watched her mouth move. 'Brilliant,' she was saying, 'brilliant.' One of her old catch-phrases, the shape of which I had almost forgotten. She smiled at Fluck sweetly, the provoking bitch. He was quite drunk by now, almost as drunk as me, and loudly inarticulate. Again I saw her try to restrain him as he drank, but he merely held his glass up towards her and proposed a toast, I think to the iguana, though his words were garbled.

'A noble beast!' he loudly concluded. Poppet leaned forward, and they not so much chinked glasses as delicately pressed them together, like hard iguana paws, and their imaginary tails curved and touched. If Destiny was rational and just, Fluck would have been a dung-beetle.

171

Dancing followed, then more games. Then dancing again. All the time Fluck took photographs, lurching from side to side of the room and displaying enormous ostentation. The worst of it was that his camera, a very 70s piece of machinery, produced instantaneous photographs which he distributed to his victims almost before they had finished blinking and scowling and averting their faces. Eventually his jovial tyranny found me out too, and he came lumbering towards me with a damp pale print in his paw.

'There you are,' Fluck said in a gabble, 'you must have thought I'd forgotten all about you, you poor suffering thing. Now, I must ask you, are you as drunk as you look? No, don't answer. This – ' he waved the photograph ' – will answer for you. Oh yes, just wait, the documentary evidence, hah!' He was very drunk.

There was nothing on the print, it was a blank white sheen, but as we watched, under the sheen a stain slowly appeared, spreading, concentrating, deepening in colour from verdigris to aqua blue to bottle-brown, and a pattern began to appear. We watched. A vertical line divided the picture into two halves, the edge of a half-opened door, letting in light to one side and casting shadow over the other, and in the shadow side a face formed, squinting blindly, mouth opened, nose in the air, an imbecile's face obviously, a buffoon, and this, it became clear, was me.

'Don't you look *beautiful*?' Fluck purred monstrously, then pealing with laughter. Someone peered over his shoulder and also began to giggle. 'Oh, isn't he the sweetest thing?' Fluck warbled. 'He reminds me of those pretty boys in Persian miniatures, I always think so. Which, my dear, makes you a sixteenth-century catamite, as if you didn't know.'

Music started up again, loud and raucous. It seemed we had moved into the late 70s, New Wave, and Punk. Johnny Rotten was screaming 'We're so pretty', a nasal nihilistic sneer. Fluck obviously thought the words wonderfully apt.

'They're playing our tune, S. J.,' he called. 'Sing along. Pretty, pretty, pretty.' Off he stumbled into the pogo-ing centre of the room, where his soft static wobble was conspicuously out of place. 'Pretty, pretty, pretty,' I heard him cry again parrot-fashion, and then I retreated to the kitchen, suddenly thirsty.

In the kitchen, the pregnant nun had forced one of the Stardust girls up against the cooker. Their mouths were glued together and her blouse was bunched round her neck. Naturally they did not notice me at first, but when I wrenched open the fridge door, the poor girl gave a squeak of alarm and the pregnant nun spun round, his face smeared over with her lipstick zigzag.

'Don't mind us, all right?' he said threateningly, staring. He looked younger than before, and thinner. He seemed to have been delivered of his pregnancy. I held up two cans of lager to indicate the innocence of my motives, kicked shut the fridge door, and departed.

The next thing I knew, I was stomping with Myra, I don't know why. I had lost track of Fluck and Poppet, probably they were upstairs again, hiding amongst the filth of Fluck's studio. She would be posing for him, no doubt, every so often breaking off to step in front of the easel and drape her lovely arms round his thick neck, though he, despotic, continued to paint, sliding colours onto the canvas, the brightest, wiliest blues, wide-open yellows, naked crimson. I had seen the picture already, of course, so I knew. Foreknowing and foresuffering, that's me. Cursed with knowledge.

Myra danced from the waist down, rigidly, as if putting up a stiff resistance to the music. Around us bodies flung themselves without inhibition. One of these was Angel's, now in its element, which purported to be dancing with Moyra, though in fact they seldom coincided. Actually she never appeared to dance with anyone in particular, but languidly gyrated on her own, expending the minimum energy, and if she occasionally raised an arm into the air it was only to take a drag of her cigarette. Generally she behaved as if all eyes were on her, which probably they were, for her boob-tube, it became obvious, was at least two sizes too small, and as she lazily pendulated through ever-decreasing circles towards the end of the song, there were moments of mind-boggling suspense. By contrast I danced with a rapid awkwardness that was inappropriate but increasingly necessary. Eventually I had to stop dancing altogether and sit down.

Sitting beside me was the man who looked like an accountant.

He said into my ear, 'I've seen Gary Glitter at the Hammersmith Odeon. Have you?' I shook my head. A mistake.

'What do you do?' he asked.

'I manage to avoid him,' I said nastily.

'What is your job?' he answered, unpeturbed.

'I'm a photographer,' I said, the first thing that came into my head. There was a pause, and then I added, 'With the *Rolling Stone*.' I had once, in fact, been commissioned to write an article for the *Rolling Stone*, and although they never used it, and never again contacted me, my connection with them continued to impress me. The accountant pondered this, pressing his finger-tips together in the manner of one accustomed to refined cerebration.

'What a coincidence,' he said. 'I studied Film and Photography at Kingston Polytechnic.'

'Oh, good,' I said, thinking that nothing could be worse. 'I'm really a writer,' I said. Again the accountant pondered, finger-tips lightly straining, but before he could deliver the almost inevitable pronouncement that he was also a writer, I made my excuse to leave.

'I'm extremely drunk,' I said, getting up with an apologetic smile, 'and I have to go and vomit.' From the living-room I made indirect progress towards the downstairs lavatory, and in the hall met Poppet, who was sitting on a chair near the foot of the stairs.

She had been crying. In fact she continued to cry as I stood there, intermittently smearing fresh tears across her cheeks with the backs of her hands. But she said nothing. The situation was obviously bizarre. But because I was drunk, or almost, it did not anger or irritate me; on the contrary my sympathies were aroused. For a moment I almost forgot that her tears, like everything else, belonged to him, the gross puppet-master of her emotions, and that vengeance only, not sympathy, was mine. However, I really did need to proceed to the lavatory, and was just thinking of squeezing past her when she spoke.

'Why?' she asked, not looking at me, rubbing tears into her face. I stared at her. 'Why am I surrounded by all these stupid . . .' she broke off to sob '. . . hostility,' she said at last, with great emphasis, ungrammatically. She appeared confused. 'You

174

won't tell me,' she added, guessing correctly, and looking at me for the first time.

There was no doubt that she was in considerable anguish. I told her, as gently as I could, that I did not know what she meant. This caused her to laugh, an awful mingling of expressions on her face, and I was suddenly, graphically, made aware of the extent to which she was embroiled with Fluck. All her desperation and longing were evident in her expression.

There was another thing, too. While I stood watching her sob and rave, I noticed that her blouse was undone almost to her navel. Also her hair, usually so neat, was disarranged. Obviously this could only mean one thing, and in a state of despair I was barely able to conceal, I made for the lavatory as the terminally desperate make for their final sanctuary.

I wept myself, or very nearly, as I sat there in the dim light with the cold ceramic pressed against the back of my legs. When I felt able, I rose, washed and dried my hands, and fled back to the party. Both Poppet and the chair had vanished from the hall.

Wild scenes greeted me, truly astonishing, though I knew well enough how drunk and desperate everyone was. The music of the Rolling Stones (mid period) pounded from the stereo, producing a kind of Bacchic frenzy in the small gathering in the middle of the room. All scruples seemed to have vanished. Within the blur and whirl of dancing creatures I saw that one of the Stardust sisters had removed her blouse. She also appeared to be smoking, clumsily, a long joint. The young nun's face pressed her closely, despite the wild deviations of his arms and legs, and occasionally the two figures blended together, united for a moment, like moth and flame, before flickering apart again. Around them the others danced with no less ebullience. The fully-clothed Stardust girl was dancing with Mussolini who, although he showed clear signs of exhaustion, kept up a furious goose-stepping pace punctuated often by stiff-armed salutes and a manic facial twitch. Angel twirled with Poppet (yes, she had returned) and Myra provided an angular counterpart to her sister's fluid grace. The accountant spun on his own, with intense concentration. But, at the centre of it all, of course, jived Fluck. Rising often above the surrounding mêlée, like a whale snorting out of the sea, the expression on

175

his face suggested ecstasies and rigours of rituals lost to man. I had never seen him so seriously animated, his bulky form antic as though by electrical stimulation. Once, catching my eye as he rose above general head-level, his mouth moved as if he was trying, however helplessly, to communicate something to me, but it was the briefest of grimaces during the most deafening of songs, and I think unintentional. Others however made strident attempts to grab me and pull me into their circle, which I was keen to resist, at least until I had finished my mug of vodka (the source of lager had run dry). And thus it was, from my vantage point on the periphery of madness, that I witnessed the fall of Fluck which put an end to all the dancing.

It is conventional to say of such incidents that they were over in the blink of an eye, but Fluck's fall, although it probably lasted no more than a second, seemed to take forever, and I remember every detail of it. It began at the height of one of his ridiculous towering leaps, from which point he ponderously sank like a chimney detonated, with hideous and doleful ruin – if I may be Miltonic for a moment – until he reached and rapidly passed the point at which he should have bounced up again, subsiding instead, with a seismic ripple of aerated clothing, on top of the oblivious pregnant nun – who disappeared briefly but was discovered soon afterwards in a broken foetal position several yards away.

Naturally the nun was not the only casualty; Fluck fell with a greater consequence than that, and most people were swept aside in the wake of his fall. But none was crushed quite so completely as the nun. I once saw a drunk fall from his bar stool onto a miniature poodle, spreading his arms as he fell and squashing the poodle beyond hope of recovery, but his fall was no more dramatic than Fluck's. Shock and horror were quite properly the general reactions, and a second or two after the accident nearly everyone was gathered anxiously round the little figure in the crumpled black habit, who lay on the floor, perfectly still and white-faced, while the music – particularly lively at this point, I remember – continued to thump uselessly from the speakers. Fluck and I, however, sat apart, Fluck on the floor where he had fallen, I on the sofa, and now our eyes, for the second time that evening, met. His shone. Not with tears, I am sure, but perhaps with anger. His expression certainly was grim, even malevolent, and I half-suspected him of deliberately staging the whole drama for obscure personal reasons, just the kind of tasteless stunt he would pull. I stared back at him with equal hostility.

Somewhere in the background of my stare, meanwhile, the nun was slowly helped to his feet and gingerly propelled towards a chair. He was not, it appeared, quite dead. Fluck also began to rise, heaving himself up in a deadpan fashion, both arms bent in front of him, like a gorilla. Once risen, he did not even look over to where the nun lay slumped in his chair, but merely regarded the palms of his hands with a surly expression, like a man unused to waiting for others. How I hated him at that moment, for myself of course, but also on behalf of those he crushed, or seduced, or both, in his efforts to attract attention.

I was ready to lead the mob against him now that his true colours were revealed. But when the music finally faded out, to my astonishment there was no mob to lead. A babble of excited voices replaced the music; scrambled, gleeful chatter from one side of the room, Fluck's boom from the other. '*La belle musique est finie*,' he shouted smoothly, '*donc* it is time for another game. Come children.' And he raised his arms in a grotesque parody of parental authority. An incredible transformation had taken place; he was all shout and bullying smiles once more, disregarding the misery he had caused only a few minutes earlier. And, even more indecently, no one except me seemed to find this strange. Leaving the busted nun to struggle weakly out of his chair as best he could, the others gathered round Fluck, clamouring for the games he had promised them. Sickening. Granted that I disliked the newly crippled nun with a special intensity, I nevertheless felt outraged on his behalf, and could not countenance Fluck's glib irresponsibility as the others did. I longed to insult him, not glancingly as before, nothing so minor, but with memorable destruction. And I think it was to this end that I now began to drink with purpose, working towards a pure performance in which there would be no hesitating kindness to deflect me. While the others bickeringly devised new games, I shuttled resolutely back and forth between living-room and kitchen, acquiring the authentic automatic lurch of body and mind. But, alas, I had forgotten Fate in whose hands I was and whose arrangements coincided so infrequently with my own.

When I made my second or third return to the living-room, Fluck swept towards me and took me moistly by the hand.

'You're first,' he said loudly, proudly presenting me to the others as a dazed but victorious boxer is presented to the drunken audience. I was puzzled by this, but determined to beat Fluck at his own game, so I merely nodded and scowled. Fluck and I left the room together, and, shuttered in the hall outside, he explained the rules of the new game to me. Much of what he said I have forgotten, although I remember that, like a raving impresario, he frequently referred to me as 'darling'. 'A simple mime, darling,' he said, 'you can't go wrong.' Apparently I was to impersonate an alligator, a creature Fluck seemed to choose on a whim, and the others were to guess it. 'Don't make it too impossibly difficult,' he added, 'they're all a bit pissed, you know. *Bonne chance.*'

Back in the living-room I found everyone politely waiting for me. A memory comes back now, of a sudden warning, 'Careful S. J.!' A suppressed giggle also; perhaps I had knocked something, or someone, over. Slowly, jerkily, consciously containing the fluids I had so rapidly just drunk, I knelt. A hush fell over everyone. More slowly still I stretched out on the floor, belly down. My trousers felt tight over my buttocks, I remember that, otherwise I was not uncomfortable. But I was now aware of my ambiguous position within that silent circle of onlookers. I was the performer, I knew that, but I felt also that, in a sense, I was about to be performed upon, audiences having certain rights and expectations. I have seen Rembrandt's pictures of dissecting chambers, doctors and students ranged round the cadaver which relaxes on a table with its scalp peeled neatly back.

'Get on with it!' someone shouted. Obediently I stretched my arms out stiffly in front of me to make jaws and began to open and close them in a vertical direction, simulating, you understand, a sort of snapping. At the same time I writhed in a serpentine fashion.

'Squirrel!' someone shouted.

'Squirrel?' I exploded with indignation. 'Squirrel?' Howls of laughter were returned to me.

'Lizard!' shouted someone else. More like it, though another

178

voice butted in, 'Rabbit!' Other ludicrous and apparently hilarious suggestions followed as I furiously redoubled my snapping
and writhing. 'Hamster!' roared someone through hoots of
laughter. 'Unicorn! Mongoose! Ostrich! Otter! Prairie dog!' I
wriggled and snapped with all my might. 'Camel! Panther!
Emu! Ardvaark!'

I began, at last, exhausted, to perceive a conspiracy. It was a
put-up job. A sacrifice, if you like. Fluck was laughing with the
rest of them, his big face howling soundlessly. As I looked up
he winked at me.

'Bravo, S. J.! Keep it up!' he shouted. 'What a lot of dunces
they are.' Beside him Poppet was spluttering helplessly. I hadn't
seen her looking so happy for days. Laugh now, squirm later.
With me it was the other way round. I felt myself going cold as
I made an attempt to produce the requisite smile of dawning
realisation, the shrug of shame-faced helplessness, the shucks-
folks-I've-been-taken-for-a-ride reaction demanded by the situation. But I have problems with conventional responses. The
laughter continued as I grimly snapped and writhed, my eyes
now closed, barely enduring.

'With such delicacy and grace, S. J.,' a voice, unmistakably
Fluck's, intoned above the rest, 'you simply have to be . . . a
moth.'

The laughter intensified, reaching a neat crescendo, then
dissipated as I slowed, stopped, and lay inert.

Fluck instantly helped me to my feet (I remember his grip on
my elbow) and shared in the spontaneous applause. Like the
keeper of a performing bear. 'Wonderful,' he said, 'you were
quite wonderful. I've never seen a more identity-conscious
alligator.' Grinning congratulations followed, the pregnant nun
even slapped me on the back, while I struggled to repress the
urge to butt him in the face. Something had hardened me and I
endured all insults, if not with good grace at least with outward
indifference. I am a survivor, am I not? At least for a little while.
Presently Fluck came towards me with a consolatory glass of
vodka, desperately needed, though it irked me to take anything
from my tormentor.

'For your labours,' he said.

As I drank, seated on the sofa, Fluck organised a final party
game. Hide-and-seek. I remember the sound of his voice baying

instructions for the hiding and the seeking and the counting with the eyes closed. My eyes, I think, were already closed. Certainly I retained no visual memory of the moment but there was squabbling and chatter in the darkness around me, a clink of glasses; the air was stale and sweet. Thus the party falters, I thought, thus spirals to its dissolution. Silently I struggled to avoid slipping into a coma, the long-awaited coma in which I might forget everything that pressed in on me and for which I had to find names: vigilance, sacrifice, humiliation, revenge. The idea of a coma was immensely tempting. I could not do it any more; I was convinced I could not do it. But then I remembered details of his portrait of her, wet brush strokes forming the mouth and opening the eyes, and other details too, the shaken hair and dishevelled blouse, a glimpse of nipple, thumb-bruised to a deeper, more dangerous colour, and the pale folds of her belly as she bent on tiptoe towards him. And names for all these horrors began to occur to me.

When I opened my eyes and found everything, even the empty glass in my hand, almost invisible in the gloom of dimmed lights, it was time for Angel to shut his and begin counting. I heard him, *One, two, three*, and as everyone rushed out I slipped into the kitchen and pulled a half bottle of Scotch from behind the sink. It is odd that I knew exactly where to find it. I suppose it is possible I hid it earlier when I was custodian of the cocktail cabinet. Who knows? When I returned to the hall everyone else had vanished, as usual leaving me alone in their giggly wake. *Sixteen, seventeen, eighteen.* I put my head back round the living-room door and saw Angel standing in the middle of the empty room, hands in front of his eyes, peeking comically through chinks between his fingers. When he saw me, he lowered his hands and shooed me away furiously. *Twenty-five, twenty-six.* I lurched down the hall and began erratically to mount the stairs. *Thirty-seven, thirty-eight.* His voice was fading as I climbed towards the silent upper reaches of the house. Somewhere between the first landing and the second, it died completely, leaving only the sound of my tiptoeing steps. Occasionally I heard coughs from behind closed doors, scuffles, and once, below me, the sudden beat of running feet down the hall. Then silence. Everyone was hidden.

I am astonished to remember these moments so exactly. I was

stone drunk for the fifth consecutive night and certain details of my circumstances must surely have been sacrificed to dying brain cells. But I managed to preserve a kind of inner concentration, cold and bitter energy by which I subsisted. I no longer felt so tired. And I had my purpose, and this kept my mind clear.

On the second landing I stopped, opened my bottle with a metallic snap of the seal, and drank deeply; regarded the ladder a few yards away that led to the attic. I was sure they would never find me up there, in the inner sanctum of Art, Fluck's airless lair. I thought again of Poppet's picture, which I was going to see. Fluck and I were going to talk about it; of this I was certain. Naturally he was at this moment up there waiting for me. Poppet would not be there; I was sure of this too. I had the idea that the fate Fluck had designed for me did not include her.

I began to climb the ladder. I was halfway up it when, to my horror, I heard him come pounding up the stairs, Angel, the bloody idiot, squeaking in a high-pitched voice, 'Coming, ready or not!' I froze. But it wasn't until I heard him on the second flight of stairs immediately below that I realised he was coming straight for me. The voice of a twelve-year-old and the body of a bison. I shot off the ladder, barged two groggy steps into a wall, opened a door that appeared beside me, and fell into a room, dragging the door shut behind me. In the dark I was suddenly invisible like a torch beam switched off. But not silent, I remember. I was almost deafened by the bellowing of my coarse lungs. I could hardly hear Angel's footsteps as he thumped along the landing, and I had no doubt that he would simply open the door, flick the light switch, and haul me off. But no, Angel barely hesitated before climbing the ladder to the attic. Between breaths I heard him knock on the hatch, apparently receive an answer, and enter. There was a muffled thump as the hatch came down behind him.

My relief at not being found soon gave way to fury at having to wait for my own interview with Fluck, but by dint of continued drinking I gradually contrived to convert fury to patience. My eyes became accustomed to the dark, although I did not look about me much. I was faintly interested to note the changing relationship between dark and light shadow contained within the shape of my bottle of Scotch, but only in so far as it provided me with a rough estimate of passing time. Occasionally, to relieve the boredom and to test my nerve, I tiptoed out of the room, took a few cautious steps up the ladder, and cocked an ear towards the attic hatch. Always I heard nothing, sensed something, and scuttled abruptly back into the bedroom. More minutes passed, and the pale shadow forming the upper part of my bottle increased downwards. Often I imagined what was happening above me, Fluck and Angel deep in discussion about Poppet's picture, which stood bewitchingly on the easel between them. This hypothetical discussion was frank, erudite, and frankly impossible, Angel being a pure philistine with the aesthetic sentience of a sponge-finger, but I imagined it all the same: Fluck discoursing smugly on chiaroscuro and *sfumato* and frottage, and Angel making witty play with the theoretical points thus raised, and citing historical precedents for illuminating comparison . . . By my liquid chronometer I judged I had been there about forty minutes when I heard the attic hatch door open again, and Angel descend the ladder. It took all my self-restraint not to burst from my hiding place and rail against his inconsiderate verbosity, the bloody time-waster, but instead I opened the door a fraction and like Keyhole Kate, pressed my eye to the crack.

Imagine my surprise when I saw not Angel but Fluck backing down the ladder, swaddled up to his mucky ears in a big grimy overcoat, though recognisable all the same, despite his very unFluckian furtive tread, down the ladder and across the creaking landing floor. An espionage-type glance to the left and likewise to the right, and then he disappeared down the stairs. Without thinking, I followed him, also furtive, unswaddled. Plans change from minute to minute, but Destiny remains the same. I would have expected Fluck to understand this rather better than he seemed to.

It didn't take long to leave the house. All the rooms we passed seemed empty. I suspected that many people had forgotten about the game of hide-and-seek and had simply gone to sleep. I suppose it was past midnight. From the living-room, as I passed, I heard a dry hissing noise like sucked teeth, and hesitated long enough to see the needle of the record-player trapped in the final groove of a record. Then the front door creaked open and clicked shut and I obligingly floated forward in the established manner of cunning pursuit. There was no opportunity to pick up a coat or more alcohol. It was a question now of following hard on Fluck's heels; otherwise in the dark he would slip away and lose me, his bulky silhouette blending with the dense dark forms of blackthorn bushes, hydrangea, or the squat crab apple trees that crowded the slope to the beach. For some reason I kept hold of my bottle of Scotch, now almost certainly empty. Perhaps it had become a sort of talisman; or else a fragment I had shored against my ruin.

Thirty yards up ahead, Fluck's torch projected a tiny kite of yellow light onto trees and hedges ahead of him. I doubt whether the torch was really necessary; the moon was three-quarters full and the stars unusually bright. As we, Fluck and I, old inseparables, crept out of the garden and along the path that leads eventually down to the sea, we were surrounded by flickering pin-pricks of light, echoes of moonlight on dew, a glossy gleam off a leaf, pale puddles cracked with reflections, the distant pulsation, red to green, of an aeroplane. It was never entirely dark; I could see, for instance, that Fluck was carrying a small satchel over his shoulder, probably full of paint and paper, perhaps a book too, and an old sandwich; or more personal possessions, a lock of her hair, assorted durex . . . But there was little time to pause and sicken. Fluck walked ahead, a heavy stumbling shadow crashing loudly into ferns and brambles at the side of the narrow path, and I followed. The beam of his torch kept him from ever quite disappearing, but I could have trailed him with my eyes shut, he made so much noise. Clumsy and purposeful, he never bothered to look back, he was off on his own, remote despite his noisiness, or perhaps because of it, its enveloping circumference, and I followed him without risk of detection, almost as if Fluck were a spectacle put on for my entertainment, like the moon or stars or winking puddles. Overhead, wisps and whorls of cloud ran like skeins of mohair across the cold sky. On either side of the hedgerows were unseen quiet fields.

How short the walk seemed. Soon we turned seaward, getting a salt whack of sea air in our faces before sinking between thicker hedges of gorse. In the narrow defile Fluck all but disappeared, though I could still hear him, of course.

Perhaps out of control, he seemed to break into a heavy jog as the slope steepened, gasping whenever he stumbled, a strange sort of noise like a flat laugh, ha ha. I don't know why, but it was an awful effort to listen to him and to run at the same time. I could no longer see my feet, my platforms, precarious as stilts, tilting against loose pebbles and into cracks in the path. It was as much as I could do not to break an ankle.

Eventually we reached a sandy opening where the silhouettes of crab apple trees stood suddenly round us, arrested in postures of intent curiosity like a Greek chorus attendant on our tragedy. I suppose the nature of my pursuit made me think of this image, a very Fluckian one, now I consider it. He would have approved.

But this is where it started to go wrong. At that most fanciful moment of my otherwise unimaginative pursuit I turned from brief contemplation of the posturing trees to find Fluck gone. You can imagine how I cursed myself. Although the darkness had lifted from the slope and in the moonlight, between trees, details of the ground ahead were quite discernible, I couldn't see Fluck anywhere. Nor, more worryingly, could I hear him. Fluck had turned Puck, a baggy fairy, and somehow spirited himself away. Behind the tree where I was hidden, I rapidly considered – and dismissed – all possible plans of contingency, then blundered out into the open, tripped over a hidden root, and fell crashing to the ground. From where he was crouched, tying his shoelaces a few yards away, Fluck stared at me, terrified. His eyes bulged in his big white face, his mouth was a wide silvery drool. As I fell, I saw all this, and I felt, let me not hold it back for modesty's sake, the thrill of my power over him. Then I let out a yelp of anticipated pain, and almost simultaneously tumbled into a small sour-smelling bush, I think a laburnum.

I gathered myself together and rolled onto my knees. Fluck was still crouched staring at me.

'Ah-ha!' I said as casually as I could. Incredibly, I still had hold of my empty bottle and I waved it cheerfully at Fluck by way of greeting. He didn't seem to take this in at first, the poor frightened fool. It was a few minutes before he recovered the power of speech.

'Curious that you should pop out just then,' he said, in a

voice quavery and faint. It was Fate, actually, but I did not tell him, silently watching as he rose to his feet. 'Come to think of it,' he added more strongly, 'it is rather curious that you should pop out at all.' I shook my bottle at him again and told him I was walking off the effects.

'Yes,' said Fluck, 'the demon drink.' He did not laugh, he was too drunk himself. 'And where are you walking to, the beach?' I nodded. 'Then I suppose we shall have to walk together.' He was doing his best to sound disappointed.

The ground fell away more sharply beyond the crab apple trees, and the sandy path that reappeared was steep and crooked. After a short while, high hedges rose up on either side, blotting out the moonlight, and into the darkness we descended together in a cramped and unsteady manner, like the Butcher and the Beaver hunting the Snark, going shoulder to shoulder out of pure necessity. Fluck made no apparent attempt to moderate his flailing gait. Twice he caught me on the ankle and once trod heavily on my toe. Despite myself I roared with pain, but he did not apologise. He seemed lost in thought, though perhaps, with all his puffing and panting, he was simply too breathless to speak.

Ahead, where the path opened out to the rear of the beach, a small glow of light slowly expanded. We tottered towards it, our faces and fronts gradually illuminated as by the effects of a Rembrandt or a De La Tour.

The path, perversely, grew steeper and more treacherous still. When we had almost reached the bottom, Fluck stumbled, or else I did, and, as we fell against each other, side-swiping for some kind of support, our faces clashed. I had forgotten, until that moment, how bad Fluck's breath smelt. Now the sour heat that fanned my face reminded me; it was a garlicky, fetid stink, redolent of foody scraps lingering between teeth, bits of sausage roll, paste sandwiches, pizza, quiche. He never cleaned his teeth. When I first met him they were already half-rotten, and when he laughed he used to cover up his mouth with his hand. Evidently he had since grown out of such fastidiousness. Yet with this reeking mouth he had kissed her, and into it she had placed her sweet inventive tongue. What was I to make of this? What possible pattern of romance could I construct from such

185

details? The myth of Pasiphae and the Bull is hardly more distressing.

We disentangled ourselves and made it to the foot of the hill without further mishap. Here for a moment we stood gazing towards the shingle which divided the scrub from sand up ahead. I asked Fluck whether he was going to paint anything particular on the beach.

'Perhaps,' he said, 'we'll see.' And he walked on. Such terseness was uncharacteristic, but then he was in a difficult position. You see, after devoting the evening to my public humiliation and bringing off the final triumph of the alligator game, he had failed to bow out as neatly as planned. We were both aware of this, although he appeared more nervous than me. Scenes of my embarrassment must have been running through his mind as they ran through my own, the feebly waving arms, the writhing body, the bewildered look on my face, I remembered and regretted it all – almost, now, for his sake.

'Why the beach anyway?' I asked. 'Why not the cliff top?'

'Patience, S. J., patience,' he replied lamely. 'You will see for yourself.' But I pressed him further. 'On the beach,' he said at last, 'there is a group of rocks, you may have seen them, though you are not very observant. They are distinctive in shape.'

'Crescent-shaped,' I said.

'A half-moon. As these rocks are situated in the *middle* of the beach, they are completely covered at high tide.' He looked at his watch. 'In about three hours' time. But until then, they afford a rather enchanting view of the bay, best when the tide is rising. As now. The effects of moonlight on the water are quite extraordinary, much more exciting than from the cliff top.' He looked at me critically. 'But perhaps you do not find the effects of the moonlight *sympathique*,' he said.

I told him that I liked the work of Atkinson Grimshaw, the Victorian painter of moonlit scenes.

'I see,' said Fluck heavily. Evidently he took a dim view of Grimshaw. I should have mentioned Böcklin's 'Island of the Dead'. 'Moonlight aside,' Fluck continued, 'it is a comfortable and peaceful spot for thinking. The rocks seem to be armchair-shaped, really quite convenient. I often go there to think. I have a lot of time to think these days.' His gloominess, I thought, was typical of the drunk and the guilty. I remembered Goya too.

When we reached the shingle and began to cross it, he seemed to cheer up, though he progressed more erratically than ever, kicking up showers of stones as he lurched from side to side.

'Terrible party,' he gasped. 'I hated it.'

'Dreadful,' I agreed. He giggled and I allowed myself a grim smile. Why not? Our moods altered nothing, and whether cheerful or sad we remained bound together as before, no possibility of wriggling free and thwarting Fate. We were bound upon a wheel of fire, if I may be so bold as to borrow once more such a well-lit phrase.

'But I must admit you were a wonderful alligator,' he said slyly. 'Truly inspired. I was frightened out of my wits, you were so marvellously realistic.' I made no reply to this, but let him laugh himself out, his sniggers soon blending with the clink and scuffle of the shingle.

'Do you remember,' he said when he had got his breath back, 'our parties at college? I don't know how we used to get all those people into our rooms. That last one after Finals, wasn't it the very last day of Trinity, remember that?' I nodded. 'You were drunk then too,' he added snootily, 'correct me if I'm wrong.' It was difficult to see where this was leading, but how funny (peculiar) that I should have thought of the same party only a few hours earlier.

'I find it outrageous,' he said with sudden violence, 'how quickly they forget you. It is worse than bad-mannered, it's intolerable. I am not naturally given to sentimentality,' he added, bringing himself partially under control, 'and obviously one's friends can be quite awful enough when they *do* remember you, but to simply forget, *for no reason*, with no apology, it appals me.' He made a noise as if he were about to spit. 'Friendship should be more than biting Time can sever,' he said bitterly.

'Eliot,' I said automatically. 'One of the plays, I forget which.'

We walked on in silence for a minute or two, and then Fluck spoke again. 'It's been so nice to see *you* again,' he said, his wet smile catching the moonlight.

I recoiled, thinking he was about to press his hand into mine,

187

but he was only searching through his pockets for a handkerchief. He was growing rather too garrulous for my liking; there was a volatility about Fluck's conversation that made me nervous. He seemed to suffer a change of mood every few minutes. His gait was also volatile, the clumsy corvine waddle exaggerated by the effects of the booze. 'Whoops-a-daisy,' he said now as he slithered wildly, his flailing arms narrowly missing my head. 'Slippery stuff, isn't it?' I maintained a scornful silence, cursing him under my breath. Unfortunately, however, seconds later, when the moon momentarily disappeared behind a cloud, it was I who had the misfortune to fall. Luckily I was not hurt. Nor was Fluck, whom I had knocked to the ground.

'Careful, old son,' he said, limping over to me and fussing round. 'It's the demon drink, I'm afraid. You'll never manage to walk it off if you can't actually walk.'

'It's the platform shoes,' I said, ignoring his sympathy. 'I'm not used to them.' I thought to myself that if there was another brief eclipse of the moon I might perhaps take the opportunity to plant the toe of one of my shoes into the back of Fluck's knees. The brief but dramatic scene I imagined had the right flavour of justice.

Thankfully we soon reached the sand and I could walk, or limp, normally. One of my shoes had suffered some damage. Fluck was really quite his old self again, he had recovered from the initial shock of our meeting. He meandered happily ahead of me, often turning round to make some fatuous comment or other, as if he was taking me on a guided tour.

'Did you see my portrait of Poppet?' he asked suddenly in breezy tones. 'The finished version.'

I said that I had not. My tone was casual, but now that the subject was out in the open I felt a genuine thrill of excitement, seeing at the end of our conversation the final confession. First his, then hers. It would be just like our conversations at college, with a twist at the end. I began to concentrate on what I would have to say, thinking clearly and coldly.

'It's rather good,' said Fluck. 'It's a great pity you weren't inspired to write something of a comparative quality. Or just to write anything at all. But then you never could write; think of those poems – yuk, Keats plus Jung plus Tweety-pie. Look, there are the rocks.'

188

I could see nothing of these, but then I was not looking for them. I looked instead at Fluck, noting in advance all the details I might later need in circumstances I could not yet foresee: his thickly-overcoated slouch, the bobbing head and tangled hair, the arrhythmical stride.

'She's a very good sitter,' Fluck said over his shoulder – and at that moment, beyond him, the edge of the sea came into sight about two hundred yards away, grey moonlight fish-scaling the flickering water and reflecting off the underbellies of the nearest waves as they flapped onto the sand. Noises also became distinct, the bubble and hiss of invisible foam, a rattle of pebbles in the undertow. If I had looked back I would have seen two dark and dotted lines of footprints side by side, most of which were to be later obliterated by the incoming tide. This was another detail to remember, though I did not look back.

'But not as good as you,' Fluck concluded. What did he mean? 'And here we are. You have to climb up now, which you probably won't be able to manage, given your present disable-ments, but I will give you a hand. Watch me, I'll go first.'

The rocks stood immediately in front of us, a large black mound about fifteen feet high, giving off a fishy tang. Some-thing rose silently into the air above and flapped away.

'Watch me,' said Fluck again, and began to climb laboriously, with a great many hesitations and changes of direction. His body was huge, suspended above me, black and bulky like a full-blown sail, obscuring the paler, purpling sky. 'Watch me,' he panted yet again as he fumbled at the seaweed. 'Note my hand-holds.'

'Come on, come on,' he yelled when he was nearly at the top. 'You can't stay down there all night.' Within a minute I was beside him. A minute or slightly longer. 'Isn't this wonder-ful?' said Fluck.

The etiolated bay lay obligingly in front of us, held between two dark horns of circumscribing coast which pointed out towards the pale horizon. The sea was a grey mist, and so was the sky. It was not easy to discern where the two met; under close observation they seemed to flicker minutely together in a monochrome fizz. Immediately below us, when the eye refo-cused, I could see water already lapping against the foot of the rocks. Had we walked through water to reach the rocks? Perhaps that was why my feet were so cold.

'Lovely,' said Fluck, 'isn't it?' But bitterly chilly. The cold sky seemed to roar above us, though the breeze was slight. The difference in altitude between rocks and beach was not profound, but the drop in temperature was marked. I cursed myself for not wearing a coat. I was also newly aware of the inadequacies of 70s fashion-wear. My trousers, for instance, were tailored from the thinnest acrylic, and although they incorporated several rows of fancy pocket flaps, there were no actual pockets behind them, nothing into which I could stuff my freezing hands.

Fluck, unaffected by the cold in his outsized overcoat, was making regal gestures over the creeping waters. Creating a firmament in the midst of them perhaps. 'Splendid!' he said. 'Isn't it splendid? Beautiful and remote and here we are.' He sat, with a prissy simper of satisfaction, on his favourite rock. 'Beautiful and remote,' he continued. 'It always reminds me of those lines in *Death in Venice*, do you remember, right at the end: something, something, "the pale and lovely summoner out there smiled at him and beckoned". Do sit down, my dear, you're blocking my view.'

There was nowhere for me to sit, except perhaps for a small ledge poking up from a tangle of seaweed at Fluck's feet. I therefore declined the offer to sit, and although the darkness and the slipperiness underfoot and the cold breeze made it quite difficult to maintain a stable upright position, I stubbornly balanced to one side of Fluck's rock.

'Please yourself,' muttered Fluck. He took his satchel off his shoulder, placed it on his lap, didn't open it, and stared out to sea. From where I stood I could see his reflection steeply imaged in a rock pool at his feet, an enormous black body and tiny head. I asked him if he was going to paint a seascape.

'Have a guess,' he replied, indicating with a sweep of his hand the sea stretched out in front of him.

'You hardly ever paint what's in front of you,' I told him, 'so I expect you to paint something completely different, "Still Life with Soft Fruit" or "Field of Poppies".' Fluck snorted with amusement at this.

190

'Very good,' he said, 'quite like your old self, but unfortunately wrong. Also like your old self, ha ha.' He cackled, throwing up his arms, and his reflection in the pool obliterated itself.

'No,' he continued. 'Do you see that island out there?' He pointed into the blank distance.

'No,' I said.

'It doesn't matter, it's there all the same, a small flattish affair straight ahead of us, about a mile out. There's a ferry to it on Thursdays.'

I said that if it couldn't be seen, it proved my point about him painting what wasn't perceptibly there.

'But I'm not going to paint it *now*,' said Fluck, irritated. 'I'm going to sit here and watch it appear and then, then and only then, I might perhaps paint it. In the dawn. It's traditional, you know.' His big face, when he looked up at me, was smug. 'But as you know I'm really a portraitist,' he added after a pause.

'Yes I know.'

'As I say.'

We regarded each other, brinking the edge of the real subject of our conversation. I noticed that I was shivering. With the cold. In other circumstances I might simply have charged him with the bare facts of his sordid little adventures, and perhaps beaten him about a bit too, but I judged that the time was not quite right, and, besides, I knew that Fluck could not resist the opportunity, perhaps his first, to confess a sexual triumph. In my opinion he was greedy to tell me what he had done.

'Did you see the portraits?' he asked. 'The recent ones? I don't remember if you did or not.'

'All except the one of Poppet,' I said, managing by some fluke not to choke on her name.

'Ah, Poppet,' he said, as if thinking of her for the first time. 'That one's good. I'm pleased with that. I finished it rather recently, and didn't have time to display it with the others. You should see it, though I don't know what you'll make of it, your taste is rather . . .' he broke off '. . . what shall I say to soften the blow – your taste is rather . . . poor. Yes, poor. I think that's the word. Poor taste.'

'You have a knack . . .' I began angrily, but then stopped, not properly knowing what it was Fluck had a knack of. I think

191

now I meant to refer to his casual sadism, but for the moment it was lost. Fluck didn't appear to have heard me say anything at all. And perhaps I didn't begin to say it, only to think it, so that even my angry thoughts failed me, hanging incomplete in my head. I was familiar with this sensation from our college days, Fluck sneering at me from his armchair while I sat against the wall (always the same spot, by the stereo) failing to say what I meant, or saying what I didn't mean. I remembered his laughter, the hiccupy sort that denoted scorn, the treacly chuckle rich with sympathy. And I remembered some of his catch-phrases too: 'Incredible, S. J., you have it wrong in *every* respect . . .' 'I am *slightly* doubtful as to the quality of your logic . . .' 'If I may intrude with the truth upon your fantasy . . .' It was always late at night, and I was always tired, distracted by the rapid shadows on the wall that leapt from Fluck's slow gestures.

'But what does it matter?' asked Fluck. 'The painting is good anyway, whether you recognise it or not.' He sighed and stretched back, regarding the bay. 'Well, here we are, S. J.,' he said, 'and isn't it just like the old days? We were younger and happier then, eh? Not yet worn down by the tread of hungry generations, but bright and alert and in love with life. You disagree? Forgive me my memories; they are all I have. And surely you must at least remember our discussions, perhaps even remember them with affection. Our little talks, humble enough, no doubt, but enjoyable, eh? Didn't you enjoy them? Goodness, I was happy then; I can hardly imagine it now.' I grunted. 'And what about you, my dear,' he went on, 'in connection with that dangerous phenomenon, happiness? I've had so little chance to talk to you, and here you are married already, and settled down, and writing wonderful knowing articles for the kind of people we once were to read and admire. Are you happy?'

This question, I admit was totally unexpected, incomprehensible even. I had no idea what Fluck was after. I was a little stunned. Perhaps this was his intention.

'Perhaps,' I said cautiously.

'No need to be hasty,' said Fluck. 'Take a seat. Think it over. It's just that you've set me thinking, with all your talk about happiness this evening.'

To my astonishment I did sit, on the cold, slimy stone at

192

Fluck's feet, and at once he towered over me in his monstrous coat. Now more than ever it seemed to me that we were something like Lear and his Fool, or Quixote and Sancho Panza, or Stan and Oliver, characters in some stock duo of fiction who are combined purely to embody and enact our hopelessness and longing because some author, some representative of Fate, requires perpetual confirmation of these our human failings. Which could mean, of course, that as real people Fluck and I had no future at all, we were doomed. It is an emotive word, 'doomed'. Like the taste of medicine, it lingers in the mouth. With a tremor of real nausea I realised what this word actually meant; I *felt* it. Apart from our predestined selves I did not know *who we were*. I was in a state of extreme existential confusion, and that is no joke.

Thus paralysed, I made no answer to any of Fluck's subsequent questions. He, however, continued to talk glibly. I think perhaps he had reached the point at which he naturally began to supply both halves of the conversation, pausing only occasionally, if at all, for breath. I sat silently on my rock, feeling the damp coldness of it spread rapidly through my buttocks (towards the vulnerable heart).

It was substantially worse than, but not radically different from, our evenings' conversations at college. And some of those conversations were pretty bad. They got worse, in fact, towards the end. I remember the night I told him I was not going to New York with him; it was a night of almost pure sarcasm. Relieved only, I think, by tears.

'The desire for happiness,' Fluck was saying, 'is a dangerous mania. I think we have established that already. But happiness itself, what is that? Let us discuss it.'

I twitched on my rock, but said nothing. But Fluck wasn't waiting for an answer, merely choosing his words carefully. 'Now,' he said, pressing his fingertips together, 'I'm going to tell you what happiness means to me. You may not want to hear it, of course, but please, S. J., I beg you, pretend to listen. For old times' sake, you know.' He expected a smile and I gave him a feeble nod and he struck an attitude of pre-oratory, perhaps intended to be comical.

'Happiness,' he began preachily, 'murkiest of phenomena . . . how shall I begin? Boldly, of course. I must divide the darkness from the light. My belief is quite simply this: that there are only two categories of happiness, true and false. Real and unreal, if you like. Do you see?' I grimaced; perhaps I was permanently grimacing, on account of the terrible chill creeping through my body.

'We agree. I'm so glad. One step further now. Evidently the problem is to distinguish between these two, the true, and the false which is its counterfeit. This is hardly a new problem. Others have been here before us, grubbing round for clues, leaving their greasy fingerprints, Flaubert was one, of course, but there is simply *no* kudos in quoting Flaubert, I rather regret having done it in the first place. In a way this brings me to William Gerhardie, forgotten novelist of the twenties – though I recall mentioning him at least once over the last week; there is at least a kind of cultic distinction attached to *his* work. He is, I think, exactly the sort of cult failure we need, don't you agree?'

I had forgotten, but was now reminded, how horrible Fluck could be in full flow – that smarmy hectoring that seemed to come to me now across the years from his place in the armchair by the window overlooking the quad, deep purple sky visible through superficial reflections thrown by the electric light. His voice buzzed in my ear, then and now.

'Obviously you are familiar with Gerhardie's work already,' he was saying, 'don't let me bore you. But remind yourself of his Literary Credo, his fatuous remarks about the ego and the soul, entirely inappropriate in *his* argument, but rather useful in ours. Do you see what I'm driving at? Of course you do, a nod's as good as a wink, eh?'

He smiled and peered at me. 'Are you comfortable down there, S. J.?' Being almost frozen stiff, I made a rather strained gesture which Fluck interpreted optimistically.

'Good,' he said, settling back. 'And so, you see, real happiness is of the soul and unreal happiness is of the ego, and although you are going to interrupt and say that the soul does not exist any more, I shall say even before you do so that you are quite right, it does not exist, nor ever will. Nor can we do anything at all that isn't of the ego. These two facts are widely known, though perhaps you think it unfeeling of me to mention them together in a single breath.'

He waited for me to interject at this point, and when I didn't he continued in the same wearily brisk manner.

'Hell is other people. Let me not forget Sartre.' He giggled here, then thrust out his arms in mock supplication. 'But is there no real happiness at all, you ask me; please, not even a little? Not in life, no. Not in nasty, dirty, egotistical life, ugh.' He shuddered. 'But there is, if we are very lucky, a little of the real stuff in art; not much, I think we would agree, but a little. Enough, perhaps. In the creation of art there is sometimes to be found a modicum of the true happiness of the soul. Let's call it ecstasy.' He sounded very depressed when he said this. 'Flaubert knew this of course,' he added, 'the poor sod.'

A prolonged silence followed this, during which we both, for some reason, seemed to be holding our breaths. I listened in vain for a bird cry or the slosh of the sea but there was a buzzing in my ears which muffled everything out, the buzzing which was Fluck's voice. I was, I think, doubtful of his sanity.

Then he sighed and put his hands lazily behind his head. 'I wanted so much to tell you all this, S. J. You of all people. I do hope you are still awake.' But what had he told me? It was nothing, nothing at all.

I was staring now not at Fluck but at his reflection in the pool, flat, unsinkable shadow, and to this I nodded. I was, in fact, probably capable of making some sort of verbal response, but I bided my time.

'So there we are. But what do *you* think? *That's* what I really want to know. Lay bare your heart.' With another sigh he removed his satchel from his lap and placed it, near me, at his feet.

The coldness which had begun reasonably enough, considering my posture, in my buttocks, had by now spread to my fingertips and toes. Cold had become a positive pain, creeping through me – as Fluck's monologue had crept over me – inexorably. I told Fluck, in a few brief words, that he had been talking nonsense, though god knows I was hardly an ideal defender of happiness of any kind. He appeared delighted, and clapped his hands.

'Marvellous!' he cried. 'I always loved your independence.' I caught his eye, which was a cold glitter. I hoped mine was too.

'And your fineness of mind, of course, of course,' he added gushingly.

'In fact I don't believe,' I said with an effort, 'that *you* believe what you just said.'

'Oh but I do. I'm quite sure that *intellectually* you can demolish my little arguments with ease, but I *believe* them, oh yes, can't have you saying that I don't.' He gestured with his overcoated arms wide out. 'Art has always given me happiness. People give me the opposite. Frankly, even to try and make somebody happy is a gross and farcical mistake, excuse my vehemence. I confess it freely and without pain: no one ever made me happy, surely you know that.' At this point I gave what would have been, but for the constricting cold, a loud sneer. Fluck went on unstoppably.

'I know what you are thinking, you poor disgruntled thing, you're thinking: what about your friends? But that's not happiness, dear boy. Tenderness perhaps, at best. A wonderful tenderness, of course, but not quite happiness. We are too complicated and ordinary.' He smiled a naive, faintly puzzled smile; I saw it flash briefly in the moonlight, and then go out. He thought I believed him, but I was thinking of the happiness he had forced from Poppet, that she had given him.

'Do you think about our college days?' he asked. 'Do you? Of course you don't, why should you? But *I* think about them continually, nostalgiac that I have become. What about afterwards, though, that letter you sent me when I was in New York, probably you don't remember that either?'

I was silent, trying not to remember, remembering, cursing my memory. 'Not much,' I said, at last, into the awkward silence Fluck had created.

'No, I didn't think so,' said Fluck. He seemed to laugh soundlessly; I saw his shoulders heaving, although his face was turned away from me, back towards the cottage from which we had come. 'Your letter, yes. It was rather brief, wasn't it? But then brevity is the soul of wit.' He laughed again. 'But did you really think I would stay in New York for ever and ever? Wishful thinking in the extreme, S. J. Oh, do sit down, will you? I'm getting a crick in my neck watching you fidget like that. What are you doing now?' I must have got to my feet, probably to alleviate the numbness of the cold. I honestly don't think I could have answered Fluck even if I had wanted to. Couldn't form the words, my mouth and chin being frozen stiff. Also a degree of anger choked me. We regarded each other silently, Fluck and I, and then he leant forward and took the empty bottle out of my hand, from which it had been lightly swinging.

'No litter, please,' he murmured, putting the bottle safely into his overcoat pocket. 'Not on *my* beach.' A nervousness had crept into his voice, but with a calm hand he gently coaxed me back onto my rock. Oddly, I did not resist; nor did I even venture to speak. With that single touch he had sapped my strength. Or else the drink had. Either way, I was suddenly docile, and curiously indifferent to Fluck's lies and jibes, now about to continue at a predictable slow drawl, another monologue about to fall and smother me, as if Fluck had enticed me back ten years into our college rooms for the usual port and classical music and interminable talk about the state of the arts, his paintings, my writing, our ludicrous ambitions.

'Our college rooms,' said Fluck on cue, 'you must at least remember those. Our final year: Michaelmas, Hilary, Trinity. I call that time prelapsarian now, before New York and bedsits in brownstones and letters and all the rest of it I didn't understand, stupid American arses – I nearly said artists: *that* would have been funny – who couldn't paint, and didn't know . . . There was something about those rooms, a kind of innocence, don't you think? Do you remember the oriel windows overlooking the quad? So convenient for observing our fellow undergraduates below. They all hated us, but it didn't matter. It was you and I against the world, wasn't it, or something like that. Forgive me, S. J., for saying all this in a rush, but sometimes I can't help it, can't stop remembering, you see. And yes, goodness, I think I can actually remember every detail of the quad looking through that window. Let's see. The New Library, the mock medieval cloisters underneath – that very narrow corridor named after a very fat former dean, do you remember, quite absurd. The Old Hall opposite with portico and cupola. Lodge built up against it, a strange mixture, neo-Georgian with Elizabethan sky-scraper chimneys. Rather faceless. Do you remember it, S. J.?' I may have nodded at this, who knows? I was drifting, reverting, seeing him sitting in that horrible room.

197

I scarcely noticed when he placed his hand on my head. I was lost in the sound of his voice rising and falling around me, ceaselessly, as in benediction.

'The shadows of the chimneys on the lawn like neatly laid out planks. The shiny black windows round the portico opposite. Yes, I remember everything. Curious that you don't. You liked those evenings, didn't you, the port and cigars at least; perhaps also the conversations. I flatter myself you liked those too, the endless, endless talks we had, quite wonderful. We would talk about anything, wouldn't we – art, poetry, science, politics, always enthusiastic, sometimes with such a ferocity. Yes, I remember in particular talking about those horrid little mags that had sprung up, pretending to dispense style and taste to the wealthy and stupid; quite disgusting things – I think you wrote an article for one of them, didn't you, you turncoat? Something about me, wasn't it? Or rather not, ha ha.'

I became aware of his pudgy fingers slowly exploring my scalp, and I sat submissively, like a small schoolboy enduring in a trance the inexplicable ways of a senior, as they criss-crossed the crown of my head from ear to ear in soft clumsy palpation.

I remembered then that time years ago when I told him I did not intend to accompany him to New York. He had immediately given a loud false laugh, quite unlike his usual guffaw. 'Your little games,' he had said, 'grow ever more wounding.'

Then I told him quite matter-of-factly that I had sold my air ticket. This was not strictly true but it was convenient as a statement of intent. Fluck thought about this for a moment.

'Wounding and ingenious,' he said. Then, guessing the truth, 'I don't suppose you bought a ticket in the first place.'

I refuted this as expressively as possible. 'It's just that I've changed my mind,' I said. 'I've got other things to think about now.'

'It's not too late to buy a ticket,' said Fluck, 'even if it means flying out a day or two after me. It could be a positive advantage, in fact, I could look up an apartment before you arrive, sort out the rent and so on, I know you hate that kind of thing.'

I shook my head, continuing to stare out of the window that looked across the quad. The sight of that cupola, its mock

Roman Doric columns, would be fixed in my mind for ever, I knew that, of course.

'Everything is settled already,' Fluck went on. 'You've got the visas, haven't you? And the library pass? My uncle's a marvel, really, it was so sweet of him to help us out.' This uncle, an American, seemed to have inherited the Fluckian sense of commerce lost to the English branch of the family. Apparently he was fabulously wealthy. For no particular reason, but with a growing conviction, I doubted his existence.

'If you are worried about financial matters you shouldn't be. I'm hardly likely to let you down,' Fluck said. I replied that I had no worries of any kind. It was just that I'd changed my mind.

'But what about our collaborations?' Fluck finally pleaded. 'What about your poems and my pictures? And think of the fun we'll have in New York, we two against the world and New York the capital of it.'

I answered him briefly and unambiguously. Perhaps I was blunter than I had intended to be because Fluck was suddenly silent. When I next looked across at him he was staring at his shoes, a picture of self-pity.

'I'm just not coming,' I said, rising out of my chair as if to go, although it was well past midnight and there was nowhere to go. 'I think Poppet and I might find somewhere together after the summer,' I said.

Fluck slumped forward in his chair – he really was the most dreadful ham – and his fleshy face seemed to half-slip from his skull as he began to sob. I had been through this before, of course, and I knew to remain silent. I had been through a lot with Fluck, the sneering, the taunting, the simpering self-effacements. Even as he sobbed, he quoted. 'Lo, ever thus thou growest beautiful in silence . . . and thy tears are on my cheek.' Tennyson, much over-rated. I could stand no more. Dispassionate observers would have blamed me only for playing along with him for so long. I suppose it was because I felt sorry for him. He attempted to cover his face with his pudgy hands and failed, bits of it kept appearing between his fingers as he trembled. '*You* go,' I said.

The cupola opposite was wonderfully geometric considered against the blue-black sky, hard and precise. When I looked back at Fluck he was appealing to me mutely with a wet face, very pathetic, but really I had put up with enough. His suffering was negligible compared to mine . . .

I saw all this clearly, as in a vision which Fluck himself had conjured up, and I knew there was nothing else for it. I rose with perfect poise and taking hold of Fluck by the lapels of his overcoat, pulled him off his throne, down onto his knees. An astonished hiss escaped from him, sounding oddly like 'Oh dear', an understatement if ever I heard one, followed by a mumbling I didn't catch. Big as he was, he had no strength, or perhaps no will, and it was surprisingly easy to push him forwards into the nearest rock pool. Also I was rabidly aggressive. I threw my weight on top of him and held his head under water. He was so passive I even had opportunity as I crouched on him to look around me and take in the surrounding scene: the dark humps of rocks, the flat stretch of sand and sea glimpsed beyond, the star-ridden sky overhead. Perhaps I counted out the seconds as I pushed downwards on his head, perhaps I didn't. Three minutes passed, anyway. That's how long it takes. He didn't struggle. Only once, towards the end, his body gave a shudder, and his arms jerked out of the pool, bumping briefly against my head, and then they flopped back into the water and he was still.

I climbed off him, backed away to Fluck's rock, and sat down, my feet resting lightly on the backs of his outstretched legs. I was immediately struck by the peacefulness of his body in repose, a novel attitude for him. For once he blended in with his surroundings, calmly and without ostentation. He looked to me as if he were lying on his belly, humbly taking a drink of water from the pool, not realising as he drank that his hands had slipped into the water and his cuffs were getting wet.

In the perfect peace of that moment, regarding Fluck, his bodger's overcoat and small head floating, lines from a certain poem came into my head and I recited them out loud:

> I propped her head up as before,
> Only, this time my shoulder bore
> Her head, which droops upon it still:
> The smiling rosy little head,
> So glad it has its utmost will,

> That all it scorned at once is fled,
> And I, its love, am gained instead!
> Porphyria's love: she guessed not how
> Her darling one wish would be heard.
> And thus we sit together now,
> And all night long we have not stirred,
> And yet God has not said a word!

Beautiful lines, are they not? How they calmed and refreshed me.

I do not remember my walk back to the cottage, but I am sure I was light-hearted. It would not surprise me to learn that I frolicked all the way back along the coast, a cheerful tune on my lips. I suppose I thought that guilt would not punish me until later. Naturally I realise that my apparent insouciance after such an appalling crime may constitute an affront to some people – and if I wasn't so tired and fatalistic I might agree with them.

When I got back into the hot, brilliantly lit house, the game of hide-and-seek had apparently been interrupted by another bout of furious dancing. In the living-room the Jackson Five were baying from the stereo, a childish noise occasionally punctuated by whoops and stomping of feet. To me these frivolous sounds were a gorgeous affirmation of life, and sauntering down the hall, I even, for a moment, considered joining the wild fracas, presenting myself for my fellow-party-goers' general comment (I imagined curiosity turning slowly to horror). But I was thirsty, so I turned aside into the kitchen, where I found the second half-bottle of Scotch I had hidden. I unscrewed the cap and drank mechanically. Suddenly I felt tired, a physical ache spreading through my entire body, as after arduous wholesome labour, so without troubling the others by wishing them goodnight, I made my way upstairs to our room. But not to bed. To hide, of course. In order, you see – in keeping with common expectation – that I might then be sought out. Or do I mean found out? Technically, I had remained hidden since the game began. Soon, I felt, the dancing would end and the game would be resumed.

Although there is no longer any need to remember, my

memory of these moments, the perfunctory epilogue to all that had gone before, is excellent. I remember how, in the dark (I had not switched on the light), I put down my bottle of Scotch, gingerly, on the corner of the crowded dressing-table before reaching across to fumble with the door of the airing cupboard. I remember too the breath of hot, dry air that greeted me, and also how I rearranged the tiers of towels and linen so that I could fit above them. Then I relocated my bottle, climbed onto my perch, and swung the wooden door softly shut behind me.

Why did I do it? I mean, why did I hide in the airing cupboard? I suppose that I was cold, and wet around the edges, what with the splashing Fluck had made, however feeble. I needed drying out and heating up. There was no better place for me than an airing cupboard.

Within a quarter of an hour I had begun to suffocate. The starchy smell of linen quickly became tainted with the sharp stink of Scotch, and I found it difficult, not to say impossible, breathing this in. It scalded the insides of my nostrils and peeled my throat raw. Of course I was also sweating profusely by now, and shivering violently, I suppose with the sudden temperature change which may have caused a degree of hypothermia. I may be no doctor, but I was reasonably convinced that I was dying. Killing myself, I mean. One tends to suspect such things. Why then did I not panic, or struggle to keep breathing, or even (god forbid such simplicity!) open the airing cupboard door? Teasing questions, aren't they, unfortunately unanswerable. I can only record that during what I supposed to be my last few minutes on earth, in accordance with the usual procedure I began to review my life. I began with my childhood – but my memories of this period are poor and anyway undistinguished. Soon I was lost in a predictable daydream: a sleeping figure left his rocky bed, lifted gently, as it were, considerately, by water, drifting, bumping against obstacles, belly-down, his arms outstretched, his fingers trailing through fronds of seaweed, making slowly for the shore. There was another figure with him, oddly motionless, but whether man or woman or alien, I could not tell. It was enough for this figure to be there. Although the sky was comparatively clear and there seemed to be a breeze, the air was intolerably stuffy.

Neither figure appeared to mind this. The one continued sitting and thinking, the other sleeping and floating.

As I daydreamed I drank, failing all the time now, and soon realised that as my bottle was still rather heavy, and therefore fairly full, I had no chance of finishing it. This was a bitter blow. Death by drink had always appealed, a blaze of self-destruction. Not apparently for me. I am anyway too safe and sane and unaccomplished. But naturally, as I felt myself grow weaker and weaker, I cast around for some convenient snatch of poetry on which to expend my last breath, something lyrical and light to purge me of myself. To my annoyance the only thing that came to mind was one of Fluck's favourites, the sadly comic *Prufrock* – 'There will be time, there will be time', nonsensical under the circumstances and anyway unexciting. However it seemed to be all I could manage. I began to chant the few lines I remembered out loud, 'There will be time, there will be time', perhaps this was all I remembered, what a bore, though there was something about faces too, something about 'creating' and something else, I forget what. I fear I did not stick closely to the text, but, although my voice was cracked and vanishing, and my memory for verse all but blown, I struggled on regardless, the habit of grim determination proving impossible to break, even at this late state. 'There will be time, there will be time,' I croaked, not very loudly now, but loudly enough stupidly to attract attention to myself, and the door of the airing cupboard was suddenly yanked open from outside, and they stood there, all of them, baffled and excited and speaking at once.

'S. J.!'

'We've found you!'

'At last!'

'S. J.?'

I fell out of the cupboard onto whirling arms and shoulders, and was violently ill.

I seem to have come to the end. At last. The end for me too, I suppose, now that this note is almost finished, the longest suicide note I have ever written.

One small confession is still lacking, and that is to say, to confess, that I feel quite marvellous. Suddenly the nagging headache of uncertainty and inarticulacy has faded away. Also my rage and bitterness. The long, exhausting tussle with my memory, now over, has left me quietly recuperative. It seems that this struggle, this picking over of my agonies, has been worthwhile after all, almost cathartic, restoring to me a certain strength of spirit.

Not much further now. A few more sentences before I shuffle off. There is just one small logistical detail to clarify: why did I murder Fluck? It is a simple matter and it would be good to get it out of the way at once. I killed him out of pity. I pitied him because, of course, he failed himself in love. That, in a nutshell, is the whole story, although there may be related factors which influenced me in minor ways, for instance my insatiable hatred of the man. Also my fear of him. Envy, too, which I felt whenever I looked at one of his pictures.

To these specific factors must be added various general ones, opportunism, the desire for liberation, moral outrage, fatalism, and Fate itself. And lastly there is the matter of his seduction of Poppet.

But, really, why play Iago? Why sully myself with motive? Is it not enough that Fluck tormented me, among others, for years and years, regardless of my suffering? Left with the simple fact that I am now his murderer, I am happy.

It is time to finish. It would be unpardonable to let this drag on much longer. But I can hardly help reflecting how strangely everything has turned out. When I began this record I expected it to be the prelude to a death, now I find it is a postscript to one. And as such it is possible to view my story with a certain amount of levity. In fact, re-reading certain passages of it, it seems considerably more light-hearted in tone than I remember. Evidently, while I laboured with the composition I overlooked the essential humour of the thing, the many comical touches. Remarkably, even the traumatic last scenes seem humorous now, in their own quiet way. In particular I am amused by the picture of Fluck being plucked from his rock like a big straw doll, muttering 'Oh dear' in schoolboyish undertones while I snarl and snap in a frenzy. 'Oh dear'! – or perhaps it was 'My dear!', even funnier. Yes, even as I slid him into the deathly pool he was murmuring to himself little phrases of regret and affection, each with an Oliver Twistish simper of self-reproach. It makes me smile, really it does. And how funny to think that

after all this here I am smiling, a calm and contented kind of
smile, I can almost see it – it is not a broad and maniacal, but a
quiet twinkle rather reminiscent of the expression of Francesco
Parmigianino in the famous 'Self-Portrait in a Convex Mirror',
his masterpiece, although several of his other paintings are
almost as good and have been unjustly neglected.

FOR THE BEST IN PAPERBACKS, LOOK FOR THE 🐧

In every corner of the world, on every subject under the sun, Penguin represents quality and variety – the very best in publishing today.

For complete information about books available from Penguin – including Puffins, Penguin Classics and Arkana – and how to order them, write to us at the appropriate address below. Please note that for copyright reasons the selection of books varies from country to country.

In the United Kingdom: Please write to *Dept E.P., Penguin Books Ltd, Harmondsworth, Middlesex, UB7 0DA.*

If you have any difficulty in obtaining a title, please send your order with the correct money, plus ten per cent for postage and packaging, to *PO Box No 11, West Drayton, Middlesex*

In the United States: Please write to *Dept BA, Penguin, 299 Murray Hill Parkway, East Rutherford, New Jersey 07073*

In Canada: Please write to *Penguin Books Canada Ltd, 2801 John Street, Markham, Ontario L3R 1B4*

In Australia: Please write to the *Marketing Department, Penguin Books Australia Ltd, P.O. Box 257, Ringwood, Victoria 3134*

In New Zealand: Please write to the *Marketing Department, Penguin Books (NZ) Ltd, Private Bag, Takapuna, Auckland 9*

In India: Please write to *Penguin Overseas Ltd, 706 Eros Apartments, 56 Nehru Place, New Delhi, 110019*

In the Netherlands: Please write to *Penguin Books Netherlands B.V., Postbus 195, NL–1380AD Weesp*

In West Germany: Please write to *Penguin Books Ltd, Friedrichstrasse 10–12, D–6000 Frankfurt/Main 1*

In Spain: Please write to *Alhambra Longman S.A., Fernandez de la Hoz 9, E–28010 Madrid*

In Italy: Please write to *Penguin Italia s.r.l., Via Como 4, I-20096 Pioltello (Milano)*

In France: Please write to *Penguin Books Ltd, 39 Rue de Montmorency, F-75003 Paris*

In Japan: Please write to *Longman Penguin Japan Co Ltd, Yamaguchi Building, 2–12–9 Kanda Jimbocho, Chiyoda-Ku, Tokyo 101*